They were waiting for me in my office at the university that morning: two men in those dark overcoats and grey hats that are as good as a uniform. As I walked in one of them shut the door behind me and stood against it. The other, short and squat, with the old-fashioned wide trousers as worn by members of the Presidium, snapped his official card in its red plastic cover open in front of me.

"Morozov, Ivan Vasilevich?"

I nodded. All the drawers of my desk were open, and the papers on top had been tossed together in a heap. I couldn't begin to understand what was going on. There was no point in asking, either; these two were obviously no more than deliverymen.

T.J. BINYON
SWAN SONG

A TOM DOHERTY ASSOCIATES BOOK

SWAN SONG

Copyright © 1982 by T.J. Binyon

Reprinted by arrangement with Doubleday & Company, Inc.

First TOR printing: February 1986

A TOR Book

Published by Tom Doherty Associates
49 West 24 Street
New York, N.Y. 10010

ISBN: 0-812-58095-8
CAN. ED.: 0-812-58096-6

Printed in the United States of America

0 9 8 7 6 5 4 3 2 1

To Felicity

"Why pick on Vanka Morozov?
He's not guilty of anything."

—popular song

1

They were waiting for me in my office at the university that morning: two men in those dark overcoats and grey hats that are as good as a uniform. As I walked in one of them shut the door behind me and stood against it. The other, short and squat, with the old-fashioned wide trousers as worn by members of the Presidium, snapped his official card in its red plastic cover open in front of me.

"Morozov, Ivan Vasilevich?"

I nodded. All the drawers of my desk were open, and the papers on top had been tossed together in a heap. I couldn't begin to understand what was going on. There was no point in asking, either; these two were obviously no more than deliverymen.

We walked back along the corridor and down the stairs. As far as I knew I'd committed no offence, broken no laws. The only solution I could come up with was that my name had been found in the address-book of someone who had. If this was the case, it should be reasonably simple to clear things up. All the same I felt far from easy.

Herzen and Ogarev watched us pass through the court-yard. No surprise registered on their bronze faces, but then in the past forty-odd years they must have seen quite a number of members of the university leave the premises under police escort.

Outside, in Manezh Square, a grey Volga was waiting. I sat in the back seat, between the two agents, and the car pulled away. The back window and both side windows were curtained, and when I leant forward to look through the windscreen the man on my left put a heavy hand on my shoulder and pulled me back. I gave up trying to find out where we were going. Reassuringly, however, we seemed to be travelling away from the KGB centre on Dzerzhinsky Square.

I didn't recognise the surroundings when I got out of the car in front of a militia station some forty minutes later, but from the architecture we must have been out in one of the new suburbs, right on the very edge of Moscow. Just beyond the station the road turned into a track, deeply rutted by construction vehicles, and to one side was a stack of sewer pipes waiting to be laid.

The sergeant behind the desk put down his newspaper and got to his feet as I was brought up to him.

"Passport."

I took it out and handed it across. He leafed slowly through it, compared my face with the photograph, and then put it down in front of him. There was a list of telephone numbers under the glass top of the desk. He ran his finger down it, picked up the receiver, and dialled. For a long time there was no answer.

I noticed that there were grease-spots down the front of his uniform, and that he had been reading an article on the American presidential election campaign. I squinted over at it while we waited. The *Izvestiya* leader-writer would obviously have been reluctant to buy a second-hand car from any of the candidates.

At last someone answered. The sergeant picked up my passport. "Sixth District? Twenty-fifth here. We've got a certain Morozov, Ivan Vasilevich, registered as living on your patch." He read my address from the passport. "Could you give us what you've got on him?"

There was another wait, but a shorter one than might have been expected. The card-index system at the other station must have been organised on exemplary lines. As he listened the sergeant gave an occasional grunt and made some notes on a pad. Then he put the receiver back on the instrument and gestured for me to be taken away.

I was led down a long, green-painted passage with numbered doors on either side, taken into a small, bare room, furnished only with a table and two chairs, and told to strip.

I stared in astonishment. The command was repeated, impatiently.

I suppose I should have protested, sworn at them, asked them what in hell's name they thought they were playing at, reminded them that they weren't dealing with some recidivist just back from the camps, or a dissident who'd been discovered duplicating seditious magazines in his room, but with a politically reliable university lecturer without a black mark to his name, a candidate of sciences, no less.

Of course, I should have kicked up a row much earlier, as soon as I'd been brought into the station. Or, better still, in my room at the university, with the moral support of its familiar surroundings. I'd been too bemused to do anything then, but if I didn't do it now, I wouldn't have another chance: it's difficult to stand on one's dignity with no clothes on.

On the other hand, submission to authority and an unquestioning acquiescence in one's fate are national characteristics of the Russian intelligentsia. Take, for example, the behaviour of the Decembrist conspirators after their failure in 1825, or that of the old Communists in the purge trials in the 1930s. But perhaps this historical generalisation merely concealed the fact that I was a coward. I took off my coat and jacket and undid the belt of my trousers.

When I was naked they began to go through my clothes, tossing each garment to me when they had finished with it. My wallet, notebook and various pieces of paper were separated from the rest of my possessions and taken away, together with my briefcase.

I got dressed and sat down on a chair. The room was hot, but I kept shivering. At the same time I found myself sweating heavily. I kept wiping the palms of my hands on my trousers, but in a minute or two they were damp again.

Some time later the door was unlocked and a uniformed militiaman came in. He put a red cardboard document case down on the table in front of me and went out. I pulled it across with a vague feeling of unease. On the upper right-hand corner there was a rectangular white sticker with file number, date and the words "White Swan." They said nothing to me. The tapes were tied together too tightly. I fiddled them apart, and opened the cover.

On top lay a carbon copy on poor quality paper. The type was smudged, in places almost illegible, and here and there a hand-written emendation had been added in that shade of purple ink used only by civil service departments and demonstrators outside the American Embassy—though the latter use it to throw, rather than write with. I hesitated for a moment before picking the papers up. Presumably I was now going to find out what I was doing here. A minute later I put them down again in bewilderment.

What on earth had I to do with what was described as the deposition of Irina Aleksandrovna Kozlova, a 55-year-old teacher at a village school in the Vologda region? They must have made a mistake; I'd been given the wrong file.

After a few minutes I took the papers up again. I wasn't so entertained by my surroundings as to be able to despise reading matter. The first page of Irina Aleksandrovna's statement was missing. It began on the second page, dramatically in the middle of a sentence:

". . . into the classroom in the morning, I found only six pupils at their places. Their names are, of course, noted on the class register for that day [copy appended at end of statement]. I naturally demanded to be told where the other seventeen were. I could obtain no satisfactory answers for some time, but at last Sonya [DOLZHIKOVA, S. I.] began to cry and told me that they had all gone into the forest. I asked if they had gone to gather mushrooms. For some reason Petya [ANTONOV, P. N.] considered it necessary to laugh at this question. I sent him and the others out of the room with instructions to prepare the next lesson and questioned Sonya more closely. She is not a bright child; she has an unfortunate history: she belongs to a one-parent family and her mother [DOLZHIKOVA, Z. V.] has not the best of reputations. With much difficulty I succeeded in eliciting from the child the following information: 1. The other children had been taken by their parents into the forest to see a 'wonderful lady'; 2. Sonya had wanted to go with them, but had not been taken, because her mother was 'a sinner'; as a compensation she had been invited by Masha [there are three Mashas in the class: GUSEVA, M. T., PETROVA, M. I., PRISHVINA, M. M. It has not yet proved possible to establish which is referred to here] to come and play that evening and to meet Masha's grandmother [see previous note; identity not yet

established] who had been ill, but had been 'prayed
for' and was now much better. I then proceeded
to question the other pupils individually without
any success. The next day the whole class was
present, but despite severe questioning and the
threat of disciplinary action I could obtain no
explanation for their collective absence. Before
continuing the teaching programme I gave the
class a short talk on the duty of a Soviet citizen
to overcome obsolete family and class loyalties
for the good of the state, adding that superstition
and religion, that 'opium of the people,' were
out of place in a world which contained such
glories of Soviet science as the first sputnik and
the All-Union Exhibition of Economic Achievements, which the class had visited under my
supervision the preceding term. During that night
I was awakened several times by noises from the
street and in the morning I discovered that my
fence had been daubed with tar and a number of
obscene expressions had been written on it
[photographs appended]. I immediately made the
strongest of representations to . . .''

I was glad not to have been taught by Irina Aleksandrovna.
I knew the type only too well: stupid, narrow-minded and
prim; ferociously convinced in the rightness of their own
beliefs, and hence unmoved by logical argument, emo-
tional persuasion, or threat of violence. In crises of war
and revolution, no doubt, they become heroines, martyrs
for a cause, but in more normal times, as teachers, assistant librarians, administrators in polyclinics, or manageresses
of local post-offices, they confine themselves to delaying
and irritating the daily processes of life.

After Irina Aleksandrovna's verbosity the statement of
Petr Alekseevich Bykov, tractor-driver, 24, was pleasantly

laconic and struck me, on the whole, as offering a better literary model.

> "I was driving back from the field to the kolkhoz. I met Tolya [GUSEV, A. T., brother of GUSEVA, M. T.]. He was walking along the side of the road. I asked him where the [. . .] he was going. He told me to mind my own [. . .] business. I said that the chairman would cut off his [. . .] [. . .]. I saw more people on the road. I did not know all of them. I asked them to get out of the [. . .] way. They asked Tolya why he was talking to a [. . .] unbeliever. One of them—I think he is called Valery, I saw him once in the club [identity impossible to establish: no Valery registered in district]—shouted: 'Brothers, stone the blasphemer.' I drove across the field. One stone hit me on the shoulder. There were several dents in the petrol tank. I am not responsible for them. I drove to the kolkhoz office and looked for the chairman [KHLEBOV, Z. P.]. He wasn't there. The next day I told him I was leaving."

There were several more short statements in the file, all apparently dealing with the same events, but none of them as interesting as the first two. Khlebov, the collective farm chairman, had sensibly taken refuge in stout denial. None of the collective farm workers had been absent that day; no strangers had been seen in the vicinity; no riots had been witnessed or reported; Bykov's tractor was an old one; it was impossible to tell when the dents in the petrol tank had been made. The collective farm was run in full conformity with the laws and constitution of the Russian Soviet Federative Socialist Republic, and its members were inspired in their work by the teachings of Marx, Engels, Lenin, ''and

other great Communist thinkers.'' I liked the peasant caution of that last phrase.

After these came some grey photocopies on limp paper.
The top sheet had a superscription in handwriting: ''Extract from the interrogation of GUSEV, Anatoly Timo-
feevich, kolkhoznik, 22.'' Poor old Tolya: he wouldn't be
exchanging abuse with tractor drivers for a long time, if
ever again. I picked it up reluctantly. There was something
disagreeable about the feel of the pages; they clung together, still charged with static electricity. I separated the
first one and began to read:

"Q. Where were you going when you met Bykov?
 A. Bykov's gone, the [. . .] idolater. We got rid
    of him.
 Q. Where were you going?
 A. I was going, I was going . . .
 Q. Where were you going?
 A. I was going . . . I was going into the forest.
 Q. Why were you going into the forest?
 A. The trees, the leaves, the green leaves.
 Q. What else?
 A. The leaves, the sticky green leaves.
 Q. What else was there in the forest?
 A. The singing, the dancing.
 Q. Who was there?
    [no answer]
 Q. Who was there?
 A. The sheep, the sheep were there, the lambs
    were there. [The prisoner simulated a fainting
    fit, but was efficiently revived by the junior
    members of the interrogation team.]
 Q. Gusev, listen to me. The sheep and the lambs
    were in the forest. Was there anyone else
    there?
 A. The shepherd was there and the blessed lady.

Q. Who is the shepherd?
A. The shepherd, the shepherd. The shepherd,
   the white swan. Praise the white swan.
   [The prisoner fainted again and could not be
   revived for a considerable time. Further interrogation was postponed.]''

I turned over. The final page was headed "Extract from
a preliminary report on the interrogation of GUSEV, A.T.''

"At the beginning of the treatment the subject
was able to answer simple questions about the
village, his work, other members of the collective and so on. As the treatment progressed,
however, the subject's replies became less coherent. It was observed that whenever the interrogator returned to familiar details of the subject's
daily life more sensible answers were obtained.
However, as soon as the subject was questioned
again about the events on''—the date had been
blacked out—''his replies rapidly became unintel-
ligible, consisting for the most part of gibberish.
Though there is without doubt an element of
simulation in the subject's mental state, some
deterioration can be attested. In the opinion of
the undersigned, this is in no way due to the
treatment the subject has received, but rather to
. . .''

The bottom of the page had been torn off. I put the last
sheet down carefully on top of the rest and closed the file.
Somehow I was coming less and less to believe that the
documents had been given to me by mistake. I tied the
tapes together in a bow and pulled the loops so as to get
them equal. The door opened. I looked up. A man in
civilian clothes was smiling at me.

"Vanya!" He threw his arms wide. "How many summers, how many winters . . ."

"Alik?" I let him embrace me.

"Come on, old boy." With an arm round my shoulders he propelled me gently out into the corridor. "I'm taking you out to lunch. You haven't anything better to do, have you?"

2

"Sorry about that bureaucratic slip-up," Alik said. We were driving back into the centre of town.

"You mean you don't want to see me?"

"Of course I do. But not quite in those circumstances. I just thought we might have a friendly chat sometime about the old days. After all, quite a lot of water has passed under the bridge since then. But I accidentally happened to mention your name in quite another context, and one of my boys completely misunderstood what was going on. Dashed off, hauled you in and stripped you down before I'd heard anything about it." He laughed. "He's loyal enough, and very efficient—if he's pointed the right way—but, between you and me, not a great deal up top. As thick as a Tambov peasant, one might say." Another laugh.

I didn't believe a word of it, but I wasn't going to say anything until I found out what his game was, what the point of the whole charade had been. And if he wanted for the moment to pretend that we were friends, I wasn't going to contradict him.

The drive back seemed to take far less time than the journey out. Alik's chauffeur shot down the centre lane, passing everything on the road and being waved on by traffic policemen. We came in past the Garden ring and the Boulevard ring, turned up into Sovetskaya Square and stopped under the statue of Yury Dolgoruky.

As usual, a placard on the glass door of the Aragvi restaurant announced that there were no places inside, and a small queue of hopeful lunchers had already formed on the pavement. Alik rapped imperatively on the glass with a 20-copeck piece and a porter in a stained uniform who looked old enough to have crossed the Alps with Suvorov let us in.

We went downstairs, to that room decorated in such a way as to try and persuade the visitor that he is eating out-of-doors in Georgia, beneath an arbour covered with vines. I wondered vaguely, as I always did, whether there were any alfresco restaurants down in the south which tried to reverse the illusion for their hook-nosed, black-moustached patrons.

I looked round. Despite the notice on the door the restaurant was far from full. On our left four American exchange students—solid young men with crew-cuts—were consuming a massive meal in order to keep them going for an entire week out at the new university; beyond them two lovers were staring soulfully into each other's eyes over cooling plates of *chakhokhbili;* and beyond them again a party of Georgians had a small regiment of bottles on parade and were inspecting them individually for loose buttons, dirty belts and careless shaves. On our right there was an empty table; then a small man in a blue suit, sitting by himself, who was going red in the face from his efforts to bring a recalcitrant *shashlyk* to heel; beyond him were a couple more empty tables, and in the distance a group of Chinese tourists were eating steak by numbers.

Alik had got hold of a waiter and with his reluctant support was laying the foundations for a very reasonable lunch. He hadn't changed much. He was as thin and dark as ever, still wore his hair cropped short all over his head, and still had, I noticed, the habit of flicking the ash from his cigarette by knocking the side of his hand against the table.

If his appearance hadn't changed, his taste in clothes certainly had. He was wearing a beautifully cut dark grey flannel suit, a cream silk shirt, and a dark-blue silk tie with a thin light-blue diagonal stripe.

"I like your suit, Alik," I said.

"Italian," he said.

"And your tie?"

He squinted down at it. "An English friend gave it to me."

"He must have had a sense of humour."

"What do you mean?"

"Wearing that tie means that you belong to a select English élite, are a member of the effete and degenerate ruling class of a crumbling capitalist society—in other words a former pupil of Eton College."

His hand had gone up to cover his tie; he now brought it down again and smiled rather constrainedly. "Lucky my colleagues aren't as well up in English social minutiae as you are, Vanya," he said.

It was a petty victory, and probably an unwise one, but it made me feel better; at least I'd revenged myself slightly for the earlier humiliation.

We talked about nothing very much until the caviare came and we were half-way through the first carafe of vodka. Then Alik said: "By the way, Vanya, do you know anything about computers?"

"Not much," I said. "Arts faculties aren't encouraged to have anything to do with them. They're too expensive." I swallowed a glass of vodka and followed it with a square of toast piled high with caviare. "In any case, there's not much you can do with them in my field except construct concordances, and we've got plenty of graduate students sitting around who are fit for nothing else except filling in filing cards."

"They're marvellous machines, Vanya," he said. "Immensely powerful and at the same time unbelievably delicate." He indicated these opposed qualities with two waves of his cigarette. "We've got the use of a large one in the department, and I've been working with it quite a lot lately."

I couldn't see where he was going, but I fortified myself with another glass of vodka and some more caviare.

"I wish I could give you a better idea of what it's like to use one. Unfortunately most of the stuff I've been dealing with is classified, and of course I can't discuss that."

"Of course not," I said with some relief. "By the way, Alik, do you remember the time we . . ."

My remark was trampled over like a child's pram in front of a charge of Budenny's cavalry.

"Now I come to think of it, there is one minor project I can tell you about. As a literary man you might find it interesting."

Here it comes, I thought resignedly, and looked round for sustenance. But the vodka and caviare were finished, and our waiter appeared to have taken the afternoon off.

Alik went on: "We've been running a small test study in various areas of the Union, putting library loans through the computer."

"You mean a buzzer goes off and a red light starts blinking the moment some poor bastard is five minutes overdue in returning a copy of *How the Steel Was Tempered* to the local library?"

Alik laughed condescendingly. "No, it's not quite like that. What we're interested in doing is analysing loans by subject and author, and correlating these with data about the borrower: age, status, occupation, educational level and so on. In this way we get a lot of tabulated information which is extremely useful for the publishing organs—they can work out what the likely demand is going to be, for various categories, and can plan their norms and quotas in accordance.''

I said nothing. I could see a whole lot of other ways in which Alik's tabulated information could be used, and none of them was particularly attractive. At that moment my attention was diverted by the realisation that I'd done our waiter an injustice. I poured myself a large glass of Mukuzani and began to dismember my chicken *tabaka*.

Alik droned on. I began to think that he'd decided to bore me to death in revenge for my remarks about his tie. He was now talking about the correlations—he called them interesting—between people's jobs and the books they read.

Half an hour later I'd finished my chicken and heard far more than I ever wanted to know about the sterling good taste, in literary matters, of steel-founders, coal-miners and construction workers. I sat back and let my mind drift off to consider the problem of what on earth Alik thought he was up to. Even warmed by his food and drink I still couldn't for a moment believe that his only purpose was to meet an old friend and give him a long lecture on computer programmes. He'd always been the most devious of people. He knew perfectly well now, I was sure, that I wasn't taken in by his front. And knew, too, that I knew that. The only thing to do was to wait patiently for the punch-line. But I must, too involved with my own thoughts, at some point have ceased registering intelligent interest, for he stopped and looked at me in a pained way.

"I'm not boring you, Vanya, am I?"

"No, of course not. It's absolutely fascinating."

"I knew you'd think so." He filled up our glasses and gestured to the waiter for another bottle of wine. "As I was saying, there's remarkably little fluctuation, within certain parameters, in regional reading habits, as far as fiction is concerned. Soviet works so many per cent, classical works so many, and the rest—not a great deal—is made up of translations. The figures vary a little, of course, but not more than one or two per cent on either side of the mean.''

I nodded wisely.

''Well, I was running a programme on one region through the machine some time ago, and I came across a peculiar anomaly—works by classical authors had shot up, almost doubled in fact. I thought at first that some data had been fed in wrongly—the operator had made a mistake—but I checked back, and the figures seemed right, so I began to analyse the results more closely. Do you know what I found?''

''The *kolkhozniki* were building cow-sheds with complete sets of Tolstoy?'' I suggested. I should have remembered that he had always disliked flippant remarks.

He gave me a cold look. ''Don't be more of a buffoon than you are, Vanya. We could have this conversation somewhere else, if you'd prefer.''

I said nothing, and after a moment he went on. ''I found that the number of loans of novels by Dostoevsky had gone up by over a thousand per cent compared to the previous year, and this increase was all concentrated in one small area.''

He leant back in his chair and lit a cigarette. If this was the punch-line, I was damned if I could see the joke. Then a thought struck me.

''Where did you say this was going on?''

''I didn't, but it was in the Vologda region.''

I had been given the right file, after all. The pieces were beginning to fit together, but the message was still indecipherable. A cup of Turkish coffee and a carafe of brandy had appeared in front of me. I tried some of both, but neither made my brain any clearer.

Alik waved away some smoke, leant forward, and began to speak with more urgency. The preamble was over.

"We studied the print-out, and—"

"We?"

"I'm in Religious Affairs now. Didn't you know?"

I shook my head. Did he think I'd nothing better to do than keep tabs on his career?

"Anyway, we sent a small team up there to find out what the hell was going on. They reported back that some kind of religious revivalist movement had started up, but they couldn't find out a great deal. The locals weren't at all keen to tell them anything." He paused. "The secretary of the district executive committee had his children christened last year."

I laughed. I couldn't help it, and I knew immediately that it was a mistake.

Alik glared at me savagely. "You know what the point of all this is, don't you?"

Suddenly I felt much more sober. Yes, unfortunately I had got the point now. In the last few minutes it had all clicked into place. Perhaps I really had known what it was all about, subconsciously, right from the very beginning, from the moment I saw Alik's two goons standing inside my room. But I hadn't been able to admit this to myself; I'd repressed the knowledge, at the same time putting off the decisions that would have to be made, the responsibilities that would have to be shouldered.

"Lyuba?" I said interrogatively, with no real hope that I'd got the wrong answer to Alik's question.

"Yes, Lyuba. Our old friend Lyuba."

"I don't think her involvement can be very serious. She never—"

"Balls. She's in it right up to her pretty white neck."

I had another glass of brandy. It had as little effect as the first.

After the shock, the gentle approach. Alik put his hand

on my arm and lowered his voice. "Look, Vanya, something's got to be done, for Lyuba's sake."

He'd lost me again. I couldn't believe in the depth of his concern for Lyuba, nor could I see what I could do. "Aren't the organs dealing with it?" I asked.

He passed over my use of the derogatory term for the KGB as if he hadn't noticed it. Perhaps he actually was concerned.

"We're trying, but there's not much we can do at the moment. It's not like it was, you know. We can't round up a whole district nowadays, as Lavrenty Pavlovich used to do. And if we were to nip off the inner cadres—if we knew exactly who they were—all we'd do would be create a lot of fucking martyrs."

I sat up with a jerk. I didn't like the implications behind Alik's easy use of Beria's name and patronymic—presumably common parlance in the Dzerzhinsky Square offices. But the barriers were really down now. He was talking to me as to a colleague, who might be expected to share his nostalgia for the good old days when whole autonomous regions could be wiped away, their inhabitants deported on cattle trucks to the Far East.

He finished off his brandy and lit another cigarette. "And we can't keep this thing under wraps much longer. There was some kind of disturbance outside a church in Leningrad the other day—on some canal off the Nevsky."

"The Church of the Resurrection," I suggested. It was Lyuba's favourite church in Leningrad, built on the spot where Alexander II had been assassinated in 1881.

"Perhaps. Anyway, a couple of foreign correspondents happened to be around—probably not by coincidence—and now they'll be shoving their noses into this pile of shit."

"Who were they?" I said. I don't know why I put the question.

"One was French, the other English—or maybe American. It's not important, anyway. What is important is the way this bloody infection keeps spreading. It's been noted in a couple of other districts already. We've now got the computer programmed to recognise the symptoms—Soviet literature down, classical literature up, then the Dostoevsky explosion, then everything falls off almost to zero—I suppose they're all at home reading their damn Bibles—and then, a month or so later, the outbreaks begin. There are a few other indicators, but they're not so important. But it's not infallible. It didn't tell us anything about Leningrad, for a start. And even if we know where and when, we've no idea how or why." He stopped and bared his teeth at me. "That's what I'm programming you to find out, Vanya."

Here was the crunch, and the brandy had run out, just when I needed it the most.

"You've been keeping in touch with Lyuba; she'll talk to you. All we need is some solid information about what's going on, and what the magic charm is. Then we'll move in quietly, sweep the whole mess up without any fuss, and set up an ideological re-education campaign in the region."

"And Lyuba?"

"I'll see she's all right. My word as a pioneer." He smiled.

The use of the childhood oath almost had me believing him. But not quite.

"But, Alik, I've not seen her for a long time. If she's in as deep as you say she is, she may have changed, she might not—"

The old school friend vanished in a moment and the KGB man returned. He gripped my wrist tightly. "She'd better, you bastard. Do you want to see her in a cell in the Lubyanka, or in a strait-jacket at the Serbsky being pumped full of drugs, or marching across the taiga with her hair shaved off and a number on her back?"

The implacable images rolled towards me like a column

of tanks. I felt weak and giddy. The palms of my hands were sweating again. I tried to blot out Alik's words by conjuring up another vision of the future: Lyuba's head on the pillow beside me; Lyuba in an apron, cooking *pelmeni;* Lyuba taking young Vanka to school; a grey-haired Lyuba sitting opposite me, knitting . . . but these ridiculous stereotypes of bourgeois bliss were so insubstantial, so unlike the actual state of affairs that they faded as soon as they appeared, withered by the breath of reality. I had to do what Alik wanted; become a *seksot,* an informer. In order to save Lyuba I had to betray her. And even then the two sides of the equation were not equal, only approximate. My betrayal would be certain; her salvation only unsure. What kind of future could be built on this foundation?

I wiped my face with the sleeve of my jacket. "All right," I said. "I'll do my best."

Alik patted me on the shoulder. "Good man," he said, and, shoving his brandy glass over to me: "Here, drink this."

A feeble thought struggled to the surface of my mind. "But what about my work, my pupils. The professor . . ."

"I'll take care of all that." He looked at his watch. "You'd better leave this day week. The fifteenth. I'll send some details over to you. Come on."

I followed him down the passage between the tables towards the stairway. The restaurant was almost empty. The red-faced man in the blue suit, exhausted by his earlier struggles, had gone to sleep over a large plate of ice-cream. The Georgians, too, were still there, though their regiment had now suffered as many casualties as Napoleon's army on the retreat from Moscow.

As we turned a corner of the stairs a thought occurred to me. "You called it the White Swan file."

He nodded. "Someone did. It's easier to refer to a title than to some bloody long number. And it's appropriate enough. All the village idiots we sweep up can't do anything but babble about a white swan, whatever it might be."

"You don't think it might be some kind of literary allusion?"

He looked down at me coldly. Posed against the marble stair, and lit from behind by two scallop-shaped sconces, his figure had a minatory, though at the same time slightly theatrical air.

"Forget about literature for the next week or two, Vanya. This is life. Something you don't know much about. You should be grateful to me. I'm giving you the chance to have a few real experiences for once. It's great out there. You'll enjoy it."

He pushed through the door ahead of me, and then waited on the pavement outside. The queue had disappeared. It was already beginning to get dark.

"I'll be in touch," Alik said. "By the way, don't forget to do your bit for cultural relations this evening."

I looked at him in surprise. He grinned and tapped his nose with a gloved forefinger. As I watched him stride away up Stoleshnikov Pereulok the door crashed open behind me and the small, red-faced man who'd been in the restaurant came out as though shot from a gun. He had the look of a man who's suddenly woken up to discover that he's slept through the last opportunity of claiming his winnings from the State Lottery Board. He scurried off in Alik's wake.

I looked after him, and thought for a moment I saw Alik again, standing in front of a brightly-lit bookshop window, talking to a thickset, dark man who was dressed, like Alik himself, smartly enough to be taken for a foreign diplomat. My view was obscured for a moment by a passing truck, and when I could see again the couple had gone.

3

It was a cold evening, though not unduly so for the beginning of March. As I walked home the sharp air began to clear some of the muzziness from my brain. The whole episode had been so contrived, so like a charade, that I found it hard to believe in the existence of any real danger. Alik had put on a good performance, but all the same it was obvious that he'd been telling me only part of the story. Unfortunately, though I'd denied it at the time, I had no real doubt that Lyuba was involved. She had written me some pretty peculiar letters from the Vologda region, when she'd been working there as a schoolteacher. Come to think of it, I ought to have another look at them: they'd certainly be more comprehensible now I knew what was going on, and they might even throw some light on the situation.

From my point of view, almost the most disquieting of Alik's remarks had been his parting shot. I didn't like to think that he'd been keeping so close a watch on me as to know all the details of my social life. Or, more reassuringly, maybe he'd just arranged for me to be sent an invitation to this evening's party in aid of Anglo-American cultural relations with the Soviet Union. Whatever the explanation, it was, I saw, one party which I wouldn't be able to skip.

That winter I was living in an old building off the Malaya Bronnaya, in a flat which before the revolution had probably belonged to a doctor, lawyer, or some other member of the liberal intelligentsia—that class which had bowed to its own belief in the theory of evolution by becoming extinct after the revolution. A faint odour of high-minded political and literary discussions still hung about the tall rooms with their moulded cornices, in one of which—saved by direct intervention from above, or, more likely, the presence during troubled times of a commissar with a taste for cut glass—a crystal chandelier still hung.

Now, however, I shared it with a woman who worked in the restoration department of the Andrey Rublev museum and her two young children; an editorial assistant on some technical journal associated with the steel industry; a bookkeeper from GUM and an assorted horde of mothers-in-law, aunts, distant relations and hangers-on: the whole creating, in a somewhat smaller space, a world not unlike that of a nineteenth-century country landowner's mansion, as depicted by Saltykov-Shchedrin in one of his darker moods. But for the servants, of course.

As usual, a heated conversation was in progress in the communal kitchen. I tossed a greeting in the direction of the debaters as I passed, and received a few absent-minded acknowledgements.

My room seemed undisturbed. If Alik's men had turned it over in my absence, they'd been uncharacteristically tidy about it.

I was going to be late if I didn't hurry. I changed into my only suit. It was a heavy grey tweed, with the label of a Cambridge tailor in the inside pocket. It had belonged to an English graduate student, who'd parted from it in exchange for the five ·volume edition of Khlebnikov's works and a couple of those early Futurist poetry brochures—the ones with the Larionov and Goncharova illustrations. It would have been impossible to say who was more satisfied with the deal: an example of the barter economy at its best.

Before leaving I crossed over to the bookshelf, took out volume 6, L–M, of the Academy dictionary and riffled quickly through the pages. A few letters and a postcard fell out. I picked them up and put them in my pocket. There was no time to read them now, but maybe I'd have a moment later on.

I took a trolley along the boulevard and then walked down Kalinin Street to the House of Friendship, built, as the guidebooks will tell you, in the late nineteenth century by a namesake of mine, the textile magnate Morozov. Dusk toned down the lunatic exuberance of the façade. I turned in up the steps.

A plump blonde in a tight black overall leant over the cloakroom counter to take my coat and gave me a cold plastic token and a warm, gold-filled smile.

The large conference room downstairs was packed out. Comparative cultural references burst around me like shrapnel as I edged my way cautiously into the crowd. Five minutes later I was standing by myself with a large glass of grape juice, wondering what on earth I was doing here, when someone tapped me on the shoulder. I turned and saw one of the organisers, a vague acquaintance from the university, whose name I could never remember.

"Nicola, let me introduce you to Ivan Morozov, who teaches English literature at the university. Vanya, this is Nicola Booth. She writes novels. I expect you've read some of them."

Having effected, like some social Michurin, an experimental cross-fertilisation of species, he drifted back into the crowd, leaving the artist and the critic face to face—a situation to be avoided, except on paper.

Nicola Booth might have been the British Council's flavour of the month, but I had never heard of her and was, moreover, unaccustomed to this kind of confrontation. I liked my authors dead and buried, preferably far away on the shores of misty Albion. Miss Booth, however, was very much alive, and there was nothing at all misty about her, even though she had come dressed—right down to the button boots—ready to leap at a moment's notice into the part of Madame Ranevskaya in *The Cherry Orchard*.

She submitted me to a short sharp interrogation on the department and on my work and then, perhaps disappointed that I wasn't teaching a course on the English novel from Jane Austen to Nicola Booth, by way of George Eliot and Virginia Woolf, asked me whether there were any Russian writers present. I looked round. A minor poet was standing alone by the bar, sipping a glass of wine and possibly contemplating an ode on the latest of our cosmonauts, while farther away a middle-aged novelist had cornered a pretty secretary from the British Embassy and seemed from the vigour of his gestures to be explaining something other than socialist realism to her.

I mentioned his name to Miss Booth, adding that his last book had been a historical novel set in the seventeenth century.

"Really? I've never tried to write that kind of thing myself. The thought of all the research is terribly off-putting. I much prefer to write about people I know." She eyed me consideringly, perhaps envisaging a walk-on part for a Russian academic in her next novel, and went on:

"Tell me about life here."

"Life?"

"Yes, you know. Where's the best place to shop, where

do you go for a night out, where do you take the girl friend. That kind of thing.''

"The boulevards in the summer, the metro stations in the winter. But it's rather a large subject.''

"For a gathering like this? Perhaps you're right. We can take it up if we meet again in different circumstances.'' She gave me a sly look. "But what shall we talk about instead?''

"I could ask you how you're enjoying yourself in Russia.''

"Safe, but hardly original. But I don't mind repeating myself. I'm having a ball.'' She told me about her visits to the ballet, the theatre, and the opera; and how wonderful the French Impressionists in the Pushkin museum were. We chatted on amicably enough until another member of her delegation turned up and took her away to meet someone more important.

It was becoming apparent that I wasn't going to get through the evening on grape-juice alone. I picked my way through to the bar, exchanging nods with a couple of acquaintances, and brought up behind a tall woman with long black hair who was giving an energetic lecture to a small audience consisting of two men: one small and thin, with thick horn-rimmed glasses and a leather jacket, the other burly, wearing a dark suit in some synthetic material with a Re-elect the President button on the lapel.

"There were two things I was trying to do in that film. I wanted the hero's experience of war to be both individual and general. Not only the expression of his own emotions, but, through him, of everything we felt at the time—in Leningrad under siege, in the ruins of Stalingrad, as partisans in the Ukraine.''

The man in glasses had been nodding his head as he listened. "Yes, yes, I see. It comes through, too. But there's one thing I'm going to have to ask you. Even if I have to apologise in advance for doing so. Isn't it a bit unusual, even here, for a woman to direct a war film? How did you manage with the brutal and insolent soldiery?''

I leant forward over Tanya's shoulder.

"She shot them all."

''You bastard, Vanya. You startled me. And who would have expected to find you here, anyway?'' There was something slightly off-key about her remark, but before I could analyse it she went on: ''This is John Wilson, who is going to interview me for English television, and—'' But the American had lost himself in the crowd. She shrugged her shoulders. ''Not one of your admirers, Vanya. I never caught his name, anyway.''

We talked about her next project for some time. She was hoping to make a historical epic about Emelyan Pugachev, the Cossack leader who led a popular revolt against Catherine the Great in the 1770s, declaring himself to be Emperor Peter III. Knowing Tanya as I did, I wasn't too surprised that she should have chosen a story which ends up with the male hero being put in a cage and then publicly quartered on the orders of a dominant female.

It sounded as though it was going to be a prestige production, with hundreds of horses, thousands of Cossacks, and, no doubt, long helicopter shots of the opposing armies together with—what annoys me most in this kind of film—cannon balls pretending to be mortar shells and exploding in pretty puffs of white smoke. Pugachev was to be played by a popular young actor as, I gathered, a cross between Valentino's Sheikh and Vladimir Mayakovsky.

''The script's got outline approval,'' Tanya said. ''I'm going down to the country next month to scout out some locations. Why don't you come with me, Vanya? It would be just like old times.''

The crowd at the far end of the room shifted into an orderly arrangement, like iron filings under a magnet, as the Minister of Culture, flanked by some attendant *chinovniki,* came in. Tanya, highly sensitised to this kind of force field, even over a distance of twenty metres with her back to the door responded to the attraction and was drawn away.

I'd rather taken to Wilson. He had that look of resigned melancholy common to those whose jobs consist of short bursts of frenzied activity alternating with long periods of excruciating boredom. I asked him how he was getting on with the programme he was making. He replied diplomatically; but, after we'd settled down at the bar with a bottle of vodka, gradually warmed to a despondent heat about the bureaucratic inefficiency and obstructiveness with which he'd had to deal. I comforted him with a couple of Radio Armenia anecdotes, and when he eventually left he pressed a Manchester telephone number on me, together with an invitation to visit him any time I happened to be in England. I had about as much chance of making use of either as he had of filming a KGB interrogation, but I thanked him politely and watched him stagger off towards his bed in the Hotel Rossiya.

The minister had now left, and the party had thinned considerably. I watched Tanya's elegant legs crossing the floor towards me with something more than just aesthetic appreciation. She came up, put her arm through mine and leant gently against me.

"Are you going to take me home, Vanya?"

"Not if you still live out in Cheremushki."

She laughed and pressed my arm more closely to her right breast.

4

Outside a light, powdery snow had begun to fall. We walked up to Arbat Square and found a taxi on the rank outside the metro station. The evening had decidedly taken a turn for the better.

Tanya was no longer living in her old apartment out in the suburbs, but on top of a newish block just off Kutuzovsky Prospect. Her apartment had everything the apartment of a successful young film director should have, and exhibited the currently modish mixture of Slav and Western artefacts: peasant embroidery on the walls and pine furniture from one of the Baltic republics; a large West German television set staring blankly across the room at a nice seventeenth-century icon of the Virgin and Child, school of Ushakov; a couple of abstract paintings, a child's head in clay and some coarsely decorated Ukrainian pottery; a bookcase full of Western art books and books on the cinema; and, scattered on the floor by the Japanese music centre, a pile of the latest American and European records, with the new Bob Dylan album on top.

I sat down and began flipping through a large, lavishly illustrated book on the American cinema in the 1930s. I was just admiring a still showing Bela Lugosi ranting at Arlene Francis over a benchful of chemical apparatus when Tanya came up behind me and bit me on the back of the neck.

"Am I going to have to drag you into my bedroom and undress you?"

"No, we'll undress each other."

"You can't undress me."

"Why not?"

She showed me.

Later on she lay above me, propped on her elbows, looking down into my face. "You don't change much, do you, Vanya," she said. "Preserved from time up in your little ivory tower. I could almost fall in love with you all over again."

I said nothing. She certainly had changed, in the years that I had known her, but not, as far as my most recent experiences were concerned, in any way one would wish to complain about. She gave me a kiss, rolled off me, and took a cigarette from the bedside table. We lay there in companionable silence for a bit, then she stubbed out her cigarette and got up.

I put on my trousers and followed her into the kitchen. She gave me the coffee and I sat down at a small plastic-covered table with the grinder between my knees. In front of me on the wall was a large bulletin board covered with press photos, clippings from newspapers and magazines, and assorted souvenirs: Tanya talking to François Truffaut at the Cannes film festival; Tanya receiving an award from the Estonian Academy of Arts; Tanya in dark glasses waving to reporters as she emerged from the door of a TU-104 at Orly airport; Tanya on the set of her latest film,

standing on the platform of a Katyusha rocket launcher
surrounded by a crowd of actors and technicians; notices
of her films in Russian, English, French, German, Italian
and Armenian; a menu from the Shota Rustaveli restaurant
in Tbilisi, covered with the signatures of the collective of
the Georgian film institute, and inscribed: "In memory of
an enjoyable and mutually productive meeting with our
beautiful and talented colleague, Comrade T. F. Tatarinova."
I grinned a bit over that one. I'd tried Georgian hospitality
myself.

I had finished grinding the coffee and was still working
my way down the board when my eye was caught by a
cracked old photograph, half-hidden behind a piece from
Time magazine on the Soviet Union's exciting new young
generation of film-makers. I unpinned it carefully and put
it down on the table.

A slightly overweight fair-haired young man in a check
shirt and a pair of Polish jeans, holding a large fish on his
outstretched hands, smiled happily and naively up at the
camera. Behind him and to his left a thin girl in a bikini
was leaning against the shoulder of a dark young man in a
pair of shorts who had his arm round her waist. Both
confronted the camera with an expression of cool awareness.

"I didn't know you had this. Where did you get it from?"

She came over from the stove and stood behind me.
"You gave it to me. Don't you remember?"

"No, I don't. And where's Lyuba?"

"She took the photo, you fool. Do you want black or
white coffee?"

She sat down and reached across to pick up the photograph. "Mmm, it's not at all bad of me," she said. "And
you look perfectly sweet, my love, with your huge fish.
How long ago was it? Twelve years?"

"About that."

"I wonder what Lyuba's doing now. Do you ever see
her? I always thought you rather fancied her."

"She went into school-teaching. Then she was sent off to somewhere on the periphery. I haven't seen her for ages." I hoped I'd thrown the line away convincingly. Tanya gave me a rather quizzical look, but didn't pursue the topic. She turned back to the photograph and ran a sharp pink nail down Alik's torso.

"Alik's very dull nowadays," she said. "I met him at some official lunch the other day, and all he could talk about were his chances of being posted to the West. He did ask after you, though, and said something about looking you up soon."

"He shouldn't have much difficulty in finding me," I said.

She laughed. "No, I expect he's got great fat files on both of us."

Soon afterwards we went back to bed. Tanya fell asleep almost immediately, but I lay awake, looking out through the window at the glittering bulk of the new university, topped with its immense red star.

Some time later I got up quietly and went into the kitchen again. The only thing I could find to drink was an almost full bottle of Moldavian vermouth. I took a mouthful and realised why Tanya and her friends had spurned it. I sat down at the table and took out Lyuba's letters.

She'd sent me the first just after she'd been transferred to the Vologda region. I skimmed through it quickly. Descriptions of the village, the school, the surrounding scenery, local characters. It was long and detailed, but there was nothing of particular interest in it.

There had been a long gap before the second letter had arrived. It began: "Dear Vanka-Vstanka, I think—don't dare laugh—that I am undergoing the pangs of a spiritual rebirth. From being a 'lady of little faith' I am rapidly becoming a 'believing woman' under the guidance of an unknown Father Z."

I brooded over this for some time. Here was Alik's

Dostoevsky motif, straight out of the pages of *The Brothers Karamazov*.

The last letter was the one I remembered. It had come about a year ago. There was no salutation or date. It began directly: "Hosanna, hosanna, we praise. The Lord hath not forsaken us: to that witnesseth one who with her own eyes hath seen, with her own fingers hath touched . . ." I went on down the page. "Blessed be the name of the Lord, for his Kingdom is at hand . . . we have cast off the flesh of corruption, and walk abroad clad in the raiment of the spirit . . . He maketh the halt and the lame to walk, the blind to see . . ." I turned it over. It ended: "In blissful expectation of an imminent Second Coming your sister in Christ Mariya (in the world Lebedeva, Lyubov Dmitrievna) kisses you."

I put it down gently on the table and closed my eyes. Perhaps I should have done something at the time, but what? I'd seen Lyuba go through plenty of short-lived enthusiasms before—some literary, some artistic, some even political—and I'd supinely let myself imagine that this was another of the same kind, exacerbated perhaps by loneliness, by the change in her situation. I'd even pretended to myself that I wasn't sure whether the letter was serious or a joke—a parody, a pastiche. But the repression had been a conscious one. I'd hidden from myself the realisation that something I'd always thought possible had now happened: Lyuba's deep yearning for fulfillment had finally led her, after so many temporary resting places, to religion.

I'd written to her a day or two later and my letter had come back annotated with the words: "Moved, without leaving a forwarding address." Since then I'd heard nothing until quite recently, when I'd received a postcard from Leningrad.

On one side was a photograph of the Bronze Horseman, Falconet's statue of Peter the Great. I turned it over. On the verso was a short and inscrutable message: "Rejoice, rejoice, for the end of the reign of Antichrist is nigh." There was no sender's name or address, but Lyuba's handwriting was unmistakable.

I poured myself another glass of vermouth and sat there thinking, putting together Lyuba's letters with the information from Alik's file. It didn't add up to a great deal. The references to the white swan still worried me. The myth of Leda and Zeus struggled through from my memory, but I pushed it firmly back. That obviously belonged to a different system of symbolic references. What seemed to be involved here was some dark and tangled off-shoot of an obscure schismatic theology, not the sunlit clarity of Hellenic myth.

Sects such as these were, I thought, the ultimate expression of that other, hidden side of the Russian psyche; the Russia of Dostoevsky, rather than Turgenev, of Leskov, rather than Chekhov. The contrast between the two was still visible—all around me, indeed, in the furnishings of Tanya's apartment, or in Alik's attempt to write faith into a computer programme. In the nineteenth century they'd called themselves Slavophiles and Westernisers, but the conflict went back much further than that, further even than Peter the Great's attempts to drag the Russian state into Europe by shaving the beards of his boyars. I remembered a sentence from Pushkin's unfinished history of Peter's reign. "The people," he had written, "considered Peter to be Antichrist." Which took me back to Lyuba's postcard and bore out my reasoning. But the message remained enigmatic.

The photograph of Tanya, Alik and myself was still lying in front of me. I picked it up and looked at it again. Despite everything, it had been a good summer; perhaps the best in my life.

It was Tanya who had suggested that we should spend that vacation in the country. We'd gone to bed one afternoon in her room in the student hostel. "Let's ask Alik to bring someone," she'd said as we lay there. "We might get bored by ourselves." Nothing seemed less likely to me at that moment, but I was too besotted to argue. And if we had to have someone, it might as well be Alik.

We'd known each other for a long time; both embassy children, we'd followed each other from one tight little Soviet enclave abroad to another. That's how I'd picked up my English, first in Washington, then in London. Alik had been a lazy, indifferent pupil at the foreign schools, but influential connections had eventually got him into the institute. I'd had to take a stiff entrance examination. A kind of affectionate contempt, I suppose, was what I felt for him then.

I'd borrowed a Czech motor-bike—a Jawa—from a friend. We left on it early one morning in June, and arrived at the farm just after midday. It was boiling hot. I'd been sweating buckets all the way down, not only from the heat, but also from the thought that one of the traffic policemen who lurked in couples at almost every bridge or crossroads on the highway would stop us with a wave of his white baton, and discover that I had no driver's licence. A great feeling of peace and relief descended on me as we came off the road and wound our way through the birches to the shore of the lake. The water was very clear and cool. Afterwards we went up to the abandoned chicken-hut where we were going to camp and ate bread and sausage and drank Zhigulevskoe beer.

The next day Alik arrived with Lyuba. I'd never met her before; she didn't belong to our social set. I never found out how Alik had met her. Thin, blonde, with huge, slightly protuberant grey eyes, she was very unlike the kind of girl he usually had in tow. Up to then his taste had run to plump Georgians or Armenians, with melting dark eyes and slightly moustached upper lips.

We fished, in the most primitive way imaginable, drag-

ging a long net through the water and up on to the shore;
lay in the sun; read; walked through the woods; talked
interminably in the evenings; once went to a film-show in
the club of the nearest village, some ten kilometres away;
once had dinner with the chairman of the collective farm—he
was the nephew of Tanya's old nurse—and his family: a
stiff, awkward occasion with too much to eat and drink.

But, all in all, it was a time of almost unimaginable
tranquillity and pleasure. Apart from a couple of winters in
early childhood spent with an old great-aunt near Ryazan,
I knew nothing of the countryside. Now I took it in with
ardour and delight.

But Tanya, of course, was right. I had been drawn to
Lyuba, very much, during that summer. Possibly as a
result, later, after we'd returned to Leningrad, Tanya and I
had drifted apart.

During the following winter Lyuba's affair with Alik
had ended—I never knew quite why—and she had gone to
pieces for a time. I hadn't been able to do much to help
her then, but afterwards we'd taken endless therapeutic
walks round Leningrad together, breathing in the misty air
and occasionally exchanging a meaningless observation.

It was then that I'd fallen irrevocably in love with her.
There'd hardly been a physical side to our relationship: it
surprised me, looking back, to think how few times we'd
been to bed together, and how unsuccessful the experiences had been. There had been an ethereal air of chaste
purity about her, which had, I suppose, appealed to the
romantic poet in me—a persona which had once existed,
but had long ago been eroded into shapelessness by the
strains of socialist competition. I'd once heard Tanya,
talking to Alik, refer to Lyuba as "your schismatic virgin"
—the expression, if meant bitchily, was undeniably appropriate and now seemed even prophetic.

Since that time the four of us had followed very different paths. Alik, determined to use life to its best advantage

for himself, had joined the party and followed his father into the Ministry of Foreign Affairs. After a posting abroad, he'd been transferred to the KGB, where he'd begun to rattle up through the hierarchy.

Lyuba, the one idealist among us, had gone starry-eyed into school-teaching like some young female Makarenko. As a reward, she'd immediately been posted about as far east as one can get without actually falling into the Bering Sea. She'd lived in a Koryak settlement, teaching Russian to the children—and some of the adults—of a reindeer-breeding collective. We'd kept in touch and when, later, she'd got a job near Tallinn in Estonia I'd gone to see her a few times during the university vacations. But somehow nothing had really come of our meetings. And then, most recently, she'd been sent up to Vologda.

Tanya, always obsessed with films and film-making—as a student she'd continually dragged me along to endless showings of Dovzhenko or Pudovkin—had fought her way through bitter skirmishes and bloody pitched battles to her canvas director's chair, leaving a trail of broken and inanimate bodies behind her.

Her career had been slow to get off the ground, but it looked as though her last film, even more of a success in the West than here, had done the trick. She'd soon be moving into the privileged stratosphere inhabited by members of the Central Committee and the Supreme Soviet, by high-ranking officers, cosmonauts, Heroes of Socialist Labour, Lenin prize laureates, world-famous musicians and ballet-dancers, celebrated scientists, economic managers, eminent—if officially approved—writers, and so on, and so on. Not forgetting, of course, their families.

Like them, she'd have access to the special departments in GUM and other stores, to the Beriozka shops, to reserved clinics, exclusive sanatoriums, luxurious dachas, closed restaurants. She'd get complimentary tickets to concerts, plays, the opera, the ballet; even to football and ice-hockey matches if she wanted them. She'd go automatically to the head of every queue, get a seat on every plane, a berth on every train. She'd be able to travel where she wanted, when she wanted, in the Union; would be able to visit the West with the minimum of delay and the maximum comfort.

I knew what it was like; I'd been on the fringe of privilege myself once. There were some things I envied her: almost unrestricted access to Western films and books, for example. But on the whole I was glad to be out of it.

Not that I'd ever made a conscious decision about the structure of my life. Up to now I'd simply always followed the line of least resistance. Drifting into graduate work rather than leave the university, I'd accomplished imperceptibly the transition from student to teacher. And any advance I'd made in the profession had come solely from seniority, rather than achievement.

This brought me back to the present and its difficulties; especially Alik's piece of moral blackmail. When I examined my feelings I had no doubt that I still loved Lyuba, even though the emotion was abstract. Going to bed with Tanya had brought no sensation of guilt in its train.

But was this love strong enough to conquer an ingrained reluctance ever to leave the spectators' seats and enter the arena? Was I really prepared to try and save Lyuba at the cost of damning myself? I was surely too old to play the knight errant; in any case the role was ridiculous in our society, my self-sacrifice would be as anachronistic as those loyalties which Irina Aleksandrovna had so rightly condemned as out-of-place in the world of the sputnik and the All-Union Exhibition of Economic Achievements.

To my surprise, I discovered that my feelings for her did provide an urgent motivation, especially since, in this instance, they ran together with an equally deep-seated dissatisfaction with the pattern of my life.

I'd quite simply had enough: enough of a life of acquaintances rather than friends; of oblique between the lines conversations, of Aesopian language; enough of talentless students, slipshod work, the absolute minimum of achievement; enough of political meetings, slogans, self-criticism and socialist competition.

I didn't want a cause; I didn't regret that I hadn't stormed the Winter Palace, or been one of the builders of Dneproges; hadn't conquered the virgin lands, or attacked a Fascist tank with a Molotov cocktail shouting "Into battle for Stalin, into battle for the Motherland." I didn't belong to the party; I'd never had the inclination or the energy to make the transition from Komsomol member to party member. On the other hand, I was very far from being a dissident. Their aims seemed to me misguided; either ludicrously utopian or verging on treason; their methods provocative and pathetic. Whatever faults—and in some cases they were glaring—our system possessed, nevertheless its basis must be right: the only possible just and equitable way of organising society, founded on a consistent, coherent and, above all, correct philosophy.

What I needed was self-redemption. I needed to stop myself becoming a hollow shell of attitudes and habits. I needed to live my own life, not a vicarious one through literature. But most of all I needed to regain my self-respect.

That I should be setting out to do so as an unpaid informer, a *stukach* for the state security organs, engaged to betray the only person for whom I really cared, seemed in keeping with the success I'd made of my life so far.

The vermouth bottle, to my surprise, was empty. I crept back into the bedroom and got into bed beside Tanya. She stirred in her sleep and muttered something undistinguishable—but whatever it was, it wasn't my name.

5

Early next morning I walked up the street to take the metro back into the centre. Kievskaya isn't my favourite station—I don't admire its Little Russian folksiness, but it does have something which sets it apart from the others: at the head of the escalators there is an eight-foot high mosaic portrait of our former leader. It must be one of the few public effigies left north of the Caucasus. Down in his native Georgia, of course, those sinisterly benevolent features look down on one wherever one goes. I don't know why this portrait, unlike all the other placards and statues, hasn't yet been removed by the Moscow city fathers. Probably because, never travelling on the metro, they've forgotten its existence. Someone once suggested, I remember, that *Evening Moscow* should run a competition in which the entrants would be invited to rearrange the mosaic so as to form the portrait of any other great Communist. Not terribly sensible, I thought, going down the escalator. Too much hair for Lenin, not enough for Marx, and no one else seems likely to be around long enough to give the winner time to chip out all the pieces and put them together again.

I got to the university just in time for my morning class. I must have looked or sounded a bit off-colour, because a bright-eyed second-year student in a tight white sweater asked me whether I was feeling ill. Perhaps she thought that her sympathy would be reflected in her end of term grades.

The common-room of the department was empty, except for Polezhaev, my colleague in Medieval English, who was sitting in a corner reading a learned journal and puffing gently on a large pipe. He nodded at me, but said nothing. It was rumoured in the department that he'd forgotten how to speak Russian, and that his wife had had to enroll in his Medieval English for beginners course in order to be able to understand what he said to her at home.

I got a glass of tea and a dry piece of cake from the buffet in the corridor and settled down with the latest number of *English Literature* to see what the opposition was getting up to. As I'd half-suspected, a rival at Tartu had hit on a subject I'd been sitting on for a couple of years, and had hammered it into the ground using all the modern technological resources of neo-structuralist criticism.

I was rather sadly admiring one of his graphs when Yuliya Semenovna put her head round the door and said that the professor wanted to see me.

I wondered what the matter was. I'd spent an unpleasant half-hour with Nikolay Stepanovich only a few days ago. He'd accused me, quite justifiably, of consistently under-fulfilling the department's norms in teaching, research and administration, and had threatened me with either a loss of status or a transfer to some provincial university. The latter alternative was not without its attractions, and I had been formulating a grateful acceptance when he'd magnani-mously inclined towards mercy and had reduced the sentence to a public confession, repentant recantation, and pledge to achieve Stakhanovite production in the future—all to be made at the departmental meeting at the end of the month. As I remembered this now, there came into my head that famous priggish remark made by the hero of an early nineteenth-century play when asked why he wouldn't enter the civil service: "I would be glad to serve, but to be servile is repugnant."

Nikolay Stepanovich was sitting behind his desk, fiddling with a fountain-pen. He looked old and grey. He shot me a quick glance as I sat down and then went back to his pen.

"I have to inform you that your application for study leave for the remainder of this term has been granted."

It took me a moment to cotton on, and then I realised that Alik had been at work already.

"It commences at the beginning of next week." He put down the pen and picked up a ruler. "But I think it would be easier for all concerned if you were to cease your teaching duties immediately."

I said I was quite happy to go on to the end of the week.

"I've already redistributed your classes among the other members of the department."

I shrugged my shoulders, thanked him and walked out. It was only when I was packing my briefcase that I realised what had caused the sudden change in his attitude towards me. He had spent a year in the camps and two in exile just after the end of the war. The source of the orders to give me leave must have been obvious to him, and now, in his mind, I'd become part of the system that had sent him off in a convoy to a year's hard labour in Karanganda. I felt sorry: I liked the old man, and had usually got on well with him. But there was no way of correcting his misapprehension.

I had lunch in a *blinnaya* and walked back to the flat, wondering how I was going to fill in the next few days before Alik sent me off—presumably to Leningrad, although of course Lyuba might have moved on since her postcard. Teaching uninspired students how Dickens faithfully reflects the shortcomings of nineteenth-century English society might not be everybody's idea of a good time—it wasn't even mine: give me a beach in Sochi and a pile of Agatha Christies any day—but it would at least have given my mind something to do besides churning through the same problems again and again, like—I thought of Alik's interminable introduction—a computer fed with a loop of punched tape.

I went through into the kitchen to boil a kettle. The conversation there died away uneasily as I came in, and then started up again, on a hysterical note.

Five minutes later I came out, puzzled, and bumped into the bookkeeper on the landing. He drew me into a doorway.

"Two individuals came to see you this morning. They went into your room and were there for about an hour—" He scuttled away as the kitchen door opened.

At the department I was thought to be a collaborator with the organs; at home a victim of them. Either way I carried the plague. Alik was certainly doing a good job in turning me into a social leper; by the time I'd finished what he wanted me to do I wouldn't even need a bell to clear the way.

The individuals hadn't taken the trouble to conceal the fact that they'd searched my room. I didn't bother to see whether anything had gone: I'd got Lyuba's letters with me, and there was nothing else I cared about.

The table had been swept clear and a large envelope was lying on it. I opened it. On top was a type-written note informing me of the subject's last known address in Leningrad. Underneath Alik had written: "We need *facts*."

Below this were an OVIR permit for temporary residence in Leningrad, 250 roubles, a ticket for the Red Arrow, leaving Moscow on Sunday night, and a reservation for a single room at the Astoria. He hadn't booked me a sleeper, and the meal tickets were at the lowest rate.

The next morning was cold and grey. I arrived at the Lenin Library just as the doors were opened. I showed my card to the armed militiaman at the entrance and went upstairs to the subject catalogue. Some time later I moved through into the huge reading-room, almost empty at that time in the morning.

The girl at the order desk gave me a queer look as she went through my slips: the books I was ordering were very different from the ones she was accustomed to get for me. She handed back a couple of requests and told me that I'd have to get special permission to read them. I shrugged my shoulders, and said that it wasn't important. I didn't want to invoke Alik's name and become a marked man at the library as well as everywhere else.

I spent the next few days giving myself a crash course in the history of Russian sectarianism. From one point of view, of course, the exercise was a pointless one: I didn't expect to find anything that would be of any practical use. I suppose it was just the conditioned reflex of an academic confronted with something outside his sphere of knowledge; a reflex which, in itself, is perhaps only a more sophisticated form of the primitive belief that one gains power over objects by being able to call them by their correct names.

But it was one way of passing the time. I was glad to find that I'd had some distinguished predecessors in this area of research. Including Lenin's secretary, Bonch-Bruevich, who'd written a book on the subject. By the end of the week I reckoned that I'd got enough material to make a stab at one myself.

The morning before I left for Leningrad I was sitting in my pyjamas, drinking tea and trying to put some order into a mass of notes when someone banged on the door and shouted that I was wanted on the phone.

The lobby smelt even more strongly than usual of fish and boiled cabbage. I leant against the battered plaster wall and picked up the receiver.

"Morozov here."

"You don't know me, Mr. Morozov, but I think we possibly have some interests in common. I wonder whether we could meet and discuss a subject important to both of us." The speaker had a foreign accent and difficulty with his case endings.

"What subject might that be?" I said.

"I'd rather not discuss it on the telephone, but it concerns a lady friend of yours in Leningrad."

"I've got lots of lady friends, and half of them live in Leningrad."

"Come on, Mr. Morozov, don't let's waste time. The girl I'm talking about has some very old-fashioned ideas."

"Ideas?" I said.

"Beliefs, then. Do you want me to spell it out?" He paused, but I said nothing, and he went on: "If you're interested, I'll be at the sixth chess table on the left along Tverskoy Boulevard in half an hour's time."

6

It had frozen during the night, but there was a bright sun, and the air was pleasantly crisp. I walked down the Malaya Bronnaya to the corner. There was the usual morning queue outside the bread-shop, and the usual longer one outside the liquor store next door for an even more popular grain product. I crossed the street to the statue of Timiryazev, admiring again the sublime imbecility—or subtle irony—of the sculptor, which had caused him to place a scroll in his subject's hand in such a manner as to make it appear, from one angle, as if the famous botanist were emptying his bladder over the Soviet public.

Two lines of chess tables stretched away under the bare lime trees towards Pushkin Square. The first on the left was unoccupied; at the second two old age pensioners, well muffled-up, were concentrating on an end-game which, to judge by the pieces involved, must have been preceded by an encounter even more attritive than the Battle of Kursk; at the third, an infant prodigy, almost hidden by his father's fur hat, waited impatiently as his middle-aged opponent pondered a move; at the fourth a stout little man with a red face wearing a blue raincoat and a pork-pie hat was reading *Izvestiya;* the fifth was empty.

As I approached the sixth a dark, stocky man in a fur-collared overcoat and sealskin hat, cut like an army forage cap—a style favoured by diplomats and members of the Central Committee—rose to greet me.

"Mr. Morozov? I'm Martin Bradley of International Press." He held out a card. I took it, we shook hands and sat down.

"I guess maybe we ought to move these about a bit." He indicated the pieces set up on the board. I noticed that he had given me white: a courteous gesture, but one which meant that I had to move first.

Hoping for an open game, I played P-K4 and said: "What's your problem, Mr. Bradley?"

"My problem? Let's just call it an interest for the moment." He copied my move. "I'm a reporter, Mr. Morozov, and, like all reporters, I'm always looking for a good story. But I haven't got a lot going for me right now. You up in international politics?"

I shrugged.

"Well, I can tell you there's nothing happening, diplomacy-wise, between your country and mine at the moment. This new high-level conference on mutual co-operation—if that's what they call it—isn't for a few months, and God knows whether it'll ever get off the ground. In any case, that's really something for the heavy boys in foreign policy analysis—I'm strictly a grass-roots man myself. You want to make a move?"

I brought a knight out, and he followed suit on the queen's side.

"I've filed a couple of background stories: shopping in Moscow, collective farm markets, cinema-going and so on—you know the kind of stuff—but there's nothing in that. I want to get in a lot deeper.''

I moved a bishop across the board.

He went on: ''Your press agency's turning out nothing but dreck on life in the boondocks. I've got a pile of releases je high back in the office which are of less use to me than a trash-can full of used Kleenex. I'll be wearing a long white beard and drawing a pension before I ever get a story that way. So I thought I'd try something else.'' He paused and reached out towards his bishop. ''I don't suppose you're a Baptist by any chance?''

''No,'' I said.

He let go of the bishop and moved a pawn forward. ''Well, perhaps you don't know, Mr. Morozov, that the United States is one of the most god-fearing nations in the world.''

''Really?'' I withdrew my bishop.

''Yes sir. Out of 216 million Americans more than 150 million believe in God. That's what the latest Gallup poll says. And that's a damn sight larger percentage than in any other industrial nation, east or west. God's a growth industry in the States at the moment. You can't open your doors without falling over a Mormon or a Seventh Day Adventist or some jerk in a yellow robe with a shaved head, all wanting to convert you to their own patented brand of truth. If you could buy shares in religion it would be a better investment than IBM or AT&T. Even politics has gotten on to the band-waggon. In this presidential election the candidates'll probably spend more time campaigning on their knees than on their feet.'' He gave a short laugh, thought for a moment and brought out his other knight.

''So I figure, Mr. Morozov, that what I want is a good human interest story with a religious angle and possibly a little sex. The church-going folks back in Wichita will like it, the college kids who still believe in real-life romance will lap it up, even the freaks and the hippies who think that smoking grass and screwing adds up to a spiritual experience will go for it. And I figure that you can help me write it.''

I'd seen what he was leading up to some time ago, but hadn't decided how to deal with it. I castled defensively and said: "What makes you think I can be of any help to you?"

"Come on, Vanya—that's right, isn't it?—don't play games with me. You know what I'm getting at. You didn't come out here to meet me because you thought I was going to sell you a bag of peanuts. Your friend in Leningrad is well and truly mixed up in some wacky religious movement out in the sticks. And she's a natural for the kind of thing I want: 'Beautiful Russian blonde Lyuba Lebedeva, 29, today revealed to our reporter how she has turned away from the atheist and materialist doctrines of Communism to embrace a fuller spiritual life. Are there millions more like her in Russia? Turn to p. 24.' With a couple of photos it'll go like a bomb." He took my pawn with a snap.

"She's thirty-one," I said.

"No beautiful blonde is ever thirty-one in any story of mine. Look, all I want is for you to arrange me an interview with her. I'll do the rest." He took out a packet of extra-long Parliaments, offered me one, and lit one himself.

"If you know so much about her, why don't you get in touch with her directly? Why involve me?" I said. It was an interesting point, but not a substantial one: I was still playing for time.

"I know plenty about her; what I don't know is where to find her. And if I go to Leningrad and start tramping round apartment houses asking questions, pretty soon someone's going to smell a rat, and she'll vanish for good. On the other hand, I do know where to find you, and you know where to find her. It's your move, Vanya."

I brought out another pawn. "But why the hell should I help you? Have you thought what the consequences for her are likely to be? It's not just the church-going folks back in Wichita who are going to read your article, Mr. Bradley."

"Call me Martin," he said. "But be your age, Vanya. If the KGB have decided to bust her and her friends, it doesn't matter a damn what I do. But you know as well as I do that they're pretty cagey nowadays about touching people who've had a big build-up in the Western press. It's the unknown ones who get carted off to Siberia. And I guarantee you to give her the kind of treatment that'll make her look a better investment than Joan of Arc. She'll be big news by the time I've finished with her; there'll be a crowd of Western reporters beating a path to her door, and if she's not there when they call, they'll want to know the reason why." He leant back in his chair and gave me a hard brown stare. "But if you don't play ball with me, Vanya, I'll still write the article. Sure, without an interview it won't have the same bazass, but what the hell. More important for you, it'll be a darn sight less sympathetic—I may even get her age right for a start—and by the time I've finished with her the great American public won't care if she's hanged, drawn and quartered in the middle of Red Square."

He turned back to the table and moved up a second pawn to threaten my bishop.

I sat there for a bit controlling my temper. Then I said: "Look. I've got to think about this. And I can't decide anything by myself. I've got to talk to Lyuba about it and see what she thinks. Maybe she'll refuse to see you anyway."

"Sure, Vanya, sure." He got to his feet. "You take your time about it. When you're through, give me a ring. The number's on the card. But you'd better persuade your friend to see me, because I'm going back to the office now to write that other article." He held out his hand.

Before taking it I said: "Just as a matter of curiosity,
Martin, how did you dig up all this about Lyuba and my
connection with her?"

He laughed. "Things seem to be well buttoned-up in
this town, but underneath it's no different from anywhere
else. State secrets I can't guarantee, but the way I've got it
set up I can find out pretty much what I want to know
about most things in a day or two."

"But not Lyuba's age, address or telephone number," I
said.

His eyes flickered. "Well, I don't claim a hundred per
cent success rate." He laughed again. "Don't take too
long to make up your mind, Vanya." He turned and
walked away up the boulevard.

I sat on at the table thinking about the conversation.
There'd been something slightly unconvincing about Bradley, almost as if he'd modelled himself on some classic
film portrayal of a hard-bitten journalist. But perhaps all
American reporters were like that. I didn't take too seriously the belief that every Western newspaperman was
also a Western intelligence agent. And even if this were
true of Bradley, I couldn't see how his interest in Lyuba
could be anything other than journalistic. But it did pose a
problem.

It seemed unlikely that Lyuba would agree to meet him,
whatever the consequences might be. Perhaps something
would happen to divert his attention: another space shot
launched from Baykonur, another nest of hidden micro-
phones discovered in the American Embassy. But I had the
irrational feeling that nothing short of a counter-revolution
followed by the coronation of a surviving Romanov in St.
Basil's would put him off her story.

One possibility, of course, would be to tell Alik about
Bradley. I didn't imagine the organs would have much
difficulty in finding an excuse for expelling him from the
Union—dealing in currency on the black market, photo-

graphing military installations, receiving seditious *samizdat*
literature, travelling on a bus without a ticket—it would be
easy enough to frame him for any or all of them.

But he could damn Lyuba just as successfully from the
States, whereas, if he weren't expelled, and did come up
with something which gained her sympathy in the West,
this might possibly help her if Alik couldn't—or wouldn't—
keep his promise to me. On the whole it seemed best to do
nothing for the moment.

I shivered; the sun had gone in and it had grown notice-
ably colder. The man in the blue raincoat, a glutton for
punishment, had finished *Izvestiya* and begun on *Pravda*. I
moved my bishop out of danger for the last time, got up,
and walked slowly back towards the flat.

7

Nothing happened during the rest of that day. I worked a little, and in the evening watched a football match on television. Neither team looked capable of raising waves on a bowl of borsht. I sneered at them for a while and then went out and rang up Tanya.

She sounded annoyed, as though I'd disturbed her at something important. When I told her I was going to Leningrad there was a long silence.

At last she said: "Look after yourself," and hung up.

From Moscow the railway line to Leningrad runs north-west, almost dead straight. There's one noticeable kink in it, however: the story goes that when the engineers went to see the emperor to ask him where the line should run, he took a ruler from his desk and drew a straight line on the map. "Build it like this," he said. But the imperial thumb overlapped the edge of the ruler, forcing the pencil to detour round it. As does the railway.

The train was very full and far too hot. I dozed off soon

after passing Kalinin, and slept uneasily for some hours.
When I woke up I felt stiff and cramped. I went out into
the vestibule and bought a glass of tea from the conduc-
tress. Outside the sky was gradually lightening, and the
marshy northern plain, strewn with patches of ice and
snow, looked as bleak as my future.

Leningrad was cold, grey and foggy. I took a bus down
the Nevsky and got off by the old General Staff building,
under the notice that still warns citizens that the right-hand
side of the street is exposed to German bombardment. The
Astoria was five minutes away, down Gogol Street towards
St. Isaac's.

After a bath and a shave I came downstairs to look for
some breakfast. I was crossing the hall towards the restaurant when someone called my name. I turned round and
saw Nicola Booth, got up this time as Anna Karenina on
her way to the fatal rendezvous at the station.

"How fantastic! I was beginning to feel rather lost. I
don't know a soul in Leningrad. Do you mind if I come
and have a cup of coffee with you?"

I had no objection. As we sat down I asked her where
the rest of her delegation was.

"They all went back to England two days ago. I thought
I'd stay on and try and see a bit more. Some friends of
mine—actually friends of a friend—in the Embassy are
putting me up." She selected a piece of bread and nibbled
on it. "I'm spending a week here and then going back to
Moscow. But I think I prefer Leningrad. I like to think
about it as St. Petersburg. Much more romantic. I'm reading a simply marvellous book at the moment." She dug
into a large brown canvas bag decorated with a pattern of
gold monograms. "Do you know it?"

I took the book she offered and looked at the title page.
*Russia: St. Petersburg, Moscow, Kharkoff, Riga, Odessa,
the German Provinces on the Baltic, the Steppes, the*

Crimea and the Interior of the Empire. By J. G. Kohl.
London, 1842.

"And you accuse us of taking our knowledge of London
from Dickens."

She giggled. "It's not quite as bad as that. Reading it
here I can compare it with reality. And he does have some
marvellous passages."

A piece of paper marked her place. I opened the book
there, and began to read:

> Towards midnight the throng increases. In St.
> Petersburg the court appears in the imperial chapel
> in full dress; and in the provinces the governor,
> with all his adjutants and officers in their splen-
> did uniforms, attend the cathedral. The priests
> begin a mass which is but languidly performed
> or listened to, till all at once, at the hour of
> midnight, the whole scene changes. The golden
> door of the "Ikonostas" (the middle door of the
> pictorial wall that separates the Holy of Holies
> from the rest of the church) flies open, and the
> song bursts forth, "Christ is risen, Christ is risen
> from the dead!" At the same moment the illumi-
> nation of the church is completed, not only the
> lamps and great chandelier, but the countless
> tapers in the hands of the congregation, which
> have been held hitherto unlighted. The congrega-
> tion shake hands, and kiss all with whom they
> have the most distant acquaintance. "Christ is
> risen," says the saluting friend, and "Is he re-
> ally and truly risen?" answers the saluted. This
> last sentence appears to be literally that spoken
> two thousand years ago by the disciples hasten-
> ing to the empty tomb of Christ, and brings
> before our eyes in the liveliest manner, the won-
> der and excitement of the first Christians who

handed it down to us. The churches are illuminated without as well as within, and all the bells in the city ring out at once. In St. Petersburg many of the streets and public buildings are illuminated; rocket after rocket rushes along the sky, and the cannon boom at intervals, amidst all the countless bells and voices echoing each other from all sides of the broad Neva.

Amid all this tumult, a procession, headed by the priests, all bearing tapers and torches, passes round the church, and then the last ceremony, the blessing of the food, takes place about three o'clock in the morning.

"What are you reading about?"

"An old-fashioned Easter."

"There's a nice passage just there where he works out the number of kisses exchanged at Easter time." She took the book back, turned a page, and read: " 'If we suppose that every person in St. Petersburg has, upon a very moderate average, a hundred acquaintances more or less intimate, that calculation will give for St. Petersburg alone, with its half million inhabitants, a sum total of fifty million Easter embraces.' A hundred acquaintances seems rather a lot. I don't think I know more than twenty I'd like to kiss." She put the book down. "I do find it all terribly fascinating. I know things aren't at all like that now, but do you think I could possibly get to an Easter service somewhere?"

"If you're in Moscow at the right time, you could try the old believers' church at the Rogozhskoe cemetery. It's a working church, so there should be a service, but I don't know what the kissing's like."

She made a face at me and took a diary and pencil out of her bag. "What was the name?"

I repeated it, and then a thought struck me. "Do you know when Easter is?"

"Of course. It's in my diary. Here we are: Easter Sunday is April the second. I'll be back in Moscow then."

"But Orthodox Easter might not be on the same day."

"What? Oh, you mean because of the difference between old style and new style dates. There's thirteen days between them, isn't there. So today is the sixteenth new style and the twenty-ninth old style."

"No, the other way round. Old style it's the third. When they moved from the old Julian calendar to the new Gregorian one they jumped on a number of days, not back. This alters the date of Christmas—Orthodox Christmas Day is the seventh of January—but it doesn't affect Easter, because that's a moveable feast."

"Well, when is Orthodox Easter?"

"It's calculated in exactly the same way as your Easter. It's the first Sunday after the first full moon after the vernal equinox."

"You're amazingly knowledgeable. Are you sure you're not a plain-clothes priest?"

I smiled. I wasn't going to tell her that my knowledge was less than a week old. I went on. "There are two differences, though. The vernal equinox is always taken as the twenty-first of March, whatever the correct astronomical date might be. And Easter Sunday has to come after the Jewish Passover."

"Sounds reasonable. Start calculating."

I picked up the diary and opened it. "There's a new moon tomorrow. The vernal equinox is on Tuesday. And the full moon after that is—" I flipped through the pages— "Saturday the first of April. So Easter Sunday is as you said on the second. And Orthodox Easter could be on the same day. But now we're stuck. I don't know when Passover is."

She reached for the diary. "I think I saw something. Yes, here we are. Passover begins on the second, too."

"So Orthodox Easter Sunday must be the week after, the ninth."

"Bang on the button."

"What do you mean?"

She held the open diary out to me. There, under the heading "Other Religious Dates," together with Passover, the Jewish New Year, the Day of Atonement, the Islamic New Year and Ramadan, was: "Eastern Orthodox Easter—9 April."

I looked at her and we both began to laugh.

Later, when I got up to go, she put out a hand to detain me. "Are you going to be here long?"

"I'm not sure. A few days."

"Could I ask an immense favour? If you have any spare time, could you possibly bear to show me something of Leningrad? Do say yes."

I hesitated. The prospect wasn't appealing. On the other hand the authorities were unlikely to give me a black mark for escorting a respectable foreign author round the town, and it might be a useful screen for other activities. I compromised. "I'll be working in the library most of the time, but we might find an hour or two."

She gave me a brilliant smile. "I'll look forward to it."

As I went up in the lift, I took with me the unexpected discovery that Miss Booth could look extremely attractive when she wanted a favour done.

By early afternoon the fog had lifted. As the tram crossed the Palace Bridge on the way to Vasilevsky Island I looked back across the ruffled surface of the Neva to the white and gold of the Admiralty with its spire brilliant against the sky.

The address I'd been given for Lyuba was down at the western end of the island. I found it easily enough: a tall, grey, ugly, utilitarian block of flats. The cement rendering was flaking off, the concrete steps at the entrance were cracked and uneven, one of the glass panels in the door was missing, and an old out-of-order notice hung on the rusty knob of the lift.

I walked quickly up to the fifth floor and leant against the wall to get my breath. I was shaking with a mixture of excitement and apprehension. I'd acted through countless possible variations of our meeting over the last few days, but none of them had seemed at all real. I had absolutely no idea how Lyuba would react when she saw me: the scene would have to be played cold, without rehearsal.

I rang the bell and waited. The door opened.

"Lyuba—" I began, and then stopped. However much she might have changed, no transmogrification could have made her into the man facing me in the doorway.

"What do you want?" He was small and thin, with black hair growing low on his forehead and several days' growth of stubble. He was wearing a high-collared shirt, a dirty blue jacket and his trousers were tucked into high black leather boots.

"Excuse me," I said, "but do you live here?"

He giggled unexpectedly. "Yes, we, as you might say, are living here at the moment."

I was puzzled. Perhaps I'd got the wrong block of flats, but I'd checked the address carefully before coming in. "I'm sorry, I must have made a mistake . . . I was looking for someone I used to know. I thought she lived here."

There was a shout from the room behind him. "Who is it, Timosha?"

"A citizen is looking for . . . a girl he used to know," he said slowly without turning away from me.

"Bring him in."

"Come in, come in, citizen. Please come in," retreating in front of me, half-bowing as he went.

I hesitated, and then followed him into the flat. He stank of onions.

The room was bare and empty. In one corner lay a heap

of padded workmen's jackets. The only furniture was a table with four chairs round it; the one nearest to me had been pushed back, obviously by Timosha when he opened the door. The man on the left, with long shaggy red hair, sitting with his face propped on his hands, turned to look at me through his fingers, but I hardly noticed him as the huge figure on the far side of the table rose to its feet and presented itself in a bass rumble.

"Peredonov, Mikhail Evstafevich."

"Morozov," I said automatically. He must have been nearly two metres tall, and broad in proportion, with an immense chest and stomach. His shirt, high-collared like Timosha's, was embroidered with red at the neck and wrists. The front hung open, and his skin shone with sweat.

"And by name and by father? We simple people . . ."

"Ivan Vasilevich."

"So. Sit down, sit down, Ivan Vasilich, and partake of our bread and salt." He waved a majestic hand over the table, indicating four bottles of vodka—two empty, one nearly so and one full—a heap of black bread, some pickled cucumbers, onions, and two open tins of salt herring.

"No, thank you, I only wanted—"

But he'd already splashed vodka into a glass and handed it to me. He filled his own glass, clinked it with mine, and drank it off. Then he picked up a piece of bread, held it to his nose, and inhaled luxuriously.

"And so you're looking for a girl, Ivan Vasilich?"

Timosha giggled from just behind my right shoulder. I twisted round to look at him. He moved slowly away and leant against the wall. I turned back to Peredonov.

"Yes. I knew her some time ago, when I was in Leningrad, and I thought I'd try and look her up again."

"Naturally. A close acquaintance perhaps?" He smiled knowingly across at me.

"Perhaps," I said.

He put his hand on his heart. "I beg your pardon. Such a question is indelicate. As you see, I'm a little . . . No offence, I hope, Ivan Vasilich."

"None at all." I started to get up. "They gave me this address, but it must be wrong."

"Sit down, sit down, Ivan Vasilich." He leant across and put a hand as big as an elephant's foot on my arm. "May I ask the name of the lady?"

There seemed no harm in telling him. "Lebedeva, Lyubov Dmitrievna," I said. "She's blonde, medium height."

"Lyubov Dmitrievna Lebedeva," he repeated, dragging out the syllables. "A pretty name for a pretty girl."

"You know her?"

"Of course. She lived here before we moved in."

So the address had been right. I sat forward and said eagerly: "Do you know where she went?"

"In a manner of speaking, no. But drink, Ivan Vasilich!"

I poured the vodka down without thinking and coughed. He filled our glasses again.

"She hasn't left Piter—we saw her not long ago. Drink, Ivan Vasilich! This isn't Moscow vodka, you know."

I noticed without paying much attention his use of the old colloquialism for St. Petersburg. "Where was she?"

"Hopping about like a little sparrow. Carrying dishes, serving wine . . . She wouldn't speak to us, but we recognised her." He winked.

"Where was it? In a restaurant? Do you remember which?"

"Patience, patience, Ivan Vasilich! Drink!" He picked out a piece of herring on a fork and ate it delicately. "Was it on the Vyborg side? . . . The Petrograd side? . . . The islands? . . . Valerik, do you remember?"

The third man hadn't moved or spoken since I'd come in; now he just muttered an obscenity through his fingers.

Peredonov hushed him as one would a dog, and turned

back to me. "You must excuse him, Ivan Vasilich. The dark, uncultured masses . . ."

I had the feeling he was laughing at me. I said nothing and waited.

He quickly grew tired of the game. "It seems to me it was not far from here. Just round the corner in fact. What's it called? Some bird or other. Timosha?"

Timosha, not to my surprise, only giggled. I remembered I'd noticed a restaurant just before getting off the tram. I tried to visualise it. An entrance up some steps; a long line of wide windows curtained with gauze, and over them an unlit neon sign in flowing script. A moment later it came to me.

"The Seagull—is that it?"

Peredonov gave me a strange look; Timosha giggled again. "The Seagull? Perhaps . . . No, I think you're right. Strange, I thought for a moment it was called something else . . ."

I didn't really listen to what he was saying; I was too eager to get over to the restaurant and see if Lyuba was still working there. I drank my glass of vodka, thanked him and turned to go. Then a thought struck me. "If you do see her, would you ask her to give me a ring? I'm staying at the Astoria."

"Of course, Ivan Vasilich, of course. At the Astoria. Of course."

Outside afternoon had already turned to evening. I walked the four hundred metres to the granite embankment and stood looking out over the dark waters of the Gulf of Finland. In front of me, moving away down the channel, were the navigation lights of a small vessel bound out towards Kronshtadt or Vyborg, and on my left the suburbs shone thinly away along the shore, coalescing in the far distance into the glow of Petrodvorets and Lomonosov.

It seemed odd that Lyuba should have taken a job as a waitress, and even odder that, if she had, Alik was unaware of it, since she would have re-entered the bureaucratic system. But she might of course be doing it on the side, illegally, and I could see no reason why Peredonov should have lied to me . . .

Then the revelation hit me, and I banged my hand on the stone of the parapet in annoyance at my stupidity. I'd been so slow. The thought of seeing Lyuba again had blinkered me to the peculiarity of finding three peasants camping out in her old flat. And they were peasants— Peredonov's turns of phrase told me that. A sentence from Bykov's statement, referring to the leader of the gang which had stoned him, swam into my memory: "I think he is called Valery." Peredonov had addressed his silent, red-haired companion as Valerik, the diminutive of Valery. The name was a rare one, and the coincidences, taken together, were too many. Of course, the three of them were members of the sect. They knew Lyuba, and Peredonov had obviously sent me off on a false trail.

I began to walk hurriedly back towards the block of flats. I had just come to the edge of a piece of waste ground when I heard light, hurried footsteps approaching from behind. I looked back and saw Timosha trotting towards me. He was holding something which glinted as the light from the streetlamp caught it. I began to run. I'd gone some twenty metres when someone stepped out of the shadow of the building in front of me.

"You looking for us, Ivan Vasilich?"

He hit me with immense force in the stomach. I doubled up, retching. He hit me again, on the side of the head. I staggered sideways, tripped over and fell down. I heard a hoarse whisper behind me. "Hit him, hit him, the fornicator!" I was kicked very hard several times. A boot caught me on the shoulder and then on the head.

I was dimly aware that someone was squatting by me. He bent over and the stink of onions told me it was Timosha. "The knife, the knife. A lamb for the knife!"

"No. Valerik, get the car."

I felt dazed and unable to move. Figures came and went, and I heard a car draw up at the curb. Liquid dribbled out of a container. I smelt petrol.

I tried to crawl away. My left arm was numb and useless. There was the scrape of a match on a match-box and then, seconds later, something flaming arched towards me. I half-fell, half-threw myself into a shallow gully full of snow and rolled in it, beating at the flames frantically with my right hand.

Some time later I pulled myself up to my knees and was immediately and violently sick. I began to shiver uncontrollably. I crawled over to the building and propped myself against it. It was comfortably solid, and warm air was coming out of a central heating duct at ground level. After a while I stopped shivering. Sensation had returned to my left arm, but the shoulder was intensely painful. My face was bruised and cut, and a lump had formed on my temple. My right hand was burnt and my coat was ruined.

I cleaned myself up as well as I could and walked slowly down the street. A tram was standing at the terminus. I got on to the rear car, took a ticket from the machine, huddled down in a corner and went to sleep.

The bang and rattle as we moved off woke me. Luckily there weren't many passengers. I got a few odd glances: there are plenty of battered drunks wandering around Leningrad every night, but not many carry with them a powerful aroma of burnt cloth.

I was in my bathroom back at the hotel when I heard the bedroom door bang.

"Mr. Morozov, are you there? It's Nicola Booth. I knocked, but you didn't answer, and since the door was open and I could hear water running I— My God, what have you been doing? I thought you were going to read books, not fight over them."

I opened my mouth for a witty reply but nothing came
out. I sat down heavily on the bed.

"Jesus, I'm sorry. You are in a state. But you ought to
do something about it. I've got some stuff in my room.
Hang on, I'll only be a moment."

She came back with a box containing a small field
hospital and began to swab my face and hand with disinfectant. Her ministrations were gentle and surprisingly
skillful. After she'd finished I felt a lot better. I asked her
whether she'd ever been a nurse.

"No, not really, but I worked in a hospital for a time,
when I was thinking of using one as the setting for a
novel."

"Tall dark handsome surgeon—blue eyes meet brown in
the operating theatre—two hearts beat as one over the
cardiac arrest machine?"

"I know you've never heard of my books, and I don't
pretend they're great literature, but I like to think they're a
bit better than that kind of thing."

"I'm sure they are. I'd like to read them."

"I might just send you a couple when I get back to
England." She paused with her hand on the door knob. "I
dropped in on you originally because I've got two tickets
for *Khovanshchina* tomorrow. I remembered you're a
Musorgsky fan, and thought you might like to go. But
perhaps you won't feel up to it."

I said I thought I'd be walking again by then. Something was worrying me, but it was only after she'd left that
I could put my finger on it. We'd certainly talked about
the opera when we'd met in Moscow, but I couldn't
remember mentioning Musorgsky, let alone putting myself
forward as an admirer of his. Perhaps she was conflating
two different conversations.

I got the hotel operator to put a call through to Moscow.
Alik was still at his desk, but as soon as I spoke he cut me

short and told me he'd ring back. While I was waiting I thought about my three friends from the country.

They couldn't have taken me for a policeman: I hadn't produced any documents, hadn't questioned them in the right manner. They must have come to a conclusion not far from the truth—that I was an annoyingly intrusive character from Lyuba's past, and as a result they'd taken steps to warn me away from her present.

I wasn't going to tell Alik about them. It would hardly be a good idea to re-introduce myself to Lyuba by betraying her friends to the KGB.

The phone rang and I picked it up. Alik sounded strangely out-of-breath. Perhaps he'd been running errands for his boss. I told him that Lyuba had vanished, and asked him what I was supposed to do next. There was a long silence. Then he said:

"I don't think she's left Leningrad. I'll get some inquiries made. As soon as I learn anything I'll let you know." He paused. "Things are getting rather urgent, Vanya. If you want to help her, you may have to find her before someone else does."

"What do you mean, Alik? How the hell am I going to do that? There are five hundred square kilometres of Leningrad, with three million people living in them."

"Well, you'll have a lot of walking to do, won't you?" He hung up.

8

I was running along a narrow street between tall buildings; the streetlamps swayed down and pecked at me as I passed; through a window I saw into a lighted room, where Nicola was reading aloud to Alik, who lay in bed clutching two dolls dressed alike in dark overcoats and grey hats.

I was climbing up a circular stone staircase; behind me came Peredonov with a bird's head and Timosha's knife in his hand. The staircase changed into the steep slope of a forest; the pine needles and sand slid away under my feet as I tried desperately to clamber higher; I caught a root above my head and pulled myself up to see over the top; beyond, ridge upon ridge of burning candles stretched away into the distance. I felt myself letting go and fell back into a sea of flame.

I awoke soaked in sweat and lay for some time staring into the darkness and listening to the clanking of the old-fashioned radiators. It was on a pipe of the central heating system in this hotel that the poet Esenin had hanged himself late in December 1925.

In the morning I was stiff and sore, but at the same time curiously elated. I'd always despised that kind of fiction in which the resilient hero, after each reverse and physical battering, bounces elastically back more energetic than before. But I couldn't deny there was a certain similarity with my own experience. I felt more alive physically. The sun was shining. My omelette and coffee tasted marvellous. It was as if the previous night had burnt off one layer of the skin that separated me from the outside world.

It would be idle to pretend that I wasn't frightened at the thought of going up against Peredonov and his friends again, but I was determined to carry on. Former abstract considerations, in becoming real, had somehow strengthened my motivation. And the thought of danger even added a prickle of excitement, like the bubbles in champagne, or the ripples of the Neva sparkling now in the sun. But the first problem was to find Lyuba.

The Seagull restaurant had just opened when I arrived. Its big light dining-room with large windows looking out over the Bolshoy Prospect was empty, apart from a gaggle of waitresses sitting round a table in the corner, waiting for the first customers. Lyuba wasn't among them, and none of them knew her, or could remember having seen her. The restaurant administrator took a moment off from his accounts and abacus to tell me that the only Lebedeva he'd ever employed had been called Marfa Gavrilovna; she'd been engaged on supernumerary duties in the kitchen; had been sixty-five years old and had died some six months ago. He showed me her card.

I found the caretaker of the block of flats where Lyuba had lived in the basement morosely inspecting the mechanism of the lift. He was a small, shrunken man, as worse for wear as the building itself, with an empty sleeve pinned to the breast of his padded jacket and a mouth full of steel teeth. He was surly and uncommunicative at first, but after I'd convinced him that I wasn't an official of any description, and showed him a ten rouble note, he admitted that Lyuba had lived there for some time.

"With the tenant's permission," he kept repeating. "I wouldn't have allowed it, only she had the tenant's permission, in writing."

"Who is the tenant?"

"Staroverov, Father Zakhar. A fucking priest." He spat neatly into the lift shaft.

"And when did you see Comrade Lebedeva last?"

He shrugged his shoulders. "Who knows? Two, three days ago."

He denied knowledge of Peredonov and the others, and, grumbling, accompanied me up to the fifth floor. The apartment door was unlocked. Apart from the furniture I'd seen the previous night, the place was completely empty. There was a pile of rubbish in one corner. I looked through it, but there was nothing of significance, apart from a lot of empty vodka bottles. I left the caretaker standing in the middle of the room, looking about him with an avid gleam in his eyes—he'd be able to make a small killing by selling the information that there was an unoccupied apartment in the block.

I took the same tram as the night before, and, as it ground slowly along the embankment towards the centre, began to wonder what to do next.

Staroverov must be the mysterious Father Z. of Lyuba's letter. She'd used his flat as a refuge for a time. Then, for some reason—perhaps Peredonov had warned her of danger—she'd moved elsewhere. But where?

I thought of what I knew about her: her way of thought, her attitudes, her habits. They were more familiar to me than to anyone else. There was one thing of which I was certain. If she was in Leningrad, she would not remain indoors all the time. She had a passionate love for the city;

as another girl might have needed constant physical contact with her lover, so she needed a daily communion with the granite of its embankments, the stucco and stone of its buildings. And I knew, only too well, her favourite places: the Summer Garden, the Mikhaylovsky Garden, the Griboedov canal, Pushkin's house, the Church of the Resurrection, for example—all grouped together in a small area of the centre. If I were to wander around them, there was a faint chance—one in a million, one in ten million— that we might meet.

I left a note for Nicola at the hotel desk, telling her that I'd meet her at the opera, and set out. I was re-enacting, I realised, an episode from the past—at the beginning of our affair I'd once called to see Lyuba, been told she was out, and had gone off in search of her. Then the baseless optimism engendered by love had convinced me that she was bound to be round the next corner, sitting on the next bench in the gardens; now reason told me that the activity was pointless.

Khovanshchina is not my favourite among Musorgsky's operas. I prefer *Boris Godunov*. Although the composer spent years on historical research for the work, it always seems to me that the subject of *Khovanshchina* is not Russian history, but something much more vague and insubstantial: the nature of Russia itself. It is an immense tone poem, beginning as dawn breaks over the Moscow river, and ending at night, in the dark and brooding Russian forest.

I said as much to Nicola, as we joined the circle of couples perambulating slowly round the lobby during one of the intervals. She didn't pay much attention to my critical insight. She was frowning over her programme.

"This is the first time I've seen it, and I've not the slightest idea what's going on. Why is it so fearfully confused? Surely someone could have done a better libretto.''

Her face took on an abstracted look for a moment: she was re-writing the story, presenting the result to the composer in the company of Balakirev, Borodin and Rimsky-Korsakov, and being acclaimed as the greatest inspiration to a musician since George Sand. I didn't spoil the moment by reminding her that Musorgsky had been an alcoholic epileptic. We went back to our seats for the fourth act.

Prince Ivan Khovansky, at table in his richly furnished mansion outside Moscow, is being entertained by serf singing girls. To him enters a messenger bearing a warning from Prince Golitsyn: his life is in danger. Khovansky rejects the warning contemptuously, orders the messenger to be whipped, and calls for his Persian slaves to dance before him. The boyar Shaklovity brings a message from the Regent Sophia, summoning him to her presence; as he leaves he is struck down by murderers in the doorway. Standing in triumph over his corpse, Shaklovity ironically repeats a line from the aria just sung in Khovansky's honour by the serf girls: "Slava belomu lebedyu," "Glory to the white swan."

The curtain came down and the applause began. Surely it couldn't be just a coincidence. I had been right and Alik wrong. The phrase was a reference back to the world of art; it did, obviously, have a symbolic meaning. I hugged the knowledge to myself with satisfaction.

The curtain went up for the last act. Peter has overthrown his half-sister, the regent, and ascended the throne. Golitsyn, Sophia's lover, is exiled; the *streltsy*, led out to execution, are pardoned at the last moment; finally, as the trumpets of the young tsar's troops sound in the distance, Dosifey, the priest of the old believers, leads his flock on to the pyre. "We will purify ourselves through fire and flame," they sing as they perish.

We walked back to the hotel in a companionable silence. I was so grateful to Nicola for taking me to the opera and solving, if unknowingly, one riddle, that I agreed without hesitation when, before going up to her room, she asked me again to show her Leningrad.

Music was drifting out of the bar on the mezzanine. It was dimly lit, with little orange-shaded lamps on the tables. The barman was polishing glasses and benignly watching the efforts of a girl with dyed blonde hair and high patent leather boots to close a deal with a drunken German businessman. He didn't bother to put his cloth down when I came up to the bar.

"We don't take roubles, citizen. Only foreign currency."

Someone materialised beside me. "Two large whiskies, boy, and hurry them up." He turned and grinned at me. "Good to see you again, Vanya. Grab your drink and come over here."

Bradley had done a good deal of drinking already that evening. The jacket of his dark suit was flung carelessly over a chair; his tie had been pulled down and the top button of his shirt undone. There was a sheen of perspiration on his face, but his brown, boot-button eyes were as watchful as before, and there was nothing slack in the set of his mouth. He looked at me closely as I sat down.

"Been taking on your weight in wildcats, have you?"

I opened my mouth to reply, but he didn't wait for an answer.

"Never mind that. Let's keep to business. When's the interview arranged for?"

"It isn't. I haven't seen her yet."

He leant forward and prodded a hard forefinger at me. "Listen, Vanya. I was serious back there in Moscow. Just don't mess me about. I need that interview, and I need it soon."

I was beginning to get angry. "What's so flaming special about this story? There must be a thousand others just as good, if you had the energy to get off your ass and go and look for them.''

''So all right, all right.'' He made a pacifying gesture with his hands. ''I've got personal reasons, which needn't concern you. Let's just say they get more pressing all the time. So hurry it along, would you. There's nothing else you can do. I've got you in a bind, and you know it. You might as well lie back and take it easy.'' He looked at me thoughtfully, and then leant forward again and put his mouth close to my ear. ''Listen. If it's a matter of—'' he rubbed fingers and thumb together unambiguously ''—I daresay I could spring something. Or in kind, of course.''

I shook my head. He shrugged his shoulders, leant back and lit a cigarette.

I was amazed. The idea crossed my mind that the whole thing might be a plant organised by the currency section, but a moment later I rejected it. The set-up was far too complicated for their simple, exchange-rate oriented minds. And Bradley, too, wasn't the kind of person they employed for the job. I'd seen them at work on foreigners in hotel lobbies often enough to recognise the type: thin, vaguely shifty, with a wandering eye and forefinger deeply stained with nicotine. In the capitalist West they'd be working on their own account selling tips at race meetings or pornographic postcards to tourists.

But the matter must be urgent if Bradley was willing to expose himself like this. However attractive the offer might be, it was too dangerous for me to accept, but no less dangerous for him to make. Another point struck me. I remembered Alik on the telephone, telling me that someone else was looking for Lyuba. The situation would be more than a little ironic if it turned out I was working simultaneously for both sides. Bradley interrupted my thoughts.

''You want another shot, Vanya?''

When he came back he slumped down in his chair and

frowned into his glass. Perhaps the alcohol was getting to him at last.

"I've been in some holes in my time, but this . . . You don't happen to know of a strip joint around here, do you? Or a poker game I could sit in on?"

If he'd asked me the same question some ten years ago, I could have helped him. A friend of mine had run a poker game from an apartment out on the Vyborg side. "The biggest game west of the Urals," he used to call it. He kept it going for a long time—he'd got connections of course—but in the end they got him for parasitism and a few other offences. Now he was presumably running the biggest game east of the Urals and taking the zeks for their bread ration.

I told Bradley the story. He was interested and gave me one of his own in exchange. In the end we stayed on until the bar closed some time in the early hours of the morning.

9

I bought a newspaper from the kiosk in the lobby on my way through to the restaurant. The world, or at least that part of it occupied by the Union of Soviet Socialist Republics, was a good place to live in that morning.

A catalytic cracker in the new chemical complex at Aktyubinsk had come on stream six months early. The production of pig-meat in the Saratov region had gone up by over two hundred per cent in the last year. Our gallant footballers had scored a resounding victory over the national team of the Republic of Upper Volta. Soviet scientists and engineers had begun to take the first steps towards the realisation of a long-cherished dream: making the Siberian rivers flow backwards to irrigate the arid deserts of Kazakhstan. Five and a half thousand flag-waving young Pioneers had spontaneously gathered to greet our leader and the Egyptian premier during their visit to the Ukraine.

Buried deep on the back page I found a selection of foreign items. Alcoholism in France had more than dou-

bled over the past decade. The number of traffic accidents
in West Germany was greater this year than ever before.
Unemployment in Great Britain had reached record levels.
The President of the United States had scraped through—
the reports hinted darkly at the methods employed—the
New Hampshire primary election.

We walked down to Decembrists' Square and the Bronze
Horseman. The day was clear, bright and cold, with a
stiffish westerly breeze that had turned the surface of the
Neva into slate-grey and white. Nicola was bright as
the weather, and full of questions. As we came through the
garden in front of the Admiralty building she returned to
the subject of the opera.

"Apart from anything else, I didn't understand the
background."

We parted to let a toddler in a bright blue boiler suit
carrying a ball rather bigger than his head pass between us.

"Can you tell me something about it, Vanya? The
religious side, especially?"

I was only too glad to. There was no point in allowing
the fruits of my research to ripen uselessly in my brain.

We passed through into Palace Square and I called her
attention to the Alexander Column, a single piece of red
Finnish granite, thirty metres high and four in diameter,
which had been raised to its present position in August
1832 by two thousand four hundred and ninety soldiers
hauling on blocks and tackles.

At the same time I exhorted her to be clear, first of all,
on the difference between old believers—schismatics—and
sectarians. The schismatics clung to the older traditions of
Orthodoxy; the sectarians, on the other hand, professed
new beliefs, often imported from the West. Ritual was
important to the schismatics, but disregarded by the sectarians. In general, the sectarians were millenarian, optimis-
tic; the schismatics pessimistic, apocalyptic. Yet the
distinctions, though fundamental, were in practice often

illusory. The scene was confused and contradictory; the two often influenced one another, even interacted or merged together on occasion.

We came up the bank of the Moyka on to the Nevsky. I pointed out the Kazan cathedral with its huge semi-circular colonnade. My exposition would not be assisted, I told Nicola severely, by visiting the museum of the history of religion and atheism inside.

In front of the low sprawling mass of the Gostiny Dvor department store I began to delve more deeply into the schism of 1654. I spoke of the reforms introduced into the church by Nikon, sixth patriarch of Russia; of the hostility aroused by his revisions of the sacred books; of the importance of making the sign of the cross with two, rather than three fingers; of the abomination of the double, as opposed to the triple alleluia.

Past the public library we turned down into Ostrovsky Square with the huge statue of Catherine the Great surrounded by famous men of her reign—Potemkin, Betsky, Rumyantsev, Suvorov and Derzhavin. I told Nicola something of the Archpriest Avvakum, Nikon's most famous opponent. Of his *Life*, and the miracles recounted in it. Of his exile in Siberia and his eventual death at the stake in 1682.

I gave her time to admire the two identical classical façades of Architect Rossi Street, washed in yellow ochre, with the columns picked out in white.

We came out on to the bank of the Fontanka and walked up towards Anichkov Bridge with its four bronze wild horses at the ends of the parapets. I dilated on the difference between the two main groups of old believers—the *popovtsy*, or *edinovertsy*, who accepted the ministry of priests, and the *bespopovtsy*, who rejected it. I touched, briefly, on other schismatic groups: the Theodosians, the Philipists, the wanderers, the runners.

We kept on along the quay, past the building of the

State Circus, past another equestrian statue of Peter, past the vast, gloomy Engineers' Palace, where the mad Emperor Paul was assassinated in 1801.

In the Summer Garden I left the schismatics, and called Nicola's attention to a selection of sects. The *khlysty,* the flagellants, for instance, who called themselves "God's people," since their founder Daniel Filippov, an army deserter, had proclaimed himself God Sabaoth on a hillside near Vyazma in 1645.

Then there were the spirit wrestlers, the *dukhobortsy,* who had appeared in the 1730s, had emigrated to Western Canada at the end of the nineteenth century and still flourished there; the *molokane,* the milk-drinkers, so-called because they would not give up milk during Lent; the spirit-bearers, the sabbatarians; and, most peculiar of all, the *skoptsy,* the self-castrators, founded by Selivanov, another deserter from the army, in the 1770s—his desire was to establish eventually the rule of the castrated throughout the world.

At the summer palace we turned left, along the embankment of the Neva and then left again at the Lenin museum. By now I'd almost finished, but I added a few more scattered details. I mentioned glossolalia, or speaking with tongues; the orgiastic rites indulged in by some sects; the extraordinary number of prophetic sectarians produced by the town of Tambov, so that it was popularly known as Tambog—for Nicola's benefit I added the translation: "God is there."

I led her down the narrow street that runs along the side of the Griboedov canal and stopped by the Church of the Resurrection.

I had never been able to understand why it was Lyuba's favourite church in Leningrad. Built in a bogus Old Russian style, as a bad imitation of St. Basil's in Moscow, it seemed to me clumsy, heavy, and tastelessly garish.

It was still being used, as it had been ever since I'd

known it, as a warehouse, and its condition had deteriorated over the last ten years. Everywhere the mortar was crumbling away; large chunks of mosaic had fallen off, and rusty bits of guttering hung down at useless angles from the roof. It obviously wasn't considered to be an architectural monument worthy of preservation.

One of the things that had most interested me about the schismatics and sectarians was the way in which, in the seventeenth, eighteenth, even the early nineteenth century, they'd constantly supported pretenders to the throne. Not through revolutionary idealism but from a fundamental and profound conservatism. Each pretender was for them the true tsar, ruler by divine right, come to overthrow the false usurper who had broken the natural line. Some claimed to be Dmitry, the young prince allegedly murdered by Boris Godunov; others put themselves forward as Alexis, son of Peter the Great, killed by his own father; while Tanya's hero Pugachev was for many of his followers a miraculously resurrected Peter III, earlier assassinated by the lovers of his wife, Catherine.

And, of course, I added, the fact that for the greater part of the eighteenth century Russia's rulers were women must have had some correlation with the extraordinary number of pretenders during that time. For the people wanted a paternal, old Muscovite tsar, earthy and peasant-like, combining the qualities of *batyushka* and *spasitel,* father and saviour. I refrained from making the obvious further point: that the people eventually did get their true, ideal tsar—but not until 1924.

By this time I thought Nicola might have had enough. We were standing in Arts' Square, under the statue of Pushkin. I took her down Brodsky Street and into the café of the Evropeyskaya. She sank down on the banquette with a sigh of relief.

"Thanks for the lecture, Vanya, and the guided tour.

But I should have worn hiking boots, not these damned shoes. Is there any chance of something to drink?''

I signalled to the waiter. I wasn't too happy myself. With Alik telling me that time was running out and Bradley harassing me from the other side, I needed a much better lead to Lyuba than anything I'd got. I came out of my meditation to find that Nicola was speaking to me.

''. . . think that any more sightseeing I do strictly from the back seat of an Intourist limousine. But just tell me some more places to visit.'' She'd got her notebook out and was looking at me expectantly.

''In Leningrad?''

''No, outside. After all, the limo's free.''

I dictated the names of Petrodvorets, Gatchina, Pushkin, Pavlovsk and Lomonosov to her, laying heavy emphasis on the charm of the surroundings, the magnificence of the architecture, the indescribable richness of the interiors.

''Great. Thanks, Vanya.'' She mused for a moment. ''I'd really like to visit a typical Russian village. Any ideas?''

If by a typical Russian village she meant a muddy street with a few wooden huts on either side, a ruined church, a single shop with nothing in it, and a drunken peasant or two, I could suggest some places she might try. But I didn't think her Intourist driver would take her to them, and I wouldn't be likely to be patted on the head for the recommendation. The health resorts dotted up the Karelian isthmus seemed a better bet.

''Get your driver to go out along the coast road on the north of the Finnish Gulf towards Zelenogorsk and Vyborg,'' I said. ''There are some pleasant places up there—Repino, Razliv, Lisy Nos, Lakhta—''

I stopped, struck dumb by a sudden thought. Nicola eyed me curiously.

''Are you all right? You looked like a stuck pig there for a moment.''

The waiter had finally torn himself with reluctance away from an interesting conversation with his colleague and made it across to our table. He was breathing heavily by the time he arrived. He had an unpleasantly puffy, yellow face which would have looked more natural on a slab in the morgue than here. But the way I'd begun to feel I would have been happy to see him even at a later stage of decomposition. I ordered a bottle of Soviet champagne and a pineapple.

"What's the pineapple for?"

"It's something we used to do as students."

When it came I cut it in two and gouged each half out to make a goblet. I handed one to Nicola and filled it with champagne.

"Well?"

"What a sophisticated daredevil you must have been in your youth."

10

The pneumatic doors rattled together behind me and the bus moved slowly off, grinding up through the gears to disappear round the corner on its way to Zelenogorsk. I stood in the middle of Lakhta's main street and looked about me curiously. It was the first time I'd visited the resort.

The centre had been rebuilt since the war. Most of the buildings were tall, slab-sided blocks of apartments or offices, with large plate-glass shop windows on the ground floor. Here and there was a lower, ornamental nineteenth century façade, and at the end of the street stood an even older single-storey building, whose squat white columns almost hid the pleasant pink stucco of its front. There were very few people about.

The glass front of the Northern café was cantilevered out over the promenade like the nose of some gigantic bomber about to take off for a raid on Helsinki. I collected a glass of coffee and a doughnut from the self-service counter and took them to a table in the window bay, looking out to sea. It was another cold, brilliant day.

Like some ballistic missile, triggered by the chance mention of a place name while I'd been talking to Nicola, the memory had come at me without warning, out of a clear sky: Lyuba packing a suitcase, refusing to tell me why; ignoring pleas and threats. Then, finally, worn out by resistance to jealousy, making me promise not to follow her, telling me that she was going to Lakhta. To rest, she'd said. She might even have talked of making a spiritual retreat. And yesterday afternoon, in the café, I'd suddenly known with absolute certainty that this was where she was now.

I didn't want to examine that belief too closely, for it was all I had to go by. Though if true it shortened the odds considerably, it still didn't make it a walk-over. Lakhta was no Leningrad, but it still covered a fair-sized area, with its holiday villas scattered along the coast, and clustering round the lake to the north. One of these more remote districts might be the most likely place in which to find her.

I walked down the main street, and then up it again on the opposite side, peering into the shops as I passed. After I'd established that Lyuba wasn't buying a jar of pickled cucumbers, a history of the Communist Party of the Soviet Union, or a new fur hat, I began to make a series of wider casts.

Some five hours later I was leaning wearily against the wall of a shed by the railway halt east of town, cleaning the mud from my shoes. I'd been down innumerable dirty tracks, seen an infinity of villas, ranging from decrepit wooden huts with sway-backed, moss-covered roofs to trim brick erections with television aerials and newly-painted white fences. I'd interrogated countless old women, only slightly fewer younger ones, a primary school of children, nine postmen, and a war veteran who'd taken an embarrassing interest in my search, limping by my side for half a kilometre, and offering me a number of tactical suggestions, apparently based on his experience of house-to-house fighting in Stalingrad. By now, I felt, the whole of Lakhta was ringing with news of my activities. But I hadn't come across any trace of Lyuba, and the exhilaration I'd felt the day before had gradually seeped away.

A suburban electric train slid slowly past and stopped. I watched idly as a few passengers climbed down on to the side of the track, and then ducked back hurriedly behind the shed. Even when topped by a fur cap, Valery's shaggy red hair was unmistakable.

I scuttled round to the back of the shed and poked my head cautiously round the far side. For a moment I thought that he'd vanished, and then I saw him walking away down the road to the east, back towards Leningrad.

The road and railway ran together straight down the coast for a couple of kilometres. Apart from Valery, the road was empty in that direction, and neither it nor the railway offered a scrap of cover. Beyond the road, however, and between it and the sea, was a thin belt of scrub and trees. I looked out again. Valery was two hundred metres away walking briskly. The few other passengers were moving more slowly off in the opposite direction, towards Lakhta.

I ran across the road, fell into the ditch on the far side, wormed up the opposite bank, and put a bush between Valery and myself. He didn't seem to have noticed anything. I went a little deeper into the trees and, crouching low, began to move along parallel to the road.

The going was easier than I'd expected. I hurried on over the hard-packed sand, covered with pine needles, and soon heard the sound of Valery's nailed boots on the tarmac. I slowed down and kept pace with him, some fifty metres behind.

We went on in this way for about five minutes when the

sound of his steps suddenly stopped. I dropped to my
stomach and crawled nearer to the road. Valery was standing still, looking back the way he had come. Apparently
satisfied, he turned off to his right, down a path leading
towards the sea. I heard him crossing in front of me, and
followed cautiously. The land sloped down gradually from
the road to the beach, but when I reached the edge of the
scrub I found that a line of high sand-dunes cut off a view
of the sea. Valery was scrambling up their side. A moment
later he vanished over the top. I gave him a couple of
minutes and then went up on my hands and knees.

In front of me was the broad, smooth white beach,
stretching away on either hand. The light was beginning to
fade, but far away, right down at the water's edge, I could
see a thin black figure looking out over the gulf. The
distance between us was too great to make recognition
possible; nevertheless, I knew at once that it was Lyuba.

Half-way between us, sitting on a rock or a lump of
driftwood with his back towards me, was Peredonov. As I
watched, Valery reached him, squatted down by his side,
and began to talk to him. After a short conversation
Peredonov rose to his feet, stretched, and turned to look
inland.

I hurriedly withdrew my head. When I looked again
Peredonov was striding towards the dunes, while Valery
was going in the opposite direction, towards Lyuba. I slid
down the side of the sandhill and took refuge among the
trees again.

Peredonov passed, and I went quickly back to my observation post, only to return almost immediately to the shelter
of the trees. Lyuba and Valery were coming towards me.
Soon I heard them, too, moving through the wood, and
even thought that I caught a glimpse of Lyuba between the
trees. I followed.

When I got to the edge of the wood I stopped. They'd
gone over the road and the railway line and were heading

towards the forest some four hundred metres beyond. I crossed the road in my turn and waited under the shoulder of the embankment until they had entered the trees. Two minutes later I was standing under the eaves of the forest on a well-defined path which led on to the north.

It wound through the trees for some way, and then joined a ride, which ran across at a diagonal to it. I hesitated for a moment on the edge of the open space, and then saw Lyuba and Valery walking down the opposite side.

I was about to parallel their movement on my side of the clearing when I heard something move behind me. I half-turned, but at that moment an arm came round my neck and dragged me backwards. I reached up with both hands, caught something, and heaved. I might just as well have tried to lift a bulldozer. The grip tightened and something hit me shatteringly hard in the small of the back. I cried out. The next moment I was lying on the ground. A knee came down on my stomach. I curled up in agony.

Peredonov squatted beside me, took hold of the front of my coat, and pulled me up to face him.

"I didn't expect to see you in these parts, Ivan Vasilich."

I couldn't reply. He let go of me and I fell back. He ruminated on.

"When we met I saw at once that you were an *intelligent*, a man with a higher education. I was glad, because I thought I'd learn a thing or two from you. We simple people don't often hear an edifying, enlightening word. But you've disappointed me, Ivan Vasilich, disappointed me deeply." He sighed and leant back. Then he bent over me again. "They say that to a wise man one need speak only once. But in your case, as it turns out, the proverb is false. You have done me a great wrong, Ivan Vasilich, a great wrong. Because of you I must take a terrible sin on myself."

I didn't ask what commandment he contemplated violating: I was too scared that he might tell me.

Lyuba's face suddenly appeared over his shoulder.

"Misha! What are you doing?" Then she saw me. "Vanya!"

There was certainly surprise in her voice, but not, as far as I could judge, any overwhelming joy.

"Let him up, Misha."

Peredonov moved back and I struggled to my feet.

"I've got to talk to you, Lyuba. It's terribly important."

She moved back a step, and held out her hand, as if to ward me off.

"Lyuba is dead, Vanya, and the things of this world are no longer important to her. Go home, Vanya, go home and forget us."

"Lyuba, you must listen to me."

"Go home, Vanya."

She turned away, and Peredonov began to move threateningly towards me. I tried a last, despairing throw.

"For the sake of the white swan, listen to me!"

Lyuba stopped suddenly. Peredonov stood motionless, staring at me. There was a long silence. Then she spoke. "So be it. Come, Vanya."

A moment later, as I followed her back across the ride, reaction set in. I felt suddenly giddy and nearly fell. My teeth chattered. Blood thumped loudly and rapidly in my ears. I found I was muttering to myself. Then something struck me as funny and I chuckled loudly. Lyuba glanced round in surprise, and from behind Peredonov gave an admonitory growl.

It had grown dark, and when, a little later, we turned into the forest again, I continually stumbled over stones and roots, or was caught by trailing branches. To judge by the sounds coming from behind, Peredonov and Valery were experiencing the same difficulties, but in front Lyuba

floated on lightly, guided either by instinct or a sure
knowledge of the path.

We came out on a track that ran along the edge of a
deep, narrow ravine. Here we turned downhill; the going
became easier, and soon I could see lights in the distance.
For some time we went on in silence. Then Lyuba stopped,
and, motioning me to wait, walked back to join the others.
I heard an indistinct murmur of conversation. In a few
moments she came back and led me off to the left for a
couple of hundred metres to a low wooden villa which
crouched under the shelter of the pines.

I stumbled up a couple of steps to the porch, followed
her in through the two doors, and found myself in a
stiflingly hot, small, low-ceilinged room over which the
Revolution had washed without leaving any perceptible
trace of its passing.

A single light, shrouded in a brown velvet shade with a
fringe round the bottom, hung low over a table covered
with a red chenille cloth on which stood an old brass
samovar. Round the table were four heavy mahogany chairs
with red plush seats; a matching sideboard occupied the
wall to the left, and in front of me, under the shuttered
window, was a sofa covered in buttoned black oil-cloth,
which, cracked and torn in places, revealed the horsehair
stuffing beneath. The faded brown wall-paper was almost
invisible beneath a frieze of photographs, framed and un-
framed, interspersed here and there by a picture cut from a
magazine and pasted directly on to the wall. All round the
room, just beneath the ceiling, hung a series of crude
woodcuts which, as I discovered later, by daylight, repre-
sented various episodes in the lives of Russian saints.

In the corner diagonally opposite the door a small three-
cornered shelf supported a wooden icon; the figures on it
were almost indistinguishable beneath the dark, cracked
varnish. In front of it was burning a small oil-lamp.

Lyuba, on entering the room, had bowed towards it and

crossed herself. She'd then left me, going out through the farther of two doors in the right-hand wall. I could hear her moving about inside, and her movements were accompanied by the welcome clatter of kitchen utensils.

I pulled out a chair and sat down. I was beginning to feel more normal, though my reflexes were still peculiar. Sometimes I would shiver suddenly, or my leg would give a convulsive jerk, and I'd developed a more or less constant tic beneath my left eye.

Soon she came back into the room, carrying a pan full of cold boiled potatoes and a wooden plate piled with slices of black rye bread—the brotherhood of the White Swan obviously believed in simple fare—and sat down opposite me. As we ate in silence I examined her surreptitiously.

She had always been pale and thin, but now her skin had a translucent, unearthly pallor, and she was painfully gaunt. The emaciation of her face was accentuated by the fact that her once long blonde hair had been cropped close to her head. Dark shadows lay under her immense grey eyes—they seemed to have grown in size as her flesh had shrunk, and in them a strange, wandering expression alternated with a blank, impenetrable fixity.

I pushed my plate aside and began. "Lyuba. You are in great danger."

"We are all in great danger, Vanya," she said quietly, primly. "The serpent is everywhere, and his words are insidious."

I groaned inwardly: this was not going to be an easy conversation.

11

I spent three nights and three days in that cabin with Lyuba. It was a strange static period, a peculiar intermission between events. Occasionally momentary anxieties troubled me, brought on by the consciousness of passing time, or the fear that Alik might embark on some action before hearing from me. But for the most part I was content merely to be with Lyuba again in a kind of limbo, outside space and time.

Just as in Leningrad, years before, we spent our time in long walks; for kilometre on kilometre through the pine forests to the north, or down to the huge lake which lay beneath the cabin and along its marshy shore, startling the wild ducks and geese; and once we retraced the path we'd taken on the first evening back to the sea, and sat by a bonfire of driftwood under the shelter of the dunes. The weather was cold, but bright; some snow fell during the second night, but by morning the sky was clear again.

Our conversation that first evening had ended disastrously. While trying to convince Lyuba of the reality of the danger threatening her, I'd incautiously mentioned Alik's name, and she'd immediately reacted to it tempestuously, with fear and loathing.

She called him a pretender, Grishka Otrepiev, a false prince, an emissary of Antichrist. Then she rounded on me, accusing me of betraying her, Judas-like, to the forces of evil. Her speech quickly grew wild and confused, interrupted by bouts of hysterical laughter and tears.

"He will not escape the vengeance of the Lord," she screamed. "He will be cast forth into the outer darkness, will fall into the pit to burn, burn for time without end. He killed the best that was within me, the ripening seed. It is written: 'If thine own eye offend thee, then pluck it out.' " She rocked to and fro on her chair in an agony of grief.

I tried to soothe her, to comfort her, but without any success. In the end she tore herself away from me and ran into the bedroom of the hut, locking the door behind her. For a long time I lay sleepless on the horsehair couch, listening to her sobbing within.

The next morning her eyes were red-rimmed, but she was calm and withdrawn, ignoring my questions, or answering only in monosyllables. I began to talk about the past, about our experiences together, and slowly and gradually she became more animated. Occasionally I would strike a wrong note, and she would lapse into silence for a while, but as the day wore on I grew more skillful in avoiding mistakes of this kind.

By evening we were talking almost as freely and unconstrainedly as we had done years ago. Indeed, in some respects we had slipped back into our former relationship.

I began to think that by mentioning Alik I had managed to advance my cause, rather than retard it. Her hysterical fit seemed to have discharged her inner tenson. It might, probably would, build up again, but for the time being she had regained a more normal state of mind. The biblical echoes gradually vanished from her speech; she even began to look more like the Lyuba I had known.

Slowly, with infinite caution, I began to lead our conversation away from the past towards the present. I asked her about life in the Far East, and then about Tallinn.

She talked without reserve about the schools, about her colleagues, her pupils, her pedagogic successes and failures. I urged her gently forward through the years and at last, with trepidation, introduced her move to the Vologda region. As it turned out, I needn't have worried: she was perfectly willing to talk about her life there, to describe the village, the countryside, and she even showed no surprise when, by accident, I let slip the name of her fellow-mistress—Kozlova, whose deposition I had read at the militia station.

"Irina Aleksandrovna? An awful woman, and a very bad teacher. Stupid and circumscribed, with absolutely no originality in her methods, or any feeling for her pupils. I used to feel so sorry for them, sitting through endless hours of *diamat* with her. And if any of them had any talent, any spark of individuality, she tried to extinguish it, rather than encouraging it."

She stopped for a moment, looking out over the lake, black and gold in the setting sun, and then said—more to herself than to me: "I wonder how Masha's getting on. I hope she's all right."

"Masha Guseva?" I asked quietly.

"No, of course not. She was a very silly little girl, with not a thought in her head. I mean Masha Prishvina—so sweet and so pretty. She used to show me poems she'd written. Very imitative of course, but there was genuine feeling in them and something more . . . ." She stared into the distance.

Suddenly everything seemed to come together in a moment of irrational illumination. I made an intuitive, quantum leap from one set of facts to another.

"It was Masha who introduced you to Father Zakhar, wasn't it?" I said.

There was a long silence. At first I thought that, immersed in memories, she hadn't heard my question, but I didn't dare repeat it. Then I saw that she was crying, noiselessly. I cursed myself for forcing the issue, appalled by the idea of having to begin the long, stealthy approach all over again.

She turned towards me. Her eyes were wet, but she was smiling brilliantly.

"You are clever, aren't you, Vanya. Yes, it was Masha. She'd been ill, and hadn't come to school for some days. I called in to see how she was; he was sitting by her bedside, reading to her."

"You wrote me a letter about your first meeting. Do you remember? You compared yourself to that unbelieving lady in Dostoevsky's novel."

"Did I? It was wrong, all wrong. I was trying to be clever, trying to fit what I was feeling into a pattern I knew, trying to make life like literature. I learnt that from you, Vanya. You've always done it, you've always lived through books, and I know now that it's so wrong, so wrong and so defensive and barren and sterile. But then, at the beginning, I felt so terribly frightened. I'd found something within me which before I hadn't known to exist, and I was terribly frightened of what might happen."

"What did happen?"

"Nothing. But I saw suddenly that life wasn't dull and grey, but bright and vibrant and full of colour. Everything was clear, and simple, and straightforward, and beautiful. The forest is beautiful, each tree is beautiful; you, too, Vanya, are beautiful."

She jumped up from the fallen tree on which we were sitting, spun round with thrown-out arms, and ran off down the hill laughing.

The horse-hair couch had proved as uncomfortable as its

appearance suggested. Late that night I was lying on it
half-asleep, covered with a rug, my head awkwardly propped
against the wooden armrest, when I felt a light touch on
my shoulder. I opened my eyes and looked up. Lyuba was
standing by the side of the couch.

"Vanya, please." She took me by the hand and led me
into the bedroom. We sat down on the bed. I put my arm
round her shoulders. She was trembling.

"I'm so frightened, Vanya, and so ashamed. At times,
when I'm not with him, I begin to doubt. My faith is not
strong enough. What am I going to do? Please, hold me,
just hold me."

We lay down together. She buried her head in my
shoulder and began to cry. Some time later she lifted her
face to mine and kissed me.

"Thank you, Vanya."

"Lyuba, listen," I said urgently. "Give it all up. Come
back to Moscow with me. Everything will be all right. I'll
fix things. We can get married."

"You're so sweet, Vanya. But you don't really want to
marry me, do you? You can't anyway. I'm married
already."

I sat up with a jerk.

"You didn't know, did you? Nobody did. I married
Alik long ago. Then I was transferred to the Far East. He
arranged that. When I came back we met again. I became
pregnant. He made me have an abortion. And sent me to
Vologda."

"You could divorce him."

"It doesn't mean anything any longer, Vanya. It was
never a real marriage, never a marriage in the sight of
God. And since then I have been through the flames of
purification, I've purged myself of that kind of love. I
have been born again as a bride in spirit, not in flesh.
Don't ask me to come away with you, Vanya—I can't. I
know you think I've gone mad, it's all nonsense, but I

believe, I really do believe. It's the only thing that I have left. I did feel weak. Seeing you and talking of the past. But now I am strong again. Oh, Vanya, if only your eyes could be opened, if only you too could see the truth, see life as it really is, could understand.''

A nasty, underhand idea crept into my mind.

"Perhaps Father Zakhar could convert me," I said.

"If only you could meet him, Vanya. If only you would listen to his words.''

"Could I meet him? Now? Soon?''

There was a pause. I thought she might have grown suspicious of my intent, but then she said meditatively: "There is more joy in the repentance of one sinner . . . I will see, Vanya, I will see.''

A little later she fell asleep in my arms.

I'd found out a good deal about the past history of our relationship, but not nearly enough about the sect and its members. Towards the evening of the next day I began to question her more closely, but without much success.

She was willing to talk about her own spiritual progress, about the rest of the congregation in general terms, even about Father Zakhar, but I could get no specific information from her, nothing which I could offer Alik. And, as she spoke, she relapsed by degrees into her former state of feverish exaltation.

I asked her what she had done after her first meeting with Father Zakhar.

"I went to hear his words," she said. "We were his sheep, his lambs, and he was our shepherd. We all went: to hear him, to be healed and made whole. It was so difficult in the spring, when the snow had melted. The wood was so full of little streams, the ground was so marshy. But the church was always like a firm island, a rock of faith in a sea of confusion.''

I tried to find out what was going to happen next, whether any other demonstrations had been planned, but she seemed not to understand what I was talking about, answering me only with a gnomic abstraction: "Those who are worthy will see, the new kingdom will arise and the garden will bloom again."

"And the Blessed Lady?"

"When she reveals herself she will bring great good to mankind. The sick and the diseased will rise from their beds to follow her. She will transform the earth and we will be witnesses to it."

Translated into everyday speech her meaning seemed reasonably clear. It agreed, too, with some of the hints in her letter to me. And in Irina Aleksandrovna's deposition.

Finally I asked about the white swan, and about the connection with *Khovanshchina*.

I noticed that she was reluctant to talk about this. She said she knew nothing of the opera. She avoided using the phrase "white swan" herself and when I did so a peculiar expression—almost one of fastidious distaste—crossed her face. I didn't want to push her into hysteria again, but I had to find out more. When I insisted she began to move uneasily. She got up and walked about the room, looking more and more worried as she did so. Then, suddenly, she burst out.

"They are like Solomon in his dotage. He went after Ashtoreth the goddess of the Zidonians. And Chemosh, the abomination of the Moabites." Her voice stuck on a high pitch. Her eyes were vast, incandescent. "They will not see how they betray the truth, how they defile themselves and desecrate their souls. They roll and slobber in their own filth under the evil red eye of the swan. I pray nightly to be cleansed of their touch." She crossed herself with a wide, sweeping gesture, bowing towards the icon.

She began to speak faster and faster, making mistakes and slurring her words. "I fled them and their desecrations, their filth, their filth. I fled them, I fled . . ."

There was no longer any sense in what she was saying.

Her eyes flickered rapidly from one object to another, but it was obvious that she saw nothing. A thin dribble of spittle ran down from one corner of her mouth.

There was a croaking, unearthly cry. She fell to the floor. Her face was dark and congested. I pulled out my handkerchief, folded it, and forced it into her mouth. A moment later the convulsive stage began. She shook and writhed on the floor. I attempted to hold her down, but it was impossible. I could only try to make sure that the cloth remained between her teeth.

When the convulsions finally ceased, leaving her unconscious, I put her to bed and sat by her side until she passed into a deep, natural sleep.

My chief emotion was one of rage. If Alik had been there, I think I might have tried to kill him.

Lyuba's hold on reality was perhaps more precarious than that of most people, but it was Alik's treatment of her, I was sure, which had sent her over the edge and into the arms of religion. The enforced abortion was obviously still preying on her mind. I remembered that she'd made a veiled reference to it on that first, disastrous evening. And it was through him, too, I felt, that her epilepsy had been brought on. She'd certainly never had an attack before during the years I'd known her.

I largely discounted her hysterical remarks about the white swan. Innate puritanism combined with religious mania could lead to the condemnation of some very innocent activities.

Finding Lyuba had earlier seemed an insurmountable problem. But now that I had done so the difficulties had increased, rather than diminished.

She needed help, needed someone much closer to her and more involved in her fate than Peredonov and his friends. And I was only too willing to take on the responsibility. She'd turned me down once, implying that my heart wasn't in it, but she'd been wrong and I wasn't going to accept the refusal.

As far as the immediate future was concerned, however, it was obvious that if I stayed here to look after her, I wouldn't be able to satisfy either Alik or Bradley. In which case, presumably, they'd both bring their threats into effect.

But in the end the problem solved itself. When I woke the following morning Lyuba had gone.

12

Valery was sitting at the table cleaning his nails with a long Finnish knife. I asked him where Lyuba was. He gave me an evil look and said nothing. When I repeated the question he gestured angrily towards the door with his knife. I shrugged my shoulders and went out.

He led me down a path to where a battered old Pobeda pick-up had been backed in under the trees. The weather had changed. The clouds were low and grey and there was the smell of snow on the air. We bounced down a rough track and at the bottom emerged onto an unmetalled road which eventually led to the Primorsky Prospect near Staraya Derevnya. Valery drove in silence, gripping the wheel hard and peering forward with his nose almost touching the windscreen.

We ran through the outskirts of Leningrad along the bank of the Bolshaya Nevka. Just before the Stroganov bridge he pulled into the pavement. I was about to open the door and get out when he took a scrap of paper from his pocket and poked it at me. I took it. On it Lyuba had written: "Friday 24th 1800 hours. At the entrance to Kropotkinskaya metro station."

Something pricked my thigh. I looked down and saw that Valery was holding the point of his *finka* against it.

"Listen, bastard. Sister Mariya trusts you. But I don't. Neither does Mikhail Evstafich. So watch yourself. Last time you got off easily. Next time I'll gut you like a rabbit. Cut that on to your nose."

He punctuated his sentences with short jabs of his knife. I scrabbled behind me for the handle, opened the door, and fell out.

The pick-up accelerated away in a cloud of black smoke as I got to my feet. Blood was trickling down my leg. He'd got in a parting slash; there was a long, diagonal cut in my trouser, and a corresponding shallow wound underneath.

The woman on duty at the desk on my floor of the hotel gave me a queer look, but handed over my key without saying anything. Under my door I found a note from Nicola, asking me to call her when I got in. There seemed no reason not to: I had a lot of time to waste before my train left.

I went up to her room early in the afternoon. She was pleased to see me.

"Where have you been, Vanya? I thought you'd gone back to Moscow without saying good-bye, but they told me at the desk that you hadn't checked out."

I said I'd been staying with friends outside the city. I asked her how the sight-seeing tour had been.

"Marvellous. I can't thank you enough for telling me where to go."

The enthusiasm seemed a little excessive. After all, I'd given her no more information than she could have got from any guide-book, and from where I was sitting I could see at least two on her bedside table. I changed the subject

and asked her about her work. It turned out to be a good
question.

She spoke with knowledge and authority about American paperback rights, about film options, about the techniques of writing for television. I listened abstractedly,
wondering how one would go about handling in fiction the
complicated, inexplicable links of love and hatred, loyalty
and betrayal that bound Alik, Lyuba, Tanya and myself
together.

Some time later she interrupted my thoughts to ask me
whether I'd still got much to do in Leningrad.

"No, I've finished now."

"So you'll be going back soon?"

"Tonight."

"On the Red Arrow?"

"Yes."

"Amazing! Listen, Vanya, I'm going back tonight too.
And I've got an international sleeping compartment all to
myself on that train. Would you like to share it with me?"

I hesitated.

"Come on! You won't be compromised. I won't tell
anyone you spent the night with me."

She'd missed the point: whether she told anyone or not,
someone would very soon get to know that I'd shared a
compartment with her. But the thought of spending the
night lying down, rather than sitting up, even in a soft
compartment, was too tempting.

We had dinner together, and afterwards an Intourist car
took us up the Nevsky to the Moscow station. As usual,
the platform was crowded. Like some rare, exotic bird,
Nicola, in a huge Cossack fur hat and long black cloak,
picked her way delicately towards the train through the
piles of luggage—fibre suitcases held together with twine,
immense, badly wrapped brown-paper parcels, bast bags
stuffed to bursting point—on which their owners sat or
slumbered, dressed in coarse greatcoats or padded jackets,

the men in fur caps, the women with kerchiefs bound low over their foreheads and shawls round their shoulders.

Soon after we'd left Leningrad Nicola suggested that I might like to take a walk. I went out into the corridor. It had begun to snow. The wind was driving in from the east, and the windows on the left-hand side of the train were already obscured.

When I got back to the compartment Nicola was in bed, dipping further into the experiences of Mr. J. G. Kohl. She was now reading about sea-bathing on the Courland coast.

"A merry, careless, frolicsome disposition prevails everywhere," she informed me. I went through into the bathroom. A few minutes later I turned off the light and came back in. Nicola closed the book and turned towards me.

"How terribly sporting, Vanya. Do all Russians wear track suits in bed?"

I muttered something and pulled my bed open.

"Don't be offended. I like it; it's a nice change from silk pyjamas. Come and kiss me good-night."

I went across to her. She raised herself on one elbow, and the bed-clothes fell away to show plainly that what she was wearing had been designed with only one sport in mind. I bent down to kiss her cheek, but she moved her head and our lips met. Her other arm came round my neck to pull me closer to her. Her tongue flickered over my mouth.

She was using some heady foreign scent; I felt myself on the edge of a dark, delicious abyss; then, as I moved, the wound in my thigh gave a sudden twinge and the spell was broken.

I reached up, removed her arm, put it gently down beside her, and drew the bed-clothes up to her chin.

"No?"

"No."

"I've never done it on a train; and to do it on a Russian

train with a Russian man would have been too much. Are you sure, Vanya?''

"I'm sorry, Nicola." I turned the light off and got into bed.

"Don't worry if you hear me getting up. You won't have to defend yourself. I'll only be going to have a cold shower.''

I wondered what was behind this attempt at seduction. I didn't in fact think that Nicola was merely, as she had suggested, a degenerate bourgeois hedonist avid for a sensation she hadn't yet experienced. Nor could I believe that she found me irresistibly attractive. If so, her passion had cooled quickly: I could hear her calm, even breathing from the other side of the compartment.

I gave her three-quarters of an hour longer, and then slid slowly and cautiously out of bed and into the bathroom, taking with me her bag from the table under the window. I locked the door and turned the bag out on to the floor. I began to go through the contents, tossing each item back when I'd finished with it.

British passport—born in Roehampton, thirty-five years ago; brown hair, brown eyes, no distinguishing marks; lipstick; gold keyholder in the form of an N; gold propelling pencil and matching pen; Madame Rochas scent spray—I paused for a moment over that; compact; slim black leather wallet with gold edges and initials stamped in gold in one corner; travellers cheques; Intourist meal tickets; and, finally, leather address book and a small black notebook.

I sat down on the lavatory seat and flipped through the address book. There was nothing there: all the addresses were foreign ones. I put it back in the bag and turned to the notebook.

The first few pages seemed to contain jottings for a novel or story. Then came a page with a few notes on Helsinki—her party had presumably come to Russia by sea. This was followed by a page headed "Moscow." I began to read more attentively, but the remarks were nothing more than tourist impressions. I turned over and my eye was immediately caught by my own name, with a circle round it. Underneath she'd noted down a brief description and summarized our first conversation.

I leafed through some more pages of sight-seeing, and came to her move to Leningrad. She'd spread herself for a page or two on a description of her first day—no doubt some helpless heroine was about to widen her experience with a trip to the Soviet Union. At the top of the next page was the notation "Vanya—research??" followed by a few notes on what I'd told her about the sectarians. At the bottom was a Moscow telephone number. The rest of the pages were blank.

Perhaps I'd been wrong about Nicola; perhaps the frequent coincidences that attended our meetings were the result of chance, not design. I'd discovered nothing suspicious, apart from her interest in me; and an innocuous explanation could be found even for that.

As a writer she certainly didn't spare herself in the search for material. Her way of putting life at the service of literature was probably more productive than mine, but I felt that Lyuba would consider it no less culpable.

13

The Red Arrow gets in just after six in the morning. Moscow was cold, wet and dirty. I walked down from Komsomol Square past the ugly twin skyscrapers of the Ministry of Transport and the Leningrad Hotel to the Garden Ring, and took a trolleybus back to the apartment.

I had thirty-six hours to kill before the rendezvous Lyuba had appointed. I didn't want to get in touch with Alik. I had no hard facts to give him. And if he learnt that I had a meeting arranged with Father Zakhar he might be tempted to have the priest picked up. That would make it far more difficult for me to help Lyuba. I hoped that he wouldn't decide he needed a progress report from me.

Time went slowly by. I tried to do some work, but found it impossible to concentrate. Even a new Agatha Christie which I'd been saving up for a rainy day proved incapable of distracting me. I walked up and down, or lay on my bed gazing at the ceiling, trying to fit the various bits of the puzzle together. But the gaps between them were too large, and I could get no idea of the overall form of the picture. The only thing of which I was sure was that I was very much on the periphery of events, a very minor piece on the board. One of the difficulties, of course, was deciding where the board ended and the more normal—though at times equally complicated—business of life began.

Punctually at six o'clock I came out through the glass doors of the Kropotkinskaya station and looked about me expectantly. For some reason I'd thought that Father Zakhar would be wearing the robes of an Orthodox priest. I was surprised when a tall, broad man in a smart black coat with a fur collar and an Astrakhan lamb hat accosted me.

"Morozov, Ivan Vasilevich?"

"Father Zakhar?"

He smiled and held out his hand. He had a strong, square face, very pale, with intensely blue eyes. His hair was no longer than most people's, and the only thing unusual about him was his short black beard. He seemed to be in his early fifties.

"Shall we walk a little?"

We started off down the Volkhonka towards the Pushkin museum.

"And how can I help you, my young friend? I take it that, despite Lyubov Dmitrievna's hopes, you are in fact not in search of spiritual guidance?" He gave me an extraordinarily penetrating, and at the same time deeply humorous look.

I'd earlier formed a plan of campaign based on the assumption that Father Zakhar would be an ascetic, saintly, other-worldly figure. Faced with the reality, I had to abandon these preconceptions and with them my tactics. I knew at once that I could not hope to mislead him; he would see straight through any attempts I might make at dissimulation. I would have to be as frank and open as possible, reveal as much of the truth as I dared, and hope I'd be successful in concealing the remainder.

"I'm worried about Lyubov Dmitrievna," I said. "I think she may be in a very dangerous position. I want to find out just what she's got herself into."

"That sounds like an honest reply, Ivan Vasilevich, though I don't care for your choice of words. Ask, rather, to what she has willingly abandoned herself, heart and soul. Or, even better, perhaps: what higher power has chosen her as one of the elect, has inspired her with a new consciousness of self, of existence. But whichever way you were to put the question I doubt whether I could answer you, an unbeliever, in terms which you could apprehend."

I had the feeling, as earlier with Peredonov, that I was being mocked, though Father Zakhar's tone was infinitely subtler than that of his disciple.

"And if I were to ask you what your aim is," I said. "What you hope to achieve, would your answer be one that I might understand?"

"Perhaps. Let me show you something." He took me by the arm and led me aross the street. "I chose this spot for our meeting not without purpose. What do you see before you?"

In front of us a small park fell steeply away to the big open-air Moscow swimming pool. Beyond was the river, and on the far side I could see the flashing sign on the roof of the Udarnik cinema. To our left, at the bottom of the hill, were the walls and towers of the Kremlin, with the belfry of Ivan the Great rising behind.

Puzzled, I looked at him. "I can't see anything in particular."

"You must learn to see with new eyes, Ivan Vasilevich, to pierce through the veil of the phenomenal to the real substance within. Look again!" He pointed in front of us at the immense circular basin of the swimming pool. As always in winter, it was shrouded in a cloud of steam that billowed upwards from the heated surface. The vapour swirled and bubbled, occasionally lifting to allow a glimpse of the disturbed green water, lit from beneath, and the bodies of the swimmers, and then descended again to obscure them.

"You mean the open-air swimming pool?"

"Not a swimming pool, Ivan Vasilevich, but hell: the bottomless pit, filled with the souls of sinners burning in torment forevermore."

He paused for a moment. "Do you know anything of the history of Moscow, Moscow of the forty times forty belltowers? Do you know what building used to stand on the spot now occupied by this abomination?"

I didn't, but he gave me no time to say so before sweeping on.

"The Church of Christ the Saviour, the favourite church of all good Muscovites. Built to celebrate the victory God gave us over the Beast of the Apocalypse, Bonaparte. Five gilded domes it had, twelve bronze doors. Inside gold and marble. On festivals and high days three thousand seven hundred candles burnt to the glory of God within. Blasphemous hands tore it down in 1932 on the orders of an arch-priest of evil, Comrade Kaganovich. They intended to erect a monument to Satan here, a Palace of Soviets they called it. But this spot by the Moscow river is marshy, without firm foundation. The old architect knew this well. His church was a triumph of engineering, worthy to stand beside any of the creations of the left-handed smith of Tula as an example of the genius of the Russian people." He turned and began to walk down the street. I had to hurry to keep up with him.

"It floated as lightly over the marsh as the feet of Our Lord over the Sea of Galilee. It was cunningly devised, with separate inner and outer walls running together on rollers, so that if one sank, the other remained in place. When it had been razed to the ground, and the excavations for the foundations of this Palace of Soviets were being

dug, the pious and devout of Moscow would pass by; and
each would call a curse down on the sacrilegious enterprise, and would spit on it thus.'' He spat violently on the
pavement. ''I, too, came then with my parents; I called an
infant's curse down on the iconoclasts; I, too, spat into the
pit, feebly perhaps, but still with feeling. Was what happened the result of fervent prayer, was it due to the nature
of the ground, or was it caused by the two conjointly?
Who can say? But the work of the godless did not prosper.
Three times they raised the walls of their Palace, and three
times the walls collapsed into the mire. At last they abandoned it in despair. The excavation was used for what you
now call a swimming pool.''

He laughed loudly, and I laughed with him. It was an
interesting story, and one which I had not heard before.

We'd now come down on to the embankment of the
Moscow river, and had turned left to walk along under the
walls of the Kremlin.

''But are you saying anything more than that we're no
longer a religious nation—which is obvious?'' I asked.

''My anecdote conveys only half of the truth, Ivan
Vasilevich. The other half is not so easy to illustrate.
Instead of example I shall have to fall back on argument.''

We walked on for a few paces in silence and then he
began again, this time more in the tone of a teacher than of
a prophet.

''During our history we have borrowed much from the
West—ideas, artifacts, technology. Little has been of last-
ing use to us; in most cases the borrowings were hasty and
ill-considered, alien to our way of life. Without doubt, the
most pernicious doctrine to have come to us from the West
was that of individualism. Like an evil worm, it ate its
way into the fabric of our society, weakening it and eventually causing it, in a year of darkness, to collapse under
its own weight. Your Bolshevik revolution, sacrilegious
and atheistic as it was, nevertheless, through the inscruta-

ble wisdom of God, was allowed to perform one immensely important task: it turned the people of Russia back from the false teachings of Western individualism, and made our society once again that which it should never have ceased to be: a unified community. The people who built this''—he gestured up at the Kremlin tower under which we were passing—''were, like the people who built that''—he pointed backwards towards the swimming pool—''a collective. The only difference is that whereas the builders of old performed their task for the greater glory of God, those of today work only for the greater glory of man. Your socialist state is a collective, as Russia must be; but it must also be, as it ever has been, Holy Russia. And believe me, Ivan Vasilevich, it needs only a small change, infinitesimal by the side of those convulsions which have racked our country in the past, a change in men's hearts, to make our Russia holy again. Your Lenin-Ulyanov has said that socialism plus electrification equals communism; I say to you now that socialism plus faith equals the kingdom of God upon earth.''

By themselves his words might not have carried conviction, but allied with the tremendous force of his personality they were hard to resist, and I found myself struggling to preserve my scepticism.

''And how will you set about changing men's hearts?'' I asked.

''The Russian people have never ceased to believe; within their dark masses the flame of faith still burns; as yet its light is dim and feeble, visible only to him who can see beneath the outer integument of being. Your Joseph Vissarionovich, that failed priest, glimpsed this once: why else did he teach his soldiers to cry: 'Into battle for Stalin! Into battle for Mother Russia!'? He was a peasant first, a Georgian second, and a Marxist only third. But a Marxist nevertheless: he could never free himself from the dead hand of that simple-minded German-Jewish ideologue. I know no such constraints, and into my keeping has been given the means to fan the spark of faith into a blaze, a blaze which will run through the souls of the people like wind over a cornfield.''

"That's your miraculous icon, is it? The one that heals the sick. Or so your simple-minded followers believe.''

He checked in his stride and turned towards me. "You've used your time well, Ivan Vasilevich. But our Blessed Lady of Lebedevo does more than heal. When our crusade begins, she will be borne in the forefront of the host, and with her aid we will conquer the unbeliever as our ancestors conquered the pagan Tartars.''

We had reached the Beklemishev tower at the south-east corner of the Kremlin and turned up the cobbled hill past the Cathedral of St. Basil. He flung out a hand towards the squat outline of the mausoleum.

"There rests the body of your secular saint, not a single miracle to his name. If an endless procession passes by his mummified remains, how many more, think you, will come to worship at the shrine of my saint, whose miracles are many?'' He dropped his voice to a more conversational level again. "I know you read Dostoevsky, that seer of the spirit, another of our great popular geniuses. He, too, saw the truth for a moment, but then misunderstood it, or perhaps willfully concealed it, as too dangerous and incomprehensible for his generation, consumed with the fever of individualism. In his story of the Karamazov family the Grand Inquisitor speaks of freeing man from the burden of individual guilt, and of ruling humanity through 'miracle, mystery and authority.' He is the real, hidden hero of that inspired work: by comparison with him Alyosha is a buffoon, Zosima a feeble and spiritless old man. And it is his doctrine that I have taken as my own. Old Russia was ruled by the ideological triad of orthodoxy, autocracy and nationality; miracle, mystery and authority will rule the new Russia.''

We came down the slope of Red Square past the Historical Museum and turned left into the Alexandrovsky Gardens. It looked as though we were going to make a circuit of the Kremlin. For the next few minutes I pondered over what I had heard. Father Zakhar might be a lunatic, but he expressed himself with enormous, frightening power. If his vision of the new Russia ever came to pass, I thought, fanaticism and intolerance could lead to worse carnage than that which our country had experienced at the height of the Yezhovshchina. But I still hadn't discovered what role Lyuba was destined to play in all this. I asked him.

"Lyubov Dmitrievna?" he said. "Don't worry about her, Ivan Vasilevich. Her fate will be glorious, whatever form it might take. She has left your circumscribed life behind to enter a higher and freer existence." He went on, speaking almost to himself. "When we met for the first time I realised at once that the divine will had led her to me. Her very name told me that. Lyubov—love; Dmitrievna—not daughter of Dmitry, but daughter of Demeter, the Earth Mother; Lebedeva—of the family of the swan. What more fitting follower of the Lady and consort for the white swan could be found?"

I stared at him in disbelief, but he was far away from me, rapt in his visions.

"They will enter the Kremlin bare-footed and bare-headed; they will be crowned, like the emperors of old, in the Cathedral of the Ascension. Church and state will become one, the prophecies will have been fulfilled, and the glory that was *Rus* will return."

He was mad: stark, staring, raving mad, but at the same time horribly dangerous. Lyuba's situation was even worse than I'd let myself imagine.

We stopped under a streetlamp. Father Zakhar turned towards me. His face was calm again. He smiled, and despite my feelings towards him I found it impossible not to respond.

"In a moment I must leave you, Ivan Vasilevich. But before I do, is there anything else you wish to know?"

One thing had been puzzling me all along. "Why should you tell me this?" I asked. "I'm not a member of your sect, I'm not even sympathetic towards your beliefs. Aren't you afraid that I might pass on what I've learnt?"

He laughed. "To whom? What do you think would happen if you were to walk into a police-station and tell them that you've met a priest who is going to overthrow the power of the party? Or if you were to go up to Dzerzhinsky Square and report our conversation to the officer on duty? The power of faith is as incomprehensible to your bureaucrats as electricity would be to a caveman. But they will learn in the future, at the stake if necessary. Some, indeed, have learnt already. We have powerful friends in the organs, Ivan Vasilevich. At the moment I am in less danger than you are. But, in any case, the time for secrecy is past. Soon what I have told you will be trumpeted abroad, as the armies of the faithful move into battle. We are about to come among you, bringing not peace, but a sword." He gestured to a taxi that was cruising slowly past. It stopped, and I saw Timosha's face as he turned and leant back to open the rear door. Father Zakhar got in.

"Farewell, Ivan Vasilevich."

He slammed the door and the taxi moved off into the night.

14

As I put my key into the door of my room Tanya got up from the stairs where she had been sitting and came towards me.

"They told me you were back when I rang up. So I thought I'd come round and see how you were."

I got the door open and let her in. "It's nice to see you, but why the concern?"

"I felt very guilty after you'd left the other day." She cleared a pile of books off my armchair and sat down. "I thought I should have warned you."

"Warned me? What about?"

"About Alik. He got me an invitation for that party. And he gave me that photograph of you with the fish. And told me to remind you of the old days."

I found a half-empty bottle of Armenian cognac and some glasses hidden in a pile of lecture notes. "I thought it must have been something like that."

"Why?"

"I knew I hadn't given you the photo. And there was no reason to lie if you'd got it from Lyuba. So it must have been Alik." I handed her a glass. "Did he tell you to go to bed with me as well?"

"No, that was my own idea."

"And this visit?"

"My idea too." She crossed the room quickly and knelt beside my chair. "I deserved that. I should have told you. But please, Vanya, forget it now." She looked up at me. Her green eyes were full of tears.

A little later I said: "But why on earth did you do what he told you, Tanya?"

She shrugged. "Everything's very much on a knife-edge at the moment. I can't afford to offend someone in his position."

"What about the Pugachev film?"

"Not as firm as I made out. He could certainly put a stop to that if he tried. But I didn't come here to talk about my brilliant career. Tell me what happened in Leningrad. Did you see Lyuba?"

"Did Alik tell you I was going to?"

She nodded.

I hesitated for a moment. There seemed no harm in telling her. After all, the secrets I knew were other people's, not my own. She might be able to see a pattern I'd missed, or Alik might have let some detail accidentally slip while talking to her. I filled our glasses and began.

With her faculty of comprehension honed to a fine edge by years of listening to inarticulate writers at script conferences, Tanya was a stimulating and sympathetic listener. I told her about the White Swan dossier, about my lunch with Alik, about Bradley. She exclaimed with proper horror at my near escapes from injury or worse, sighed over Lyuba's plight, and waxed indignant at Father Zakhar's presumption. I said very little about Nicola.

Obviously fired by the dramatic potential of the situation, Tanya was most fascinated by the anecdote I'd just heard from Father Zakhar about the Church of Christ the Saviour.

"It's too good to be true. Your Savonarola of the steppes must have invented it."

"No. I thought that too. So I called at the library on the way back and looked it up." I took out my notebook and flipped through the pages. "This is what I found. It's about the 1933 plan for the reconstruction of Moscow:

> "The architectural centre of Moscow will be the gigantic building of the Palace of the Soviets, which has already begun to be constructed on the site of the former Church of Christ the Saviour. This majestic structure, four hundred metres high, crowned with a gigantic sculptural figure of V. I. Lenin, in the totality of its composition, architectural forms, and inner organisation, expresses the idea of the socialist epoch, represents a grandiose monument to V. I Lenin, and imprints in architectural forms the greatness and pathos of socialist construction."

For some moments we both contemplated in silence the thought of a building four hundred metres high crowned with a gigantic statue of Vladimir Ilich. Then I said:

"What should I do, Tanya? Should I tell Alik what I've found out? Or should I get in touch with Bradley? Obviously I can't arrange for him to see Lyuba, but I could give him enough material for an article or two."

"See Bradley," she said. "He's absolutely right. He can do more for Lyuba than Alik can. The organs hate messing with people who've had some exposure in the Western press. Anyway, do you trust Alik?"

There was only one answer to that. I got Bradley's card out of my wallet and went out into the hall.

The number, as I dialled it, seemed familiar, but I didn't have time to wonder why this should be so, as the journalist answered on the first ring.

"Bradley here."

I could hear music in the background. "Care for another game of chess, Martin?"

"Who the hell is this?" He sounded irritable. "You got the right number, bud?"

"We played the other day, remember?"

There was a long pause. The music was suddenly cut off. I thought he must have put his hand over the mouthpiece to talk to someone else in the room. When he spoke again he sounded much more amiable.

"Sure, Vanya. Tomorrow evening, around seven?"

"Early in the morning, if you can manage it."

"Sorry, no dice."

"All right. Seven. The same place."

When I came back into the room Tanya was standing in front of the bookcase, apparently studying my taste in literature. I told her what I'd arranged. She nodded. She took a book from the shelf, blew the dust from the top edge, opened it, closed it, and put it back in the shelf again. Then, without turning round, she said:

"Are you still very much in love with Lyuba?"

It was a question I'd asked myself several times during the last few days.

"No," I said. "Not at all. I thought I was, but I'm not. But I do feel protective towards her and responsible for her. I can't leave her on her own, leave her to Alik and Father Zakhar. I shall have to look after her if no one else does. But I'm not in love with her any longer."

"I see." She took another book out and looked at it. Then she turned to face me. She was smiling.

"Do you remember I told you I was going into the country to look at some locations for the new film?"

"Yes. Why?"

"Alik arranged it. And do you know where we're going?"

I shook my head.

"Vologda."

I had been right; she did have some information to add to what I already knew. But it didn't bring any more clarity to the picture.

"What's he playing at, Tanya? Do you have any idea?"

Her face suddenly went serious again. She lit a cigarette, and pushed back a wing of dark hair that had fallen forward over her face.

"He hates you, you know."

"*Alik* hates me?" The statement seemed unbelievable.

"He always has done. It's obvious from the way he talks about you."

"But why? What have I done to him?"

"Because you're so different from him, perhaps. He thinks you're cleverer than he is. He thinks you despise him."

I did, but I hadn't known I'd let it show.

"There's a lot of jealousy in it, too. He was livid when you took Lyuba away from him for a time. That was one of the reasons why he married her."

"I wonder why she married him."

Tanya looked at me pityingly. "She loves him."

"But I still don't see—"

"He wants to get his own back. That summer we spent together has got some kind of symbolic significance for him. He wants to recreate it in some way. Show us how much power he's got now. It's all rather frightening."

It was: very frightening. Especially since, if Tanya was right, it sounded as though Alik had gone a little mad. But something else had surprised me.

"I didn't realise you knew him so well," I said.

Tanya stubbed out her cigarette and took her time about lighting another one.

"Lyuba didn't tell you then. Too high-minded for gossip, I suppose."

"Tell me what?"

"About Alik and me. It started that summer. You were mooning about after Lyuba. Or communing with nature. I wasn't getting any fun. So Alik set out to give me some."

I watched in silence as the shattered wreckage of my memories disappeared under the waves. Tanya came up and put an arm round my neck.

"I'm sorry, Vanya. I really am. But it was all a long time ago. And I had to tell you. You'd never have trusted me if you'd found out some other way later."

Truth was more valuable than fiction. The past was dead; the present was by my side: living, vibrant, beautiful. I pulled her towards me.

She had to leave early the next morning. I walked her down to Nikitsky Gate to look for a taxi. It was cold and foggy. As we waited on the pavement an idea occurred to me.

"When are you going to Vologda?"

"Next week. Wednesday the fifth, I think."

"Can I come with you?"

"Why not? I'll get the studio to issue a permit for you."

A taxi appeared. I flagged it down. For once it stopped and the driver made no objection when I told him the destination. I opened the door. Tanya hesitated for a moment. Then she said:

"I've just put my career on the line for you, Vanya. So you'll have to win, won't you? And take care."

She got in. I shut the door and the taxi moved off.

15

The fog persisted throughout the day. Afternoon merged imperceptibly with evening. It was dark when I eventually went out. The streetlamps were dim, faintly glowing globes of yellow. It was slippery underfoot as the frost began to bite. A trolleybus slid past with the peculiar noiseless gait of its kind.

I found Bradley pacing up and down between the empty chess tables. He came hurriedly towards me and we shook hands.

"Christ, Vanya, it's cold. Can we go somewhere a little warmer to talk?"

I thought for a moment. Metro stations are good places for clandestine meetings—in the winter they're usually full of courting couples and blackmarketeers concluding deals—but there wasn't one nearby. And I didn't want to take him back to the apartment: if an uninvited guest is worse than a Tatar, as the proverb says, a foreign journalist is even less desirable.

"There's a *shashlyk* house just up the boulevard," I said.

"Fine. Lead me to it."

We started to walk in the direction of Pushkin Square. As we set off Bradley gestured towards a stout red-faced man in a blue coat, who had fallen asleep on one of the benches.

"I'll never understand you Russians," he said. "Back home no one would think of sleeping it off in Central Park on a day as cold as this. But your drunks just lie down anywhere, whatever the weather. I remember walking down Kuznetsky Most last New Year's Eve—it must have been ten or fifteen below zero—and the drunks were passed out on the pavement like railway ties. You could have got clear from one end of the street to the other without ever stepping on a paving-stone."

The *shashlychnaya* was a small, rather seedy restaurant, down a couple of steps in a semi-basement. Inside it was hot, and the air was full of smoke and the smell of cooking. I collected some food and two mugs of draught beer from the counter and took them over to Bradley, who was sitting with his back to the wall, under a brightly coloured poster inviting the tourist to visit Soviet Abkhazia. He poked at his *shashlyk* a few times with his fork, and then pushed it away.

"There's only one kind of short-order cooking that's worth eating, and this isn't it," he said. "Well, Vanya, what did you want to see me about? Have you laid on that interview with your preacher-lady for me?"

I concentrated for a moment on the improbably blue surface of Lake Ritsa. I'd given a good deal of thought to what I was going to say to him, but I wasn't at all sure that he would accept the proposition I was about to make.

"No," I said slowly, "I haven't been able to do anything about that yet."

He leant over the table and pointed his fork at me. "So

what's this about, Vanya? Are you trying to give me the run-around? That promise I made the other day still stands, you know.''

"I want to make a deal with you."

"A deal?" He relaxed back in his chair and grinned. "That's my kind of language. OK, Vanya. Lay it out on the table."

"Look," I said. "I will get you that interview with Lyuba, later. But I can give you now a whole lot of other material on the movement she's mixed up in."

"Go on."

"You'll get a much bigger story out of it. Not just one article, but a series."

"All right, that's one side of the bargain, but what's the pay-off? What do I do in return?"

"Lay off Lyuba for the moment. Write an article on the movement instead. Get your Western readers interested in that." I stopped.

"So go on. Tell me all about it."

"But do you agree? Will you write the article?"

He'd been drawing patterns idly on the plastic table top with his fork while he listened to me. Now he suddenly scraped it harshly along the edge.

"How in hell do I know what I'm going to do until I've seen the goods? Put them out in front of me and I'll tell you what they're worth."

"But if I give you everything now, what guarantee have I got that you'll use it?"

He grinned again. "None. But I'll sweeten the pot. I won't do anything about your girl friend for the moment. And if your stuff is as interesting as you say it is, I'd be a fool not to use it, wouldn't I?"

I thought for a moment, and then mentally shrugged my shoulders. I hadn't got anything else to bargain with, and this was my only chance of passing the information on.

"All right," I said. "Well, this is how it is."

I began by sketching in the background briefly. I told him something about the Old Believers and the sectarians. He shifted restlessly in his chair, and soon interrupted me.

"Jesus, Vanya. Can't you cut the historical crap and get on to the here and now?"

"But you can't understand what's happening now without knowing something about the past."

He waved a hand impatiently. "Maybe, maybe. But I don't want to understand it, I just want to know what's going on. I work for a daily paper—right?—not the New York Public Library."

"All right, but I still think—"

"I'll do the thinking. You just give me the facts."

There was no point in arguing any further, and, anyway, he was absolutely right. The historical background was irrelevant to him, and I'd only brought it in, I suppose, to regain the initiative I'd lost earlier.

I told him most of what I'd learnt and deduced about the movement. He didn't seem to be paying much attention at first, and once, when I started to explain why I thought it had taken its name from Musorgsky's opera, interrupted me again.

"Facts, Vanya, facts. Do me a favour and forget you're an academic."

His tone reminded me unpleasantly of Alik, and I hurried on to tell him about Father Zakhar, about the icon, and about the future crusade. All this certainly caught his interest. He stopped drawing on the table, leant forward, and listened intently. He made me describe Father Zakhar to him in detail, and cross-questioned me at length about my conversation with him.

I didn't tell him anything about Alik, or Lyuba, or how I'd gathered my information and come to meet Father Zakhar. And, somewhat to my surprise, he didn't seem interested in finding out. I was also rather surprised that he didn't find it necessary to take notes, so surprised indeed that I asked him about it.

"Notes? No, I never take notes." He tapped his forehead. "I've got a built-in tape-recorder up here which does the job much better. Most people, apart from politicians, clam up if you start writing down what they say. And, anyway, Vanya, in a situation like this do you really want me to get out the reporter's notebook and start making with the shorthand?"

Under his mocking gaze I felt a fool. I went on hurriedly.

Eventually I came to an end. Bradley leant back in his chair and nodded slowly to himself.

"Well, what do you think?" I said. "Will you do it?"

He didn't seem to understand me.

"Do what?"

"Will you do an article on it?"

"Oh, an article. Yes, sure I'll do one. I like it, I like it very much. It's great, way-out stuff. Something for everyone." He lapsed into thought again for a moment, and then said, almost to himself: "But I wonder what his gimmick really is? How does he work it?"

"Who?"

"Your Father Zakhar. What's his particular brand of miracle?"

"I told you. It's this icon. They believe it cures illness."

"Sure, sure. Faith healing and all that jazz. He's probably had a genuine case or two, and then worked up some more."

"How?"

"Well, you can have a stooge in the audience. He comes hopping in on crutches, throws them away at the end of the service, and dances about on legs as sound as yours. But that's strictly for the sticks. Your Russian peasant isn't the most sophisticated of audiences, but even he might find that a bit crude. No, there must be a better trick there. Like those guys in India who go around healing cataracts. They prick the lens of the eye with a thorn, the liquid runs out, forms a temporary retina and bingo! you can see. A few weeks later the liquid dries up, and then you're blind for good. But by that time the surgeon's collecting fees from grateful patients five villages away. I'd guess he's thought up something as convincing as that. But what else does he do? That's the sixty-four dollar question.''

''But why should he need to do anything else? Surely if they believe the icon actually heals the sick—''

''You don't get it, Vanya, do you? You ever heard of Lourdes, in France, where little Bernadette had her visions? They do a line in miraculous cures there. I passed through the town once, and I wouldn't go there again in a hurry. The place was packed with coaches full of cripples, all hoping their own, personal miracle was just round the corner. This Rasputin character of yours wants a procession of incurable pilgrims like he wants a hole in the head. What he needs, for what he wants to do, are plenty of strong, healthy crusaders. You see any sign of disease about those bodyguards of his? No, he must have something else going for him. Don't you have any idea what it is?''

I saw his point. It hadn't occurred to me before, but he was obviously right. The only possibility seemed to be the white swan itself. But this was unlikely if the name was only a reference to Prince Khovansky, and through him symbolically to the old medieval Russia. I told Bradley this. He grunted and was silent for a minute. Then he said:

''I'd give a whole lot for an eye-witness account of their ceremonies. I think I might just take a ride up to Vologda and nose around there on the off-chance. You can usually hear something if you get your ear close enough to the ground.''

Given the character of the movement, it didn't seem likely to me that Bradley would be any more successful

than the KGB, but I didn't tell him so. Instead I asked him
when his first article might appear.

"Why are you so keen on getting this into print, Vanya?
Especially after being so coy with your girl friend's telephone number. You've come round to my point of view,
have you? That a bit of publicity in the free press of the
Western world might just take the heat off? You could be
right. And I guess you're right too in thinking that the
balloon's going to go up pretty soon. But when? That's
what's really vital. I wish to God you'd had the sense to
ask a couple of simple questions while you had the chance."

I was conscious that I hadn't cut much of a figure in
Bradley's eyes so far, and was obscurely glad of a chance
to redeem myself.

"I think I can make a pretty good guess at zero hour," I
said.

"Why the hell didn't you say so? Come on, give!"

"It's a religious movement, so the date is likely to have
a religious significance. And the next church festival—" I
paused for a moment, but Bradley was there before I could
go on.

"Of course, Easter. That'll be it. But when the hell is
Easter here?"

I could answer that question. "The ninth of April. But
the service begins the evening before."

He got out a diary and leafed through it, muttering to
himself. "Today's the twenty-fifth. Easter in a fortnight.
And a primary at the end of the month. Perfect. Couldn't
be better." He closed the book with a snap and put it back
in his pocket. "OK, Vanya. Let's get this show on the
road." He got up. "Set up that interview in about a week's
time, if you can, and give me a ring about it. You can
always leave a message about a chess game if I'm not
there." He smiled.

I stayed in my seat. "What primary?" I said.

He looked at me blankly, and then his expression cleared.

"The next primary in this year's presidential election. I'm going back Stateside to cover the rest of the campaign. But I've got time to clear this up first. Be seeing you."

He moved briskly through the tables to the door. I followed, but was held up for a moment or two in the narrow entrance lobby by a short stout man who was having difficulty in getting his arm into the sleeve of his coat. When I came out into the night Bradley was already vanishing into the fog, about fifty metres away, up the boulevard towards Gorky Street. He stopped suddenly. I saw a movement in front of him, and a man appeared behind him, emerging from a shop doorway.

I turned quickly away and began to walk fast in the opposite direction. Two more men seemed to spring out of the pavement before me. A black van skidded to a halt on the cobbles, and then reversed, bumping up on to the pavement in front of me. The man on my left pulled the back door open. I was half-pushed, half-lifted into the dark opening. The door slammed shut behind me. There was a jarring thump as the back wheels came down off the kerb. I landed heavily on the base of my spine, biting my tongue as I did so.

16

I was furious with Alik. Did he really think he could play the same trick on me twice? I wasn't going to let myself be softened up in the same way again. Admittedly I owed him an account of my progress, but he could have sent for me in a civilised fashion if he wanted to see me.

Then a worrying thought came to me, as I remembered that Bradley had been picked up as well. Had Alik somehow got wind of the fact that I was going to tell the American about the sect? That certainly might explain the peremptory treatment. But there was no way in which he could have found out, unless Bradley himself had passed the informaton on. Or Tanya. But that was a thought I couldn't contemplate.

In any case, even if Alik didn't yet know why Bradley and I had met, he would as soon as the questioning began. Worst of all, Bradley's arrest meant that there was probably no longer any chance of getting the information out to the West.

The van stopped. The back door rattled open. I was hustled over a courtyard, across a vestibule and into a lift. It all happened too quickly for me to be able to take in my surroundings, but the shortness of the journey meant we were still somewhere near the centre.

The lift groaned its way up to the sixth floor. We walked down a corridor—I noticed with surprise that it was carpeted—to an open door at the far end. A man in army uniform stood just inside the doorway and watched us approach.

"Come in, Morozov." He waved the escort away and shut the door behind me. As I followed him across the room I noticed that he had the four stars of a captain on his shoulder-boards.

"Come over here." He looked round slowly and then picked his cap off the table and held it out towards me as though he were asking for alms. "Just empty your pockets into this, would you."

I did as he asked. He sat down and began to go through his booty, grunting and muttering to himself.

He was a large, plump young man, untidily dressed, with thinning dark curly hair and incipient jowls. His grey eyes had an unpleasant wet sheen to them, and his mouth seemed unnaturally red. The colour of his shoulder-boards and cap-band showed that he was in the security forces. Certainly in that slovenly get-up he wouldn't have lasted ten seconds in a crack regiment. He smelt very strongly of that scent which costs ten copecks a squirt in the wash-rooms of better class hotels.

The room wasn't at all what I'd expected. It had more the air of someone's private apartment than a police office. But a second glance suggested that no one actually lived here. There was a stiffness and formality about the furnishings and decorations which revealed not an individual taste, but the impersonal hand of some state enterprise, while the old-fashioned mahogany furniture with its red leather upholstery looked almost brand new.

The door opened. A short, stout man with a red face slipped unobtrusively into the room, sidled over to the captain, bent over him, whispered something, and sidled out again.

He avoided looking at me, but I recognised him immediately: the man from the *shashlychnaya* who'd held me up at the exit by his inability to get his coat on. And then, as though this one act of recognition had suddenly fed power into a portion of my brain which up to then had been switched off, images of a whole series of earlier encounters leapt up before me.

He had been, hadn't he, that drunk on the boulevard bench whom Bradley had pointed out earlier that evening. I was pretty sure, too, that he'd been somewhere around when Bradley and I met for the first time over the chessboard. And I was absolutely certain that I'd seen him in the Aragvi when I'd been there with Alik. I remembered him pushing hastily past me as I stood on the steps of the restaurant after lunch, as if he'd been following Alik, rather than me.

This last, almost careless observation struck me forcibly. There was a lot to think about in its implications. But at that moment the captain called me over.

He had a printed form in front of him and the first five minutes were taken up with personal particulars: surname, first name and patronymic; date and place of birth; education, profession, place of residence; father's name, mother's name; date and place of their birth; father's profession and social status; nationality; party membership; and so on and so on. I'd given the same information often enough before for it to be on file in the offices of every state organisation in the land, but if the captain wanted his own personal copy he was welcome to it.

He filled in the last blank space, put his pen down and sighed. I sat up straighter and wiped my hands surreptitiously on my trousers. Now the real thing was about to begin.

"I'm disappointed, Comrade Morozov, to see a man in your position mixed up in an affair of this kind. The consequences for your career could be serious."

I said nothing. He wasn't telling me anything I didn't know.

"Yes, very serious. It's not always wise for Soviet citizens to consort too freely with foreign nationals, especially if these happen to follow the same profession as your friend Mr. Bradley."

I couldn't let that pass without making some protest. "He's not a friend of mine," I said. "I hardly know him."

"Really? Yet you had a long and intimate conversation with him this evening over *shashlyk* and beer, you spend your mornings playing chess with him." He leered as he said this, perhaps hoping to astound me with the extent of his knowledge.

I said nothing. Our meeting in Leningrad had apparently escaped their attention.

He reached over and picked my wallet up. "You keep his card"—he produced it with a conjuror's flip—"carefully in your wallet." He dropped the wallet and took up my notebook. "And, for greater security, in case you lose that, in your notebook"—he opened it and held it up in front of me—"you write his telephone number."

I stared at the page in disbelief. I'd certainly never put Bradley's number in my notebook, yet there it was. Another entry on the same page caught my eye. I remembered when I'd written that, and with one recollection came the other. This was a number I'd found among Nicola's notes that night on the train.

The captain must have taken my surprise as a tribute to the psychological efficacy of his methods of interrogation. He smiled broadly. "And what subjects, might I ask, do you discuss with your American acquaintance?" He underlined the last word with heavy irony.

This was dangerous ground. I had no idea what answer Bradley might be giving to the same question. But it seemed worthwhile concealing the truth as long as possible.

"We have talked about a lot of things. About chess, about life . . ."

"About politics, perhaps?"

That was too simple a trap. "No, never about politics."

"He tells you about life in America?"

"Sometimes."

"And you tell him about life here?"

This was difficult to answer. If I wasn't careful I could easily be accused of giving enemies of the Soviet Union material for their slanders. "I try to correct some of his misapprehensions about life in our socialist society."

We both knew the worth of my statement, but to my surprise he took it at its face value and moved on to another subject.

"Perhaps you discuss literature? It's the subject you teach, after all."

I recognised the sublime KGB logic behind the statement. If I'd been a stomatologist, would he have asked me if I'd discussed teeth with Bradley?

"I think we might have done, yes."

"American literature?"

"Possibly."

"And Soviet literature as well?"

There was a slight change in the tone of his voice as he put this last question.

"I can't really remember."

He slapped the table with his hand. "Come, come, Morozov. I've been very patient with you so far. You must remember what you talked about. You don't have conversations with American journalists every day."

I was in a quandary. On the face of it this was a safe subject, far removed from Lyuba and the White Swan. But if I invented an imaginary conversation I'd soon get into difficulty.

"I don't think Bradley's very interested in literature," I said lamely. For some reason this was a fortunate remark.

He gave a nasty smile. "Mr. Bradley's very interested in literature—of a certain kind. We're not sewn with bast, you know. We know exactly what he's trying to do, and when the right moment comes we'll squash him like a cockroach." With his thumb he pressed an imaginary insect to death on the glass top of the desk. "It's bound to happen sooner or later. But there's no need for you to go down with him. I know you're a cultured, intelligent man. You move in certain circles, are given certain books to read. We can understand that. Some of us may even have read them ourselves. But do you think it's right that your friend Mr. Bradley should make large sums of money out of them?"

A buoyant tide of relief swept over me. I finally understood what he was talking about. I'd been picked up because I'd been with Bradley, not for anything I'd done myself. The arrest had nothing whatsoever to do with Alik, Lyuba or the White Swan. The red-faced man must have been following Bradley; it followed that, if he'd been at the Aragvi, it had been by pure coincidence. Or I'd been mistaken.

They thought that Bradley and I had been meeting in order to arrange the smuggling of *samizdat* manuscripts, dissident literature, out to the West. Whatever else I might be guilty of, I was whiter than driven snow as far as this crime was concerned. Of course, I'd read Pasternak, Solzhenitsyn and the others; I even knew a couple of writers who'd be lucky to get published here, and would be only too pleased if their work appeared in Zurich or New York. But that was as far as my connection went.

Nevertheless, there was still a problem. I could go along with him, make up a story, say that Bradley had asked me to put him in touch with dissident authors. If they believed me, Bradley would probably get expelled. And if that happened, he wouldn't want to do us a favour. But if I denied that this was what we'd been talking about, I'd be asked what the subject of our conversation had been.

The captain was visibly growing impatient at my hesitation. I took a quick decision.

"I think you've been misinformed, comrade captain. We never discussed the kind of literature you have in mind."

He seemed to swell in his chair. His forehead and jowls went red. "Lies!" He thumped the table with his fist. "You're aiding an enemy of the state, Morozov. I want the truth, and I want it now. I was going to be lenient with you, but—" He broke off, jumped hastily to his feet and came to attention as the door opened and a short, round man in civilian clothes came in. "Comrade general! I didn't expect—"

"All right, Boris Mikhaylovich. I'll carry on now." He took the seat the captain had vacated, arranged a silver cigarette case and lighter in front of him, and pulled over a large glass ashtray. Only then did he look over at me.

He was an old man, with sharp black eyes in a wrinkled brown face. His hair was greying bristle, trimmed close to his scalp. He was wearing a striped brown suit and a lilac shirt with a raised pattern. It was buttoned to the neck, but he wore no tie. He looked like an old tortoise. Tough, wise and horribly knowing.

He stirred my belongings, which the captain had left lying on the table, with a blunt forefinger.

"Yours?"

I nodded and he pushed them across.

"I'm Manilov. I had you picked up. Wanted to have a look at you. There are some funny things going on at the moment, and you're in the middle of them."

He stopped and lit a cigarette. He held it upright between second finger and thumb, as men smoke who are more used to hand-rolled cigarettes, loosely packed with coarse *makhorka,* than the factory-made kind.

"Didn't get on very well with Lapshin, did you? Bit of an idiot. Thinks anyone who meets a foreigner is trying to get a book published." He caught my look of surprise and gave a bark of laughter. "I've been listening to you. The room's wired. And watching you. Closed circuit television as well." He pointed towards what I'd taken to be a spotlight on the wall, illuminating a full-size reproduction of Repin's famous picture *Zaporozhe Cossacks Drafting a Reply to the Turkish Sultan.* "We're old, but we try to keep up-to-date."

He flicked the ash from his cigarette with a gesture strangely similar to Alik's. "But Lapshin's right about one thing. Not a good idea to have much to do with Bradley. Not a proper journalist, you know."

"You mean he's a spy?" I couldn't keep the incredulity out of my voice.

"Spy? What's that? Don't know what that is. He's a *pomoyshchik:* a garbage man. Collects all kinds of rubbish. Sends it home. Might be a diamond in it. Most probably not."

I couldn't see why he was being so open with me. But my puzzlement was overshadowed by despair. Bradley obviously had no intention of ever writing an article on the White Swan. He'd only promised to do so in order to get the information out of me.

Manilov misunderstood my change of expression. "Don't worry. Not going to put you in jail. Not yet, anyway."

I tried to look reassured.

He went on. "Why don't we throw him out? That's what you want to know. Very useful to us. Very useful to know what he's asking questions about. Tells us what interests them in Washington."

I was completely bewildered. Manilov's words had the

same effect as that produced by tapping a kaleidoscope. Everything I'd learnt suddenly became unrecognisable, settling into a new, complicated pattern. Could the CIA really be interested in the White Swan? Were they possibly lunatic enough to believe that Father Zakhar's scheme stood a chance of success?

"What could I know that would be important to him?" I said.

Manilov lit another cigarette, blew out a cloud of smoke and squinted at me through it. "Might not know it was important. Probably wouldn't. Just an odd detail. Something to fill out a picture." He knocked his hand against the edge of the table to shake the ash from his cigarette. "What was he interested in?"

There was no point in defending Bradley any longer, but what would the consequences be for Lyuba if I told Manilov everything?

"I don't think—"

Manilov went on as if he hadn't noticed that I was replying. "The *shashlychnaya*. Whose idea?"

"Mine."

"Georgian food. Did he like it?"

"No."

"What did he ask about? National minorities? Tatars?"

"No."

"Uzbeks?"

"No."

"Kazakhs?"

"No." I was completely at a loss. The questioning had taken an absolutely incomprehensible turn. But I was happy for it to go on in this way.

Manilov was silent for a moment, then he began again. "Holy books. Did he mention them?"

"What?"

"The Koran, the Bible. Ask about buying them, importing them?"

"No." I began to cringe inwardly. Manilov appeared to be approaching the truth gradually, in an indirect fashion.

"Moslems?"

"No."

"Religion?"

"No."

"Religious manifestations?"

"No." To my ears the last two negatives had sounded horribly false. It seemed impossible that he would not have noticed the difference, but he seemed to have lost all interest in the conversation. He was leaning back in his chair, staring abstractedly in front of him. There was a long pause. Then he sat up abruptly and stubbed out his cigarette.

"Thank you, Morozov. That's all."

"I can go?" I couldn't really believe it was over.

"When you like. But stay away from Bradley."

The warning was superfluous. I'd already decided never to see Bradley again if I could help it. I got slowly to my feet.

I was half-way to the door when he spoke again. "See much of Alik these days, do you?"

I swivelled round and stared at him. He was smiling sagely at me through the smoke of another cigarette. Then the smile vanished.

"Keep away from him, too. Sympathise with you. But it's a very nasty business. A dirty business. Nothing you can do to make things better. You'll harm yourself. And others as well. Go back to your literature. The dead aren't as dangerous as the living." He waved his hand in dismissal.

17

During the next week I stuck religiously to Manilov's instructions. To my relief I heard nothing from Alik or Bradley. I spent my days in the Lenin Library, and my evenings in the apartment. I saw a good deal of Tanya, though not as much as I would have liked. She was busy with rough cuts in the studio that week.

That moment of doubt in her, immediately after my arrest, had been the last of its kind. We were now cautiously engaged in re-establishing our old relationship. This time round it promised to be better, more mutually satisfying.

But overshadowing everything was the worry of what might be happening to Lyuba. I should have been glad to have so much uninterrupted time to give to my work, but attempts to study were a dismal failure. Time after time I found myself, instead of sitting at my desk, walking up and down the long dreary smoking-room on the top floor of the library, going over the same thoughts.

To begin with I tried to make myself believe that Manilov was in control of the situation. But I couldn't succeed in doing this for long. Why had his questions dealt with such irrelevant topics? Why had he stopped so soon, when in a few more minutes he could have cracked me open like a ripe sunflower seed, and extracted all I knew? Had he got everything he wanted from Bradley, or was he not interested in the White Swan? Had Bradley even been arrested? What was this dirty, nasty business? I began dimly to see Lyuba and myself, even Father Zakhar and his icon, as playing out a game which was only tangentially connected to some much vaster and more dangerous struggle.

Worst of all was the feeling of helplessness. There was nothing I could do to change or influence the course of events. I was several times tempted to arrange a meeting with Nicola—she'd given me the address of her friends at the embassy just before we'd parted. Though there could be an innocent explanation for her possession of Bradley's telephone number, I was inclined to think that she too was somehow involved. Some of her remarks had been too knowledgeable, too percipient and pertinent to be those of a mere bystander. But her involvement semed even less central than mine; she wouldn't be able to help me find Lyuba. And for the moment I'd had enough of consorting with foreigners. I think that, in the end, despite Manilov's warning, I would have tried to get in touch with Alik. But in the event it proved unnecessary.

Over a week had gone by since my meeting with Bradley. The cold spell had continued, bringing with it what I hoped was the last snowfall of the year. Walking back to the Malaya Bronnaya early one afternoon after another pointless session in the library I'd passed a gang of women clearing the snow and ice from the pavement. One of them, straightening up and stretching as I passed, had shown me a profile as pure and as innocent as Lyuba's.

When I was called to the telephone soon after getting back to my room I knew who the caller must be.

Her voice at the other end of the line was thin and high-pitched. "Vanya? I must see you." She sounded terrified.

"Where are you?"

"The Leningrad station."

"Stay there. I'll meet you in the buffet." I put down the receiver and hurried back to my room.

It took me just over half an hour to get to the station. She was sitting in a corner of the buffet, infinitely frail and woebegone. Her face was thinner than ever and looked tiny under the heavy fur hat. A small suitcase stood at her feet and she was clasping a handbag in her lap. She tried to smile at me. I sat down and put my hand on her arm. It was tense and rigid.

"What's the matter, Lyuba? What are you doing here?"

"He came to see me."

"Who?"

"The Evil One. He was clothed in human form, but I recognised him."

I thought for a moment, and then took a guess. "Alik?"

She shuddered. "His name is anathema. Yes, he. Grishka the pretender."

Bit by bit I got her story out of her. Alik had turned up at the dacha in Lakhta the previous evening. His appearance had thrown her into a state of fear which his behaviour had rapidly turned to panic. What he'd actually done or said I was unable to discover: it was something which Lyuba found so terrifying that she was only able to refer to it obliquely. He'd left late at night, threatening to return again the next morning. But Lyuba had slipped out of the house after he'd gone, had made her way through the forest to Leningrad and had then caught the train to Moscow. As she talked she threw hurried, jerky glances around her, like a bird. She looked as though she might be on the verge of another attack.

I was surprised that Alik had managed to get to her past Peredonov and the others. I asked her about this.

"They are no longer with me," she said. "The master called his servants. They have gone on ahead to prepare the way. Now I must follow. But he, Grishka, has sent his dark emissaries after me. Help me, Vanya, help me to escape them."

I thought for a moment. This sounded very like paranoia, but on the other hand Alik *had* known where to find her, and it seemed quite likely that he would be having her followed. She took my hesitation for disbelief.

"It is true, Vanya, true. I know that it is written that the wicked flee where no man pursueth, but I have seen them like black ravens behind me, their sulphurous breath has scorched my raiment."

"Are they here now?"

She looked slowly round the buffet. It was almost empty. A group of Red Army soldiers in greatcoats, their kitbags piled in a heap, were drinking beer at one of the tables over a quiet game of *shtoss*. At another an old woman with a cloth scarf tied over her head was knitting away at a small pink garment, perhaps destined for a new granddaughter. By the far wall a severe-looking young woman, wearing thick, horn-rimmed spectacles with her hair tied back in a bun, was reading some technical journal.

"No, they have vanished. Your coming has driven them away. But they will return. Help me, please help me." She clutched my arm.

"Where must you go?"

"Some of the righteous live in Moscow." She opened her bag and showed me a scrap of paper with something— presumably an address—written on it. I reached out, but she put it quickly away again.

"They will help me on my way. But I must be free before I can go to them."

"And where will they take you?"

She looked at me in surprise. "To the church in Vologda, of course."

I sighed. The last thing I wanted was for her to join Father Zakhar's crusade. And why, when she'd fled the sect with disgust earlier, was she now so eager to return to it?

Suddenly her hand shot out over my shoulder. "There! Behind you! The ravens are returning one by one."

I twisted hastily round and met the surprised gaze of a respectable-looking middle-aged citizen in a black coat and Astrakhan fur hat who was standing at the counter. He was certainly wearing the devil's colours, but otherwise bore no particular resemblance to a plain-clothes policeman. Now he'd appeared, however, it did seem worthwhile finding out whether Lyuba was right in thinking she was being followed. If it did nothing else, the activity might allay her anxiety. And when she was calmer, I hoped to be able to persuade her not to leave Moscow. If necessary, I'd have to use force to keep her with me.

I picked up her bag, took her by the arm, and led her out of the buffet. Out of the corner of my eye I saw the man in the black coat put down his sandwich and turn after us. It looked as though it wasn't just paranoia, after all.

As we crossed the station concourse I found myself wishing I'd paid more attention a few years ago, when a drunken dissident cornered me at a party and insisted on telling me about all the techniques he'd evolved to evade pursuit. Only one or two of the simplest stuck in my mind. But I did remember quite well something else that he'd said.

"If they pull their fingers out and put on a full-scale operation, with ten or a dozen *chekisty,* four or five cars, radios and all the rest, you haven't a hope in hell of getting away." He waggled his empty glass at me. "But if they do that, you'll never know they're there. So it doesn't matter anyway."

Since Lyuba had recognised a follower, it looked as though Alik was only employing a small team. The first thing to do was to identify them.

We dived into the metro station. I fed a couple of coins into the turnstile and hurried Lyuba down the long escalator. When we reached the bottom I turned and looked back, but black coat wasn't to be seen. We took a circle train, going west. I wanted to be on the line that runs north out to Khimki. The stations on it offer much less cover than most.

I thought I caught a glimpse of black coat behind us as we went through the interchange at Belorusskaya, but the figure vanished immediately in the crowd. We were now on the line I'd chosen, and it was time to begin.

I got us off the train at Aeroport, the second station north. It's never very busy, and today was no exception.

We stood on the platform and let a few trains go by in either direction. I spotted black coat quite soon. He'd changed his Astrakhan hat for a flat cap, and was trying to conceal himself behind one of the fluted chromium-plated pillars that separate the up and down platforms. But, as I'd known when I'd chosen the station, they're too slender to be used in that way. Unlike, for instance, the squat Ukrainian columns of Kievskaya, behind which a regiment of Indian elephants could keep out of sight.

A moment later I discovered his colleague, and my heart leapt up. It was the senior of the two men who'd picked me up from my office at the faculty: the one Alik had described as being "as thick as a Tambov peasant." I hoped devoutly that this was meiosis, rather than hyperbole.

I went on watching for a few minutes more, but couldn't see anyone else suspicious. Alik was certainly cheeseparing on this operation. Perhaps he thought Lyuba was an

easy quarry. The next step was to disabuse him of that
notion.

I waited until I could hear the next train approaching—it
happened to be going south—and then took Lyuba over to
the north-bound platform. When the train pulled in on the
opposite side I hung on until the last moment before
running over to it and pulling her in. As I'd half-expected,
this elementary tactic didn't fool anyone. One of the agents
was in our compartment; the other had got in higher up.

Lyuba had said hardly a word since we'd started off, but
was looking a little better: perhaps the exercise was doing
her good. I put the suitcase into her hand and told her to
get out at the next station, but not to move away from the
door.

The train slid into Dinamo and stopped. The doors
opened. Lyuba got out. So did my acquaintance. Black
coat stayed put. There was a hiss of air as the doors began
to close. They met my foot and jerked open again. I leant
out and pulled Lyuba back into the carriage. The doors
slammed shut and the train moved off, leaving the Tambov
peasant behind on the platform.

The easy success made me feel light-hearted and ab-
surdly pleased with myself. Then I glanced across at the
other agent and came down to earth with a bump. He was
not at all pleased with events. In fact, he looked positively
murderous. It would probably be wise not to let him catch
us alone down a dark alley.

I sat down next to Lyuba on the bench and considered
our next move. The metro had done us proud, but we
ought to get off it now. If we went on changing trains we
might allow the other *chekist* to catch up with us. And we
ought to keep moving as fast as possible, so that black coat
wouldn't have time to whistle up reinforcements. The only
difficulty was to think of some way of eluding him in the
open air.

Belorusskaya came again and went, followed by Maya-

kovskaya. At Sverdlov Square I jerked Lyuba to her feet
and out of the carriage. We came up into the open air by
the side of the Bolshoy. I ran her down the side of the
square past the information booths and the *pirozhki* sellers.

The Metropole Hotel opposite seemed a promising refuge for a moment, but then I remembered there was only
one way in and out. Instead we turned right, down Okhotny
Ryad, past Union House, where Lenin had lain in state in
1924—a particularly useless piece of information to come
into my mind at that moment—and the ugly grey mass of
the State Planning Office. After we'd crossed Gorky Street
I quickened our pace.

We shot into the courtyard of the old university, and ran
up the steps to the entrance. The door-keeper recognised
me, but cast a surprised look at Lyuba.

"A colleague from Tallinn. For the seminar this evening," I said, and pulled her past him, up the wide
staircase to the first floor. As we turned into the corridor I
heard him below.

"Where are you going, citizen? Entry is forbidden to
nonmembers of the university," followed by a voice raised
in expostulation.

The first door along the corridor was locked. The second gave under my hand. It was a small storeroom. I
tumbled Lyuba inside, followed her, and shut the door
behind us. The room was pitch-dark and smelt of mouldering
paper. I put my arm round Lyuba and held her to me. She
was breathing in great gasps.

A moment later I heard footsteps rushing up the stairs.
They came on down the corridor more slowly and stopped.
The handle of the first door was rattled. Lyuba shuddered.
I put my hand over her mouth.

I was in a raging fury at my own incompetence. Alik's
agents might be stupid, but catching us was easier than
shooting fish in a barrel. I'd shown less street sense than a
ten-year-old. Any Moscow child could have made the

chase last at least three times as long, and would probably have got away in the end as well. But I'd simply succumbed to panic and had, like a fool, run in a straight line towards a familiar bolt-hole, which proved to be a trap.

The footsteps began again, slowly. They stopped outside our door. In my mind's eye I could see the hand reaching out for the knob. The frustrations of the last few weeks, feelings of helplessness and inadequacy, all came to the boil together.

I pulled the door open, reached out, heaved the man into the storeroom and kicked the door shut again.

Holding him by the lapels, I smashed him repeatedly against the wall. There was a series of subsidiary bangs and crashes as shelves gave way and decanted their contents on to the floor.

He hit out and kicked, but there was no force behind his blows. Perhaps he was encumbered by his overcoat, or perhaps the first impact against the wall had hurt him badly.

I began to cough and couldn't stop. I could hear Lyuba also coughing behind me. In front of me the man was making a kind of wheezing rattle. It suddenly cut off. He sagged towards me. I let go hurriedly. There was a rustling sigh, and something heavy landed on my foot.

Stepping back, I collided with Lyuba. I put my arm round her again. She was trembling violently. I opened the door, found the light switch, and closed the door again.

The air was thick with dust. The floor was covered in a sea of books and papers. My opponent was lying half on his side with his head propped against the wall and his knees bent. He was breathing shallowly. A thin trickle of blood ran from his nose down his cheek. A layer of dust had already settled on his face. He seemed suddenly to have shrunk. His coat had become several sizes too big for him. Lying there, he was a small, sad, old man with bad teeth and a hole in the bottom of one of his shoes.

I switched the light off and closed the door quietly. A quarter of an hour later I was buying us each 250 grams of champagne from the soda-fountain on the ground floor of GUM.

When I sat down opposite Lyuba she leant forward and took my hand in hers. For a moment or two she said nothing. Then she whispered: "Thank you, Vanya, thank you. You've been a veritable David."

It seemed an opportune moment to try and persuade her to stay in Moscow.

"What's going to happen in Vologda, Lyuba?"

"Didn't the master tell you?"

"Not really, no."

She was silent for a moment, as though debating whether to tell me or not. I drank some champagne. It was horrible. Lyuba reached a decision and began to speak, slowly and quietly.

"A new era will begin. The radiance that was dimmed will shine out again, brighter than ever before. A truth will be proclaimed which will echo over all the land, rejoicing men's hearts and making them whole once more. The miracle of this Easter will be surpassed only by that of the other Easter, the first of all."

As she spoke her voice became firmer and louder, her gaze rapt and ecstatic. She was looking out over my shoulder into the cavernous, noisy interior of the department store, filled with crowds of shoppers, but she obviously saw and heard nothing of what was before her; her mind was filled with the intensity of her inner vision.

I reached out, gripped her hand, and squeezed it hard. She came slowly back to reality, and looked down in surprise. I let go; the marks of my fingers stood out on her skin.

"You mustn't go there. It's too dangerous. You must stay here with me."

She astonished me by laughing. "Dangerous? There

will be no danger, Vanya. Because I am frightened here, alone, surrounded by evil, does not mean that I will be frightened there, among the hosts of the faithful. And how can I not go? When the White Swan is crowned, must not his affianced bride be by his side?"

"I thought the White Swan was a filthy abomination. Like Chemosh of the Moabites, or Ashtoreth of the Zidonians."

"Don't mock, Vanya. These things are beyond your understanding. Earlier I was wrong, as was explained to me. Spirit and flesh must go hand in hand. Without a soul the body dies; but without physical integument the soul is impotent. The Blessed Lady and the White Swan are two faces of one and the same truth."

She'd recovered completely from the semi-hysterical state she had been in at the station. But she had changed since Lakhta. She had become more remote, less human. And was obviously not going to listen to any argument I could put forward.

I finished my champagne and got to my feet. "All right," I said. "I'll take you to your friends, and then we'll say goodbye."

Lyuba remained in her seat and looked at me with a smile. "No, Vanya. With the help of God I will make my own way there. You have helped me much and I will pray that you too may come to see the light. But we must part now; I must be alone."

She'd seen through my subterfuge with ridiculous ease, and if she refused to go any further with me there was nothing I could do. Her unreasoning faith, together with her bland dismissal of my help, annoyed me intensely. For a moment I contemplated the idea of taking her at her word and leaving her. Then I looked down. Her short blonde hair clung damply to her forehead, accentuating the hollowness of her temples. She was holding the champagne glass in her hands, and was gazing into the wine. I knew that, no matter how irritated I might be by the irrationality of her behaviour or the senselessness of her beliefs, I could never abandon her. I sighed and sat down again.

"Let me come with you to Vologda, Lyuba."

"Come with me?" She sounded surprised. She looked at me and then shook her head. "No, it is not permitted. You are not yet numbered among us. I cannot reveal our secrets to the uninitiated."

"But—" I looked away for a moment, trying to think of some argument which might persuade her, and saw something which immediately altered the situation: a young woman in thick horn-rimmed glasses with her hair caught back in a bun was standing on the far side of the glass partition which separated the bar from the rest of the store, and was looking through at us.

I touched Lyuba's arm. "One of your ravens has caught up with us again. We'd better go."

Her face changed immediately. She looked almost as frightened as when I'd first seen her, and rose to follow me without a word.

It was dark outside. I thought for a moment, and then led off down towards the district that lies behind the Red Square, *Kitaygorod*, the Chinatown of medieval Moscow. There were very few people about.

Still flushed with success from the two earlier encounters, I didn't think we'd have much difficulty in throwing off this pursuer. For five minutes we twisted and turned at random. But the clacking of high heels never lagged far behind. Finally, as we were going down a deserted sidestreet, I pressed Lyuba's suitcase into her hand and told her to wait for me round the next corner.

I dragged off my coat, draped it over my shoulders, stuffed my hat in my pocket and began to lurch back the way we'd come. I rounded a corner and saw the agent hurrying towards me under the high brick wall of a churchyard. As we drew level I staggered across her path and tripped her. She fell. I bent down, snatched her spectacles and bag, and ran back. As I ran, I crammed the spectacles inside the bag and threw both over the wall.

When I reached the corner where I'd asked Lyuba to wait I stopped and called softly. I expected to see her step out of one of the dark entries, but no one appeared. I called louder, with no result. Perhaps she'd misunderstood me. I went on to the end of the street and tried again. A quarter of an hour later I gave up. She had vanished completely.

18

I was coming out through the courtyard of the apartment house when they jumped me. In retrospect, of course, it was stupid to have gone back to my room. But if I was going to Vologda I needed warm clothes. In any case, after my success as bully-boy and bag-snatcher I was feeling ten feet tall and almost invincible.

I was jammed up in a corner of the yard with my suitcase pressed painfully into my stomach. A torch was shining in my eyes.

"I don't expect he knows who we are, Fedya."

"Or what we're doing here."

"We might be common criminals, *blatnye*, after his wallet and everything else. Or just *makhnovtsy*, with bicycle chains in our pockets, looking for a black or a yid or a queer to beat up."

"Perhaps you'd better show him who we are, Sasha."

But I already knew only too well who they were. I didn't need the beam from Sasha's torch turned on their

159

faces to recognise Alik's original two *chekisty*, the Tambov peasant and his junior partner.

"When we're keeping an eye on a *gavrik*, we don't like him to play silly buggers with us."

"He knows we're there, and he ought to behave in a gentlemanly way about it. Not fuck us about by jumping on and off trains like a yo-yo."

Their cross-talk act was getting on my nerves, as it was no doubt intended to. "You're wasting your talents here," I said. "You ought to be down by the river, on the stage at the Variety Theatre. You'd go like a bomb." I winced as the torch caught me on the side of the head.

"And we don't like them to talk back, do we, Fedya?"

There was a short silence, and then Sasha said reminiscently: "Do you remember the diplomat, Fedya?"

"The Fritz?"

"No, the wop. The one with the sense of humour." He turned to me. "He had the same ideas as you. Every time he was a subject, nothing but fun and games. Into the metro, out of the metro. Into GUM, up and down the stairs, out by the back door. He'd get in a taxi, slide out of the far door, run through the park, take a bus a couple of stops and then change to a tram going the other way. Oh, he was a laugh a minute, *il commendatore*."

"Until we caught up with him in Sokolniki Park. That was a real laugh, now."

"He went out there one fine day to meet the girl friend. A typist from the American embassy with tits like railway buffers. But he met us instead. They swept him up and sent him back home on the next plane."

I didn't find the story as amusing as they did. It was probably a good thing that as yet they apparently hadn't heard about their two colleagues.

A car stopped in the road outside. I heard a door open and then slam shut. Someone walked briskly along the pavement, turned in under the courtyard arch. The footsteps hesitated.

"This way, comrade colonel!"

Sasha shone the torch in that direction and I saw Alik. He was in uniform and looked furious.

"You fool, Vanya." He struck me across the face with his gloves. "You knew my men. Didn't you realise I was protecting her? I told you someone else was involved."

"Were you protecting her in the same way when she was in Lakhta? Or when you sent her to Kamchatka to talk to the reindeer?"

He looked as though he was going to hit me again, but restrained himself. "Are you going to believe her stories? A hysteric with religious mania?"

"And epilepsy. Don't forget the epilepsy."

He made a gesture of annoyance. "And epilepsy. I tried to get her to go into a sanatorium, but . . ." Then, leaning towards me: "Where is she now? Do you know that, at least?"

I couldn't see that I would do her any harm by telling the truth. "No, I don't. She got away from me as well."

He swore loudly and obscenely. "I flush her out of hiding in Lakhta, she runs straight into your arms and you lose her. And you think you can protect her better than I can." He took a few steps backwards and forwards, slapping his gloves against the thigh of his breeches. "What happened?"

"I left her for a moment. When I came back she'd gone." It sounded very lame. Even through the dark I could feel the force of Alik's sneer. "She had a Moscow address to go to. Some fellow sectarians," I added.

"And then?"

"She was going to Vologda."

"Vologda." He repeated the name slowly, voluptuously. "Perhaps you've not done too badly after all." He turned away and began to walk back across the courtyard. Over his shoulder he said: "Where do all roads lead to, Vanya? Rome, is it?"

He was just about to go through the arch when Sasha came loudly to attention. "Comrade colonel!"

"Yes?"

"Your friend here."

"I'll leave him to you. But not too rough. He works with his brain, not his muscles."

The two agents had given me a fair amount of freedom during the conversation with Alik, and they hadn't yet closed in again. Sasha, moreover, had just turned away from me to ask for instructions.

I swung the suitcase at Fedya as hard as I could and heard him grunt as it hit him. I came out of the corner, caught him with my shoulder, and spun him aside. The only advantage I had was an intimate knowledge of the courtyard's geography. I skidded wide round an outbuilding and then cut in again towards the back entrance. There was a resounding multiple crash: either Sasha, or Fedya—or, preferably, both—had collided with the row of garbage cans. As I pulled the gate open I heard Alik laughing. A moment later I was out of sight in the tangle of alleys behind Aleksey Tolstoy Street.

I had to ring the bell a couple of times before Tanya came to the door. She held a yellow towelling robe together at the neck and blinked sleepily at the harsh light in the corridor.

"You didn't tell me you were going to be as late as this when you rang up."

"I'm sorry." I followed her inside, put my suitcase down and took my coat off. "I've had an eventful evening."

"Tell me about it in bed. We've a plane to catch in the morning, remember?"

She dropped the robe to the floor and slipped into bed. I undressed slowly and got in beside her. As always, her skin radiated a dry, stimulating heat, giving the impression that for her normal body temperature was naturally several degrees above 37 centigrade.

"Well?" she asked.

As I told her what had happened I felt her grow tense in my arms. When I finished she let out a long sigh and relaxed. Then she pulled my head down and put her lips to my ear.

Sometime afterwards she asked me to light her a cigarette. As I passed it over to her she said: "Will there be any trouble?"

"I don't think so. It was a private affair of Alik's. If they take me in again I'll simply tell Manilov everything."

"If you get to see him."

"True, but whatever happens, it's not going to be nine grams in the back of the neck."

She smoked in silence for a time. Then she said: "What a *psikh* he is!"

"Alik?"

"Yes."

"Crazy like a fox, perhaps."

"Perhaps." She reached over and stubbed her cigarette out on the bedside table. "But did you ever consider that Alik might have got religion, too?"

I laughed. "Are you serious?"

"Why not?"

"Well, to begin with, nothing except the real, the concrete, the tangible, has ever existed for him. His whole career has been dedicated to seeing that Aleksey Petrovich Ostroumov gets the best of everything our society and the party can give him. Why would he throw all this up for some imaginary benefit in the hereafter? He's never done a single generous unselfish action in his life. Or thought of doing one. He's simply not the stuff religious converts are made of."

"What about his attitude to Lyuba?"

She went on before I had time to say anything. "Don't you see. In fact, it's people like that, apparently the least likely ones, who do suddenly change from unbelief to belief. We've all got some way of expressing our spiritual side. If not religion, then love, or art, or music, or literature. Even making films. But they haven't. And so it fills up inside them. Until something gives way, it all comes pouring out and their character reverses itself completely.''

"Lyuba was saying something like that earlier."

"There you are then."

"The way you describe it, it sounds like an example of what mathematicians call catastrophe theory."

"Really? I was thinking more of Central American war-whistles. I was reading about them the other day." She put a hand out of bed and rummaged around in the pile of books and magazines on the floor, finally coming back with a small volume with a torn and dirty paper cover. "They're huge earthenware jars, with lots of pipes and mouths and funnels. You put them under a spring or a waterfall—or pour water in, if you like. When they're full, some valve operates. All the water suddenly sluices out through the stops, whistling and booming and gurgling. I'd like one in the bathroom. Here, read it.'' She riffled through the book and passed it to me, with her finger marking the place.

"What is it?"

"A translation of some English romantic novel. Type of Aleksandr Grin. They thought it might make a film."

"Would it?"

"Perhaps, but not here." She kissed me and lay down, pulling the blanket up.

I read the passage she'd indicated, and then looked at the title, mentally translating the Russian version back into English: *Lost Endeavour*.

19

I had a row of seats all to myself on the plane, and I used the first part of the flight to catch up on some of the sleep I'd missed. Tanya had dragged me out of bed at six and had hustled me down to a minibus that was waiting to take us to the airport. After a bit the stewardess came round with coffee and I began to wake up.

In the row behind me Lyova and Petya, the two cameramen, and Stasik, the sound engineer, were deep in a game of poker. They'd been playing ever since I first met them, and I could see no reason why they should ever stop. I'd earlier declined an invitation to take a hand, and had politely been put down as a middle-aged non-union member with no sporting instincts.

Tanya was sitting on the other side of the gangway, going through a script and making notes on it with a variety of different coloured ball-point pens. She looked up and caught my eye. I moved across and joined her.

"Is that the script?"

"No, it's my laundry list. Aren't you awake yet, Vanya?"

"Is it any good?"

"It needs a lot done to it. The dialogue is almost as bad as yours, but I think the basic movement and rhythm are about right. I'm just making some notes about locations."

"That's all you're doing? Looking for locations?"

"Why?"

"Do you need two cameramen? And a sound engineer? And all that paraphernalia?" The back of the minibus had been piled high with cameras, tape recorders and other equipment.

"No, but this is how Alik arranged it. I don't need a technical assistant either. Which is what you're listed as."

"Why should he want you to bring all this?"

"There's only one reason, isn't there?'

At Vologda airport a bus which looked as though it might have been new about the time of the first Five Year Plan was waiting for us. We rattled into town over a pot-holed road, past rows of wooden huts followed by the usual ubiquitous slab-sided blocks of flats. The sky was grey and it was very cold.

The hotel had been smart, but a long time ago. Inside it was dark and musty. The chairs in the lobby were all protected by white dust covers, which would probably only be removed if the Council of Ministers were to hold a meeting there.

I felt depressed and low on initiative. Now that I was here, I had no idea of what to do next. Back in Moscow I'd had a vague conception of myself as a knight, girding on his armour in order to go and rescue a maiden from a dragon. But now the enterprise seemed a forlorn hope, doomed to disaster. The immense rolling expanses of pine forest I'd seen from the plane had been frighteningly vast. A whole religion could have got lost in them, let alone a sect.

Alik would be turning up at any moment. Whether he was a believer or not, his presence would add a further complication to the situation. I must have been mad, too, to think that coming as a member of a film crew would be a good way of blending unobtrusively with the background. As soon as the cameras came out we'd be signing autographs for the whole of the local population.

I was deep in gloom when Tanya appeared, looking harassed.

"They'd got the numbers wrong, of course. They always do. And though they've found us a jeep and a camera truck, there aren't any drivers. They say there aren't any available in the district."

We went outside to inspect the jeep. It was just a battered old *gazik*, but the tires looked new and the engine started at the first turn of the key. The sun had broken through the cloud and there was a strong smell of wood smoke in the air. I sniffed it with relish. It took me back to my childhood; to winters in Ryazan; to snow and brilliant sunshine; to a happy, carefree, uncomplicated existence. I began to feel better.

"Let's go for a drive."

Tanya nodded vigorously in reply. She was wearing a red ski outfit which might have passed without notice on the slopes of Gstaad, but which here had already collected a small crowd. Her nose was pink with cold.

We drove back past the airport and on to the north-east. The main road had been cleared, but when it turned left I told Tanya to keep straight on, and we bumped up on to a surface of hard-packed snow and ice.

"Where are we going?"

"I thought we might go and look for the church."

"You know where it is?"

"Lyuba gave me directions when we were in Lakhta. It shouldn't be too difficult to find."

We drove on. To our left there was open country. On

our right the pine forest went up, ridge upon ridge, to the horizon. We passed through a small village. A knot of people outside the store stared at us curiously, and a small boy ran into the road and threw a snowball at the car. He was probably one of Lyuba's pupils: she should have taught him to be more polite to strangers.

A few kilometres further on the road divided.

"Which way, Vanya?"

"Keep to the right."

She turned the wheel too sharply. We skidded across the track and into the soft snow at the side. The back wheels spun uselessly and the jeep stopped. She put the engine into neutral and turned to me.

"What do we do now?"

"Try it in four wheel drive."

"How do I do that?"

I reached over and fiddled with the levers. There was a chunk as the drive engaged. She put the car back into gear and we crawled slowly out on to the road.

A power transmission line ran along the road here. Half an hour later, when it turned off abruptly down into a valley, I told Tanya to stop.

"According to Lyuba, somewhere here there's a path. I'm going to walk up there and see what's happening."

A little further on there was a clearing by the side of the road, full of huge stacks of logs. We ran the jeep in between them, and walked back. The path wasn't difficult to find. A lot of people had passed that way recently. We started off up the hill.

Forty minutes later we were still climbing. I was sweating profusely and wished I'd put on another pair of socks. My right heel was loose in my boot, and I was gradually rubbing a blister on it. A few hundred metres further on the path ran diagonally up a steep incline and then levelled out. I stopped at the top and waited for Tanya. She came up panting and threw herself down beside me.

"Are we nearly there?"

"About half-way. But look." I scratched a rough map in the snow. "We've reached the top of this ridge. As far as I can make out it runs back south-east, parallel to the road we left the jeep on, swings round to the west, and then north-west, making a kind of horseshoe enclosing a valley. The church should be somewhere down there, at the head of the valley. A track runs in at the bottom end from the village we passed, and we probably could have driven all the way up. But our entrance would have been rather public."

"So what do we do now?"

"I want to follow the ridge round. From somewhere on it we might get a view of what's down below."

Once off the path the going was much more difficult. Sometimes the frozen surface of the snow bore our weight, but more often we were forced to wade through it. However, it was never very deep under the trees, and the occasional bare stretch of ground had been swept clear by the wind. Once Tanya fell with a shriek up to her waist in a hidden gully. I went back to help her out, and, looking back the way we had come, saw that we were leaving a pretty obvious trail behind.

For some time it seemed that we would never get a look into the valley. The ground fell away too gradually, so that the view was obstructed by the trees on the slopes below us. All I could see was the distant ridge that formed the other edge of the basin. As we went on, however, we swung round gradually to the right, and the slope on that side grew steeper.

A little later I suddenly came out on to a slippery ledge of rock. On my right a cliff fell perpendicularly away into the valley, with a steep snow-covered slope at its foot. I stepped back into the trees and waited for Tanya. A few moments later we were both lying on the edge of the cliff, looking down into the valley.

It was like an immense scoop taken out of the landscape. The forest covered the floor and rose up the sides, but directly before us was a large, man-made clearing, roughly oval in shape, the site of Father Zakhar's *skit*, his hidden monastery. I stared at it in amazement—I'd never really believed in its existence.

Nearest to us, at the south-eastern end of the valley, was the church. It seemed almost near enough to touch. It was a tall wooden building with a single onion dome covered with cunningly worked, overlapping wooden scales. Once it had been gilded. To one side was a free-standing belfry with a gallery and small spire. Further away, in the middle of the clearing was a cluster of long low buildings with overhanging eaves. A stockade had earlier surrounded the whole complex, but now it was ruinous, with great gaps in it. From the buildings a track led down to what had presumably once been a gatehouse. A stump still survived, but the rest of the tower had gone. Beyond the gatehouse the track continued on down the valley.

There could be no doubt that the followers of the White Swan were in residence. Smoke was blowing away from the chimneys, some lorries were parked in the square, and figures were moving about among the buildings. By my side Tanya had begun to make impatient noises. We wriggled back from the brink, and I began to wonder what to do next.

20

It was still early in the evening when I began to make my way down into the valley. Tanya hadn't wanted me to go. She'd said that it was madness; that I'd get badly hurt, if not worse; that I'd not be able to do anything, certainly not be able to help Lyuba. Tears had even been brought into play.

In my heart of hearts I agreed with her. I hadn't been successful with Lyuba in Moscow. It would be even more difficult here, surrounded by her fellow believers. But with Easter less than a week away, it seemed impossible not to try something.

At last Tanya had given me an angry kiss and started off down the hill towards the jeep. She'd turned after a minute to shout something to me.

"What?"

"I said: what shall I do when you don't come back?"

"Tell the police."

She waved a hand exasperatedly and a moment later vanished among the trees.

The slope was steeper on this side of the ridge and the path led downwards in a series of zig-zags. It levelled off on the valley floor and wound its way through the pines. I crossed a stream by a wooden footbridge and further on came to the track we'd seen from the top of the cliff. I turned to the left, up towards the monastery. If one behaves like a spy, one can expect rough treatment. The best way is to march in by the front door. It gives a spurious air of legitimacy to one's actions.

At close quarters the gatehouse was even more of a ruin than it had seemed from above. It was little more than a heap of rotten logs, piled almost haphazardly one on another. As I drew level with it two men in *tulupy,* rough sheepskin coats, came quietly out from behind it and stopped in front of me. One was carrying a shot-gun. The other addressed me.

"Where are you going, friend?"

"The White Swan has sent for me."

They exchanged looks.

"Your name?"

"Morozov, Ivan Vasilevich."

The one who had spoken jerked his head at me and we set off up the track. The buildings further up were in much better repair than the gatehouse. Here and there bright new logs had been inserted into the dark timber of the old walls. The roofs also showed patches of new work. There were hardly any windows in the outside walls, but each building had a timber ramp, leading up to heavy double doors.

We passed through a gap in the middle of the range and came out into a square, facing the church. I looked about me curiously.

The square was symmetrical, in the shape of one L faced by its mirror image. The walls on this side were pierced with small, low windows with doors at regular intervals between them. Both doors and windows had

ornamentally carved lintels, and a carved frieze ran round
under the eaves. Four or five women were unloading
crates from the lorries, and carrying them into the building
on my right.

My guide urged me diagonally across the square towards
the end of the left-hand range. He opened a door and we
went inside. I found myself in a narrow, bare entrance
hall. It was pleasantly warm, but smelt strongly of manure. He vanished into an inner room. A moment later he
came out and held the door for me to go in. Father Zakhar,
in priest's robes, was standing on the far side of a table
covered with papers. He didn't seem surprised to see me.

"Welcome, Ivan Vasilevich, welcome to our abode."

If the passage had been warm, the room was almost
unsufferably hot, and the cause was easy to discover. In
one corner a big brick stove, with a built-in bed over it,
was roaring away. I took off my coat.

"I see that it wasn't in vain that I cast the seed before
you in Moscow, since you have now come to join the
army of the faithful, taking the name of the White Swan
as your password."

I found his air of mocking superiority extremely annoying.

"No, I haven't come to join you," I said. "As you well
know." I sat down. "But I am quite interested in your
little sect. As an anomalous survival from our distant
past."

"An anomalous survival. From our distant past. Well,
well."

"You must admit that such superstitions are out of place
in the world of the sputnik and the All-Union Exhibition of
Economic Achievements."

For a fraction of a second he looked startled, then roared
with laughter, slapping his thigh with his hand. "You
worried me for a moment, Ivan Vasilevich. Until I
recognised the style of Irina Aleksandrovna, our local
freethinker."

"You know Kozlova then?"

"Of course. She's the village school-teacher. We've had many a spirited ideological debate." He laughed again. "But what interests you about our church? As an anomalous survival, of course."

"How did it begin?"

"How did it begin?" He shrugged his shoulders. "With the first day of creation. But in your terms, from your limited view of history, it began nearly a decade ago, when we were first led here out of the wilderness. A little later the miraculous quality of our Blessed Lady was revealed to us. And since her fame has spread and grown in such a fashion, that we are now at the dawn of a new age."

"And the White Swan?"

"What of the White Swan?"

I had to ask the question that had been itching in my mind since that evening in Leningrad. "What's the connection with the opera? Why did you take that phrase from it?"

"The opera?"

"Musorgsky. *Khovanshchina.*"

"I don't understand you, Ivan Vasilevich. The White Swan is the White Swan. You will be able to see him, magnificent in flight and vigorous in his masculinity. A mystery play, perhaps, but no opera." He paused for a moment, and then said quietly: "Why did you come, my friend?"

"To take Lyuba back with me. To tell you to call the whole thing off."

"As blunt as before. Even dangerously so. But go on. I will be interested to hear your arguments."

I got up and leant forward with my hands on the table. "You haven't got a chance of achieving anything but disaster. And you must know it. You may start something here, with the locals, for a day at the most. But the authorities will find out. The army and police will move in. You'll be rolled up into a neat little parcel before you've finished your first hymn.''

"You place no reliance on the power of faith, Ivan Vasilevich?''

He was mocking me again.

I began to get angry. "Do you think that tanks and machine-gun bullets can be stopped by prayers? You may want a martyr's crown for yourself, but what about your followers? How many of your flock, do you think, will be left alive to purge a tenner or so in the camps?''

He listened to me calmly. "To die in a righteous cause may be more blessed than to live in a world full of evil. And perhaps you underestimate the force of prayer. But we do not rely on it alone.''

"On what then," I said. "The help of your friends in the KGB?''

"Yes.''

As I gaped at him in astonishment, he went across to an alcove and drew a curtain aside. Behind was a squat grey radio transceiver. He patted its top, and then turned back to me.

"With this I can exchange messages with your friend Aleksey Petrovich.''

"Alik?''

He nodded. "And through him I can communicate with his superiors. As I told you before, we have influence in high places. Others, too, await with longing the transformation of our society. We have laid our plans for it together. So your tanks and machine-guns will go into battle under our banner, not against us.''

I stared dumbly at him. The whole idea was too preposterous to believe in for a moment. But the set stood there, winking at me ironically with its green eye.

Father Zakhar smiled in satisfaction. Then he went over to the door, opened it, and called out. I heard footsteps in the corridor. A low-voiced conversation followed. He came back into the room.

"You must go now. I have much to do. But we will see each other again several times before the trumpets begin to sound."

Still in a daze, I followed his gesture and moved towards the door. On the threshold I stopped and turned towards him again. But before I could say anything someone seized my collar from behind and dragged me out of the room. I twisted round and looked up into Peredonov's face.

He kicked the door shut and grinned down at me. Then he planted a huge hand on my chest and pushed. I flew backwards down the corridor, caught my heel on something in the floor, and crashed to the ground. He followed and stood over me.

"You're a fool, Ivan Vasilevich. A meddler, a busy-body. I should have wrung your neck the first time we met."

He unlatched a door and pushed me through. I fell down a couple of steps. The smell of manure was much stronger here, and when I picked myself up I realised why. The rear half of the building was one long, dimly-lit barn, which must have run the entire length of the range. The near end was piled high with hay, and down one side stood a row of cows in stalls.

I didn't have time to take a more extensive survey. Peredonov grabbed me by the neck and ran me along in front of him. After a few steps he stopped, and with his other hand fumbled at something near his feet. Then he straightened up, bringing with him a trap-door. It was only too obvious where I was supposed to go. I didn't wait to be thrown down the hole, but lowered myself into it down a short ladder. The trap-door slammed down. After a minute it opened again to let in a small cartload of hay. Then it shut. I heard Peredonov push the bar across, and then his footsteps receded down the barn.

The cellar was pitch-dark and seemed, when I began to grope my way about, to be full of hard, knobbly objects. The floor was earth; three of the walls were brick; the fourth—on the side of the living-quarters—was made of rough planks, as was the ceiling. I dragged the hay over to the wooden wall and made myself a nest in it. I was very much alone with my thoughts.

I certainly had enough to chew on. I hadn't taken Tanya's speculations about Alik seriously, and the revelation that he was a member of the sect had come as a numbing shock. Now, looking at the news more calmly, I saw that it did explain quite a lot. But not the riddle of his relations with Lyuba. Nor the question as to why he should have dragged me into the affair.

Though the hay was doing a reasonable job in keeping me warm, it was no feather bed, and I pitied the cow that had to chew on it. More than half seemed to be dry thistles or brambles. I shifted around to get more comfortable, but only jabbed a few more spikes into my legs. I gave up and went back to my thoughts.

Something was very wrong somewhere. The whole scenario was cock-eyed. You can't get history to run backwards—try re-inventing the matchlock and see how many armies rush to adopt it. Socialism must turn into communism. A reactionary counter-revolution, especially one based on Father Zakhar's peculiar social philosophy, just couldn't succeed. No one in the higher ranks of the KGB could have forgotten enough Marxism-Leninism not to see that. And it's not a service that encourages visionaries, either. I could have been persuaded by one convert, perhaps, but I couldn't swallow a whole crew of them. There was only one answer. Father Zakhar had told me the truth, but only as much of it as he knew. Someone was feeding him a story. He was being used, just as much as I was, and probably by the same person.

There was some satisfaction in coming to this conclusion, but not a great deal. For the moment I couldn't think of any way of using it. Father Zakhar certainly wouldn't listen to any arguments. It was too necessary for him to believe that he did have supporters in the organs.

The trap creaked open and a light shone into the cellar. Peredonov came down the steps carrying a lantern. I shrank back against the wall. He looked round, put the lamp down on a crate, and tossed me my coat. Then he reached up, brought down a tray of food, and passed it over to me. I relaxed slightly. I was ravenously hungry. The soup was hot and good, and the bread blacker and more tasty than any from a state bakery.

As I ate, I glanced around. The cellar was about four metres long and three wide, full of old farm tools, lumber, and broken crates. Peredonov dragged one up, sat down and watched me eat. After a bit he brought a bottle out of the front of his shirt, took a drink, wiped the bottle's mouth with his sleeve, and handed it across.

As he leant forward I caught a whiff of his breath and understood the reason for his benevolence. I put the bottle to my lips, drank, and almost dropped it in a fit of coughing and spluttering.

"What is it?" I asked.

He winked. "The real stuff. *Samogon*. We make it ourselves."

I tried again, more carefully. It would probably make my toe-nails fall off, but it was doing a good deal to reconcile me with my situation. A little later I was almost ready to consider Peredonov a friend.

"Do you come from these parts, Mikhail Evstafevich?"

He spat scornfully. "No, I'm a Tambov man." He repossessed the bottle, gargled some down, and laughed. "You know the saying, don't you? 'He drinks like a Tambov peasant'?"

I nodded abstractedly. Tambov seemed to have been in the news a lot recently. A province of simpletons, a province of prophetic sectarians, and now a province of drunks. There might be a connection between the three.

"Have you known Father Zakhar long?"

"Long enough."

"Have you been here since the beginning?"

"On and off. I was working in Siberia when I was called here." He sighed and took another drink. "The women out there. As large and as juicy as Antonov apples."

I let him get over his memories, and then put my foot delicately on what might prove to be a thin piece of ice.

"You're a sensible man, Mikhail Evstafevich. You've seen a lot of life. Do you really think anything is going to come of all this?"

He stiffened in the act of handing me the bottle, and I thought for a moment that the ice had given way. Then he sat back again, resting the bottle on his knee. I let my breath out.

"What do you know of Russia, Ivan Vasilich? You're a townsman, an *intelligent*." He picked a hunk of bread up off the tray and held it and the bottle up in front of him. "Black bread and *samogon*. The flesh and blood of real Russia. And you eat white bread and drink foreign wines. What do you know of Russia?"

He got up and stood over me. The lantern between us threw a huge, menacing, bear-like shadow on the opposite wall. He thrust a hand towards me, but it was only a gesture, not a blow.

"You despise the peasants, because you don't understand them and fear them. And you are right to fear us. I know Mother Russia as a man knows the palm of his own hand. I can tell you what the dark masses feel, what they talk about in their huts at night."

"And what do they want?"

He kicked up some dirt from the floor. "They want this. The earth, the black soil of Mother Russia. And they thirst for faith, like one crying for water in the desert. We will

give it to them. We will give them their land, will quench
their thirst with the tears of Christ, and they will follow us
and the unbelievers will fall like corn before the sickle. So
it will be.''

He stopped. He was breathing heavily. He wiped the
sweat from his face with his sleeve. The gesture seemed to
bring about an abrupt change of mood. He smiled ironically. ''Such, at least, is my humble view, Ivan Vasilevich.''

He bent down and picked up the vodka bottle and the
lantern.

''Are you leaving me here?''

''That is the order.''

A moment later the trap-door shut and I was in darkness
again. I wrapped myself up in my coat and got back into
the hay. I was half-asleep when a memory drifted unbid-
den into my mind. Last year I'd been talking to an old
peasant in Suzdal, the heartland of medieval Russia. Things
had never been the same there, he'd complained, since the
invasion. And he hadn't meant the Germans, who'd been
there in 1941, but the Tatars, who'd burnt the town in
1238.

At the time I'd thought it was amusing, but now I took
it more seriously. Perhaps Father Zakhar and Peredonov
were right; perhaps the essential nature of Russia hadn't
been changed by anything we'd done since 1917. And
perhaps there was a reservoir of dark, primordial forces
below the surface, below the five-year plans and the computers and the space shots, forces which might suddenly
burst through into the light under someone's guidance.

21

The sound of the trap-door being opened woke me. A dim light fell into my dungeon. Someone leant over the opening and beckoned to me. I crawled awkwardly up the ladder. I was infernally cold and very stiff. At the top I found the peasant who had taken me up to the monastery the previous afternoon. He led me through the living-quarters and out on to the square. It was still early. The sun hadn't risen, and a thick mist filled the valley.

We walked down the side of the building and turned in at another door. It led into a corridor which looked exactly similar to the first one. My guide showed me in to the room on the left and went out. I heard the lock click shut behind him.

I was in what might once have been the abbot's parlour. Faded red hangings, torn and spotted with mould, covered the walls. In the middle stood a heavy mahogany table. Both it, and the chairs round it, were thick with dust. The end of the room was piled high with broken furniture and

other odds and ends. The one small window looked out on
to the square. I could have broken the glass and got out
without much difficulty, but what would have been the
point? I might manage to escape, but without doing what
I'd come here to do. The room was blessedly warm. I
pulled out a chair and sat down.

A few minutes later the door opened and a peasant girl
came in with a tray. She set it down on the table, glanced
sideways at me; and went out giggling. For the moment I
was too occupied with the food to wonder what had amused
her. There was more of the black bread I'd had the night
before, cheese, and, best of all, a jug of coffee—horribly
weak, but hot and very sweet.

When I had finished I fell to considering what I should
do now. But it was only too obvious that I could make no
plans until I knew what Father Zakhar had in store for me.
Time passed slowly by. Outside the sun had come up and
the mist was beginning to thin. I could see the pines on the
far ridge where Tanya and I had been the day before. I
wondered how she had passed the night.

On the other side of the square members of the sect
began to move about, busy with something or other. I
grew bored and sleepy. After a while, for want of anything
else to do, I began to rummage among the rubbish at the
end of the room.

It was a peculiar collection of junk. Between the depar-
ture of the original inhabitants of the *skit* and the advent of
Father Zakhar's followers the buildings must have had a
number of other occupants: a detachment of White soldiers
during the Civil War, followed later by foresters and
kolkhozniki.

I found, among other things, a couple of empty ammu-
nition boxes which had once held—according to the legend
burnt into the lid in pre-revolutionary script—7.62mm car-
tridges for the Nagant rifle; a tangle of leather straps and
tarnished brass buckles which turned out to be an officer's

sword-belt; a number of books—the Bible and a volume of Gumilev's poems among them—all with their pages gutted, presumably for the making of cigarettes; a stack of copies of the local newspaper, *Vologdsky Kray,* dating from 1932; an exercise book, containing someone's notes on the diseases of cattle—another hand had filled the blank pages with obscene rhymes and lewd drawings; and a bundle of badly typed and duplicated *trudoden* chits, tied together with baler twine.

There was nothing of any use to me, and my activities had raised a good deal of dust. I pulled an old tin trunk full of moth-eaten army blankets to one side. It had been standing next to a large cupboard, whose door must have been released by the movement, for it swung slowly open and I saw my reflection in a cracked and blackened mirror fastened to the inside. It was not surprising that the girl had found my appearance amusing. I had a black eye from Peredonov's handling the previous evening, and my hair was full of hayseeds and pieces of straw. I was cleaning myself up as best I could when the door opened again and Lyuba came in.

She looked a very different person from the frail waif I'd seen only a couple of days ago in Moscow; different too from the pale, neurotic girl in the villa in Lakhta. She seemed, in some indefinable way, to have filled out; there was colour in her cheeks; she moved with a strong, confident grace. In her peasant dress, with a kerchief bound low on her forehead, she could almost have posed for one of those posters on which a peasant woman and a Red Army soldier jointly hold aloft with their left arms the hammer and sickle banner, while at the same time their right hands point proudly into the radiant future.

She took me by the hand, looked into my eyes for a moment—a slightly glazed expression in her exophthalmic stare was the only sign of anything abnormal—and kissed me.

"I'm glad you're here, Vanya. It's good that you are with us. I'm to look after you today. Come. I'll show you everything."

Outside the light on the snow was dazzling. The sun was still low, only just above the eastern ridge. The dome of the church sparkled and shone in the light, almost as though it were gilded once more. We turned in that direction and began to walk slowly up the valley. When we'd gone a few hundred metres, I looked back and saw that the man who'd released me from the cellar was coming along behind us. It seemed that Lyuba was not the only person who had been deputed to look after me.

In front of the church a large area of snow had been trampled down. Its massive west porch had canted slightly sideways, but it still looked solid enough to last for another few hundred years. We went up the steps and Lyuba pulled open the heavy door.

After the brilliance outside the interior seemed very dark. It was very quiet. There was a strange, musty smell in the air. Lyuba took a candle out of a box, lit it, and placed it on a stand which stood to the left of the entrance. She crossed herself and her lips moved silently.

My eyes gradually became accustomed to the gloom. I looked around with absorbed fascination. Unlike the few other working churches I'd visited, the walls and ceiling were not covered with frescoes. The wood had been left bare, though decorations had been carved in the main beams and in the four huge pillars that held up the dome. The iconostasis was of simple, almost rough construction, with only three or four small, crudely painted icons hanging on it. Above the altar gates, however, was another, larger one, swathed in sacking. I asked Lyuba what it was. She crossed herself again.

"The miraculous icon of the Blessed Lady of Lebedevo," she said in a whisper. "She will be unveiled on Easter eve, at midnight."

Intense curiosity gripped me as I looked at it. I longed to see beneath the sacking. And it was, of course, the key to the whole situation. If it were to be hidden or destroyed Father Zakhar's crusade would collapse.

But when, half an hour later, we walked back down the valley, everything seemed so normal and undisturbed that I found it hard to believe in the real existence of any threat. The mingled smell of woodsmoke and baking bread rose to meet us. A couple of peasants shouted friendly greetings, and further along two small children stopped playing for a moment to look at us in solemn curiosity as we passed. By my side Lyuba was talking gaily about ordinary, everyday matters. The memory of the dark fanaticism of the night before receded into the distance, became pale and insubstantial in the morning air.

We passed the buildings and took a path leading north, down the west side of the valley, opposite the ridge on which I'd been the day before. As we went through the stockade I glanced round and saw that our follower was still with us.

We passed in under the trees. It was much colder in their shadow. I shivered involuntarily. Suddenly all the signs reversed themselves in my mind. The peace and tranquillity of the valley were no longer real, but an illusion, concealing something monstrous and terrible. Tyutchev's lines describing the day as "a gold-woven veil thrown over the abyss of night" floated into my mind.

The danger did exist. In three days' time death and destruction could tear this peaceful scene apart. And it seemed that I was the only person who was in a position to do anything about it. I felt an appalling emptiness in the pit of my stomach. My hands were wet again. I wanted to run away, hide, get into bed and pull the covers up over my head.

It seemed so unfair that the responsibility should rest on me alone. And what had happened to the doctrine of the unimportance of the individual in history? But perhaps I was panicking without cause, perhaps Alik or Manilov or the local party secretary—in fiction it would certainly be him—had already taken measures to avert the possible catastrophe.

We sat down on a pile of logs in the sun and Lyuba asked me rather timidly whether anything was wrong.

"I'm frightened, Lyuba. Frightened of what's going to happen."

"But if only you believed, you would see that there is no cause for fear. The revelation is almost upon us, the new age is about to dawn."

Her language was becoming incantatory. I didn't want her to fall into another ecstatic trance. I took hold of her shoulder and shook her. Out of the corner of my eye I saw the man who had been following us start to his feet. I let go, and he squatted down again slowly.

"Listen, Lyuba. There's not going to be any revelation. Or any new age. The whole thing's a fake. Father Zakhar has tricked you."

"I won't listen to you, Vanya. You don't know what you're saying." She started to get up. I grabbed her arm and pulled her down.

"He's in touch with the KGB. With Alik. With Alik, do you hear?" Surely the name would affect her as it had affected her before.

She stared at me for a moment, and then burst out laughing. It was the last reaction I'd expected.

"Poor Vanya. I know you care for me, and you try so hard to help me. And I'm grateful, really I am. I never really thanked you for what you did in Moscow, but I do now." She kissed my cheek. "But it was all unnecessary, all a misunderstanding. Everything's been explained to me now. Haven't you noticed that I've changed? The cloud that hung over me has vanished, as though by a miracle. Satan had set a cunning snare for my feet. I was deluded

by a false visage. But now I know the truth, and I am so
happy.''

''What is the truth?''

''Alik, my Aleksey is the true tsarevich, not the pretender I believed him to be. In him lives again that prince
done to death by his father, Peter-Antichrist. He is Aleksey
reborn. He is the sun and hope of *Rus,* of old Russia.
Those whom we fled from in Moscow were his messen-
gers, sent to protect me, not to harm me. When the White
Swan has conquered, the new Patriarch will crown him
tsar and consecrate our marriage in one glorious ceremony.
And you will witness our triumph, Vanya; you too will be
there. We shall have need of your counsel when our reign
begins.''

There was nothing more to be said. I had played my
card and had it trumped. No wonder Lyuba looked so
much better. Love and religion were no longer pulling her
in different directions; they had become united.

But her psychological state was unimportant beside the
piece of information she'd given me. If I'd finally managed to accept the idea, with some unvoiced reservations,
that Alik had taken to religion, could I really believe, in
addition, that he saw himself as the future Tsar of All
Russia? What credentials did he have to establish his
legitimacy? How was Father Zakhar going to persuade his
followers that here was the true heir of the Romanovs? The
whole thing was moving into the realm of fantasy, and the
trouble was that the mess wasn't going to be cleared up by
men in white coats and ambulances, but by soldiers in
armoured troop carriers.

We walked back to the settlement in silence. I was shut
into the abbot's parlour again, and a little later brought
some food. I dozed uneasily throughout the afternoon and
early evening, always conscious of the sounds around me.
Occasionally someone walked down the corridor; outside a

lorry or two came and went; sometimes I heard a shout, or a short, muffled conversation.

An hour or two after sunset I realised that something unusual was going on in the square. I got up and looked out of the window. A small crowd had congregated on the far side and more people were arriving to join it. I wondered what was happening. The room had grown very stuffy. I had a headache and was extremely thirsty. I was still watching the crowd when the door opened behind me. I turned round and saw Father Zakhar. He was followed by the girl I'd seen before. She put two glasses of tea down on the table and went out. Father Zakhar sat down and motioned me to a chair opposite.

"How are you, Ivan Vasilevich? I hope you are enjoying your stay with us."

He pushed one of the glasses across the table to me. I picked it up and sipped it. Like the coffee, it was hot and extremely sweet. The glass-holder was an old one. It seemed to be silver, with an incised design of branches and leaves. Father Zakhar noticed my interest.

"It's a pleasant piece, isn't it? Early nineteenth century. Tula work, I think."

I put it down. "I suppose it's no use trying to convince you again that your plans are insane, that they're bound to fail?"

He laughed. "No use at all, Ivan Vasilevich. No use at all."

"I hope you're not depending too much on Alik's help. I've known him for a long time, and I'd trust him about as far as I could throw this table."

"You might be unjust to Aleksey Petrovich. You only see with the eyes of the intellect, not with those of the spirit. You are too close to the ground, too borne down by the things of this world. You must learn to soar aloft on the wings of faith."

The tea had grown cooler now and I drank it thankfully

as I listened to him. He went on for some time in much the same vein. I had no doubt that he was right. If I had faith, then I would see everything from a different point of view. But I couldn't achieve faith through an act of will, or a logical process of thought. And even if I were to believe, I'd have a hard job convincing myself that Alik was a suitable candidate for a throne. The mere fact of belief doesn't, in itself, imply a complete abdication of rational judgement.

I thought of putting this point of view to Father Zakhar, but it didn't seem worthwhile. For some reason I was beginning to feel curiously uninvolved in the whole situation. It struck me that the fact that Father Zakhar seemed to trust Alik so implicitly ought to be extraordinarily interesting and revealing, but I could summon up no more than a mild curiosity in it.

I turned the glass-holder to and fro in my hands, letting it catch the light, and saw how marvellously intricate and detailed the design was. The branches flowed organically one into another, the leaves swayed and rustled in the evening breeze.

Father Zakhar was saying something. I looked up and saw him staring at me.

"I'm inviting you to take part in one of our ceremonies. Will you come?"

He rose to his feet and I followed. Outside the sky seemed no more than a few metres over my head: black velvet sewn with a myriad blindingly bright diamonds. As I looked up, I could feel the movement of the earth on its axis.

The cold air cleared my brain for an instant, and I realised that the tea must have contained some hallucinogenic drug. It hadn't affected me physically—not yet at least—but I couldn't concentrate on what was going on. I fought for control, but my will was impotent and I seemed to hear the sound of a snapping string as I let go and abandoned myself to sensation. In some strange way I was simultaneously within my body and outside it, viewing my behaviour dispassionately, without any particular interest.

We passed into a huge barn, dimly lit by oil lamps hanging round the walls. It was full of people, who stood there in silence. My senses had become preternaturally acute. I could hear the rustle of clothing, the sound of breathing, the crepitation of a burning wick. I could smell incense, sweat, onions, vodka, black bread, cheap scent and damp cloth.

A flame flared up in front, revealing Father Zakhar with his arms stretched above his head.

"Behold the White Swan!"

"We behold him!"

He moved aside, and from behind him, out of the darkness, swam the White Swan, a huge, majestic bird. It raised and lowered its wings. Its neck uncurled, its head moved from side to side as if seeking something. I saw a gleaming yellow eye. There was something indescribably frightening and evil about its gaze: not human, and at the same time not bird-like. I felt an unreasoning horror, but I could not have moved to save my life. I heard someone near me draw in their breath sharply. There was a feeling of almost unbearable tension which seemed to last forever. The light suddenly went out, and the bird vanished. I heard Father Zakhar again:

"Praise the White Swan!"

"We praise him!"

There was a short pause, and then the whole congregation began to move slowly round the floor, chanting in unison "Glory to the White Swan," each syllable coinciding with a step. I found myself moving with them, echoing the chant.

"Glory to the White Swan. Glory to the White Swan. Glory to the White Swan."

The building shook beneath our feet. Very gradually the pace quickened.

"Glory to the White Swan. Glory to the White Swan. Glory to the White Swan."

We were moving faster. The huge circle had broken up into smaller groups, each revolving on itself.

"Glory to the White Swan. Glory to the White Swan. Glory to the White Swan."

The syllables were running into one another and their note was rising. From a slow thudding, the sound of steps had turned into a medley of syncopated patterings. I felt someone clutch at me from behind, and I caught hold of the body in front of me.

"Glory to the White Swan! Glory to the White Swan! Glory to the White Swan!"

The words had become almost indistinguishable. There was a rank, musk-like odour on the air, the smell of animal lust. Somewhere a woman screamed, not in fear, but in pleasure.

As if this had been a signal, a tongue of fire shot up again. I saw the tall white neck. The beak drove down and the flame went out. I heard bodies falling to the ground around me.

A hand in my hair wrenched my head round. I saw a broad face running with sweat, high cheekbones, slant eyes. Her dress hung open. My hand cupped a heavy breast, fastened on an erect nipple. A flame leapt through my groin. Then there was nothing but sensation, darkness shot through with streaks of fire.

22

I had a splitting headache, a foul taste in my mouth and
no idea where I was. Then, as I turned over, I heard
crackling beneath me and realised that I was back in the
cellar on my bed of hay. The only thing I wanted to do
was to go back to sleep in the hope that I'd feel better
when I woke the next time. But I forced myself to sit up
and groped around for my coat. The candles I'd stolen
from the box in the church were still in the pocket. I took
one out, lit it, and stuck it upright on a box with a dab of
its own wax. It was nearly two in the morning.

The trap-door, I'd noticed, was flush with the floor of
the barn. It rested on a narrow lip which ran round inside
the opening, and was secured not by a bolt, but by a bar,
pivoted in the middle, which slotted under two wooden
lugs screwed to the floor on either side of the door. Both
lugs and bar looked very solid, and I thought that it might
be easier to force the hinge side of the trap-door open. I
began to look through the debris in search of a suitable
instrument.

Everything I found at first was either too thick or too thin, but after some minutes I discovered a broken spade without a handle which seemed made for the job.

I jammed the blade in between lip and trap-door, underneath where I imagined a hinge to be, and put my weight on the other end. The hatch groaned, but held fast. I tried again, under the other hinge. There was a sudden crack, as something gave way, and I fell down. It wasn't the hinge, however. The edge of the lip had split away right across the opening, and there was no longer anything to lever against.

I moved to the other end of the hatch, but the steps on that side which sloped down into the cellar got in my way, making it impossible for me to apply my full weight to the lever. Nevertheless, I worked on for some time until it became obvious that this method wasn't going to answer. I was out of breath, sweating profusely, and my knuckles were torn and bleeding.

I took another candle and examined the trap-door more closely. But it was an extremely solid piece of work and I could see no way of breaking through it. The ceiling, too, seemed unassailable. The joists were so deep and set so closely together that I couldn't get my spade in to prise the floorboards up. The hinges of the trap were the only weak point. I inspected my resources again.

A little later I'd assembled three logs in the space under the trap. I chose the thickest to act as a fulcrum, and placed the longest at right angles across it. I then tried to balance the third—which was almost as long as the cellar was high—on the end of the lever, so that it came immediately beneath the hinge of the trap. The contraption was difficult to set up. I had to try to hold down the lever with one foot, while putting the upright in place. Eventually I got it arranged, felt my way cautiously to the end of the lever, and threw my weight on to it. The other end slipped sideways from under the upright, and I collected a few more bruises in another fall.

I set the thing up again—it went without a hitch this time—and tried again, putting the pressure on very gradually. In the end I was standing on the log, with my hands above my head on a joist, pushing downwards as hard as I could. The hinge protested loudly, and then there was a sudden crash as it gave way. The other went much more easily.

I put on my coat, picked up my spade and swung myself up on to the floor of the barn. The large doors weren't locked. I ran down the ramp and turned right, up towards the church.

It seemed best not to approach it directly, by the path Lyuba and I had taken that morning. I circled cautiously round, keeping to the edge of the clearing, and only approached the church when I had got round to its eastern side. Its huge bulk loomed over me, seeming twice as large as it had done during the day.

Turning to the right, I began to move round it. Just before I got to the north-west corner I thought I heard something. I dropped to my knees and put my head slowly round. I smelt tobacco and saw the red end of a cigarette. Someone was sitting on the steps of the porch. I withdrew my head and cursed Father Zakhar's foresight.

A few minutes later I heard the man get to his feet, hawk loudly and spit. Then footsteps came towards me. I flattened myself against the wall. They stopped. I waited a moment and then risked a glance. He was standing with his back towards me, in the classical attitude of a man about to empty his bladder.

I took a step out and hit him on the side of the head with the flat of the spade. He staggered. I hit him again, and then, as he dropped to his knees, again on the back of the head. He collapsed in the snow.

I ran round him and up the porch steps. The church door

was unlocked. I groped around in the dark, lit a candle, and hurried down to the iconostasis. The icon was too high for me to reach, but when I pushed it up with the spade it fell off its hook, and I only just managed to prevent it falling to the floor.

Outside the guard was lying where I'd left him. I took his hat—I'd lost mine somewhere during the evening—and propped him up against the wall of the church.

As I began to climb up the west side of the valley I found the icon an appalling nuisance. It was too big to go under one arm; I had to carry it in both hands and hadn't got an arm free to help myself up with. This was hopeless, and I soon resorted to dragging it along behind me. Even so I fell repeatedly, and at times seemed to be slipping back faster than I was climbing up. But I had to take the icon with me: the track I was leaving was all too easy to follow, and if I hid it somewhere on the way it would be discovered immediately. I toyed with the idea of breaking it up and throwing the pieces away separately, but I knew that I'd only be able to bring myself to do that as a final resort. Miraculous or not, it was presumably still a work of art.

I wondered how long it would be before the guard came round and gave the alarm. Ten minutes? Half an hour? An hour? I looked down at the monastery, but there were no lights, and I could hear nothing. Whatever time I'd got, it probably wasn't enough. I couldn't hope to outrun local peasants on their own ground. And they didn't even have to follow me. Once they'd found out the direction I'd taken they could drive round and come into the forest further down, cutting me off from Vologda. Perhaps it would have been more cunning to hide the icon some-where and leave by the valley road. Its surface was too hard-packed to take a trail. But it was much too late to put that idea into effect now.

At last I reached the top and threw myself down, gasping. A moment later I rolled over and looked down into the valley. There was still no sign that anything was happening.

I began to work a hole through one edge of the hessian envelope that covered the icon. I could make a sling with my belt and then carry the thing over my shoulder. When the hole was large enough I put my finger and thumb through and took hold of the end of the belt. I could feel the rough back of the boards on which the icon was painted. I pulled the belt through, buckled it, and slung the package on my shoulder. While doing this, I tried to work out the best route for me to take.

The valley in which the monastery lay was cut into the north-western slope of a spine which ran roughly south-west from a knot of hills down towards Vologda, losing height as it came. Other considerations apart, the two most sensible alternatives were—either to turn right, down into the main valley, along which Tanya and I had driven; or left, up on to the summit of the spine. In either case it should be easy enough to find one's way back to Vologda.

But there were disadvantages to either course. If I went left, I'd be going back towards the monastery for part of the way, rather than away from it; if I went right I'd be going towards the sectarians as they came up the road to look for me.

The third course was to keep straight on, crossing each successive reentrant at right angles. If I did that, I should still be able to find my way, and it would keep me off the beaten track. It would involve a lot of hill work, but nevertheless it seemed the best solution.

I jogtrotted down the slope. The snow was sufficiently frozen to bear my weight, but the trail I was leaving was still distressingly obvious. It was an absolutely still night.

I reached the bottom of the valley, crossed a frozen stream, and started up the other side. This climb wasn't as steep as the preceding one, but it seemed interminable. My

calf muscles were in knots long before I reached the top.
As I staggered up the final incline, I wondered whether it
was worth going on. Surely I was bound to be caught, and
I might as well sit and wait for my pursuers, instead of
trying to outrun them.

When I reached the top I leant against a tree to recover.
If I lay down I probably wouldn't be able to get up again.
But what I saw when I raised my head revitalised me. In
the distance was a glow in the sky which could only be
Vologda. And it looked as though it was downhill all the
way from where I stood.

Half an hour later I came to the road. It ran across in
front of me, at right angles to my line of march. It was the
obvious place for the troops of the White Swan to be
posted. I got down on all fours and crawled slowly towards
it, moving carefully from one tree to another.

The road was cut into the side of the hill. On my side
there was a bank about two metres high, and on the other
the forest fell away again. If they were waiting for me,
they'd be in the trees on the far side, hoping to see me as I
crossed the road. I lay there for a long time, staring into
the trees beyond, but it was hopeless. There could be an
entire tank division hidden there for all I knew.

I heard a hum in the distance. It grew nearer and turned
into the sound of a heavy engine labouring along in bottom
gear. A pair of headlights appeared. The beam lit up the
bank and the woods behind me and then moved on to the
other side of the road as the vehicle came round a curve.
The driver changed down, the engine note dropped, and
the truck gathered speed down the road towards me. Just
when it came level I dropped down the bank, ran across
the road as it passed, and clapped down in the shadow of
the nearest tree. The noise of the engine gradually died
away.

I felt dreadfully exposed as I lay there. It was a situation
out of a childhood nightmare. At any moment the *baba-*

yaga, the horrible bird-woman of the folk-tales, would come silently up on her long crane's legs to pounce on me from behind and dig her sharp beak, running with the blood of her previous victim, into the back of my neck. I cowered down into the earth. I knew that in a minute my nerve would break. I'd have to leap to my feet and run off, even though my reason told me that would be the stupidest thing I could do. I put a knuckle into my mouth and bit it as hard as I could. Gradually the feeling passed.

Five minutes later I raised my head and looked around cautiously. I hadn't heard anything since the truck had gone and I couldn't see anything suspicious. I got slowly to my feet. There were no shouts of discovery, no one rushed out at me from behind a tree. I waited a minute or two longer and then started off again.

I was convinced that they were playing with me. At any moment, I thought, there'd be the familiar sensation as Peredonov's arm came round my neck again. At the thought I involuntarily quickened my pace, first to a trot, then to a run. Soon I was tearing frantically down the hill, with the icon flapping and bumping on my hip.

I crashed through a clump of low bushes, tripped, and fell down a steep bank. The fall knocked all the breath out of me. I lay there for some moments, trying to listen for sounds of pursuit above the noise of my gasps. But there was nothing to be heard. The night was as silent as before. The icon had fallen a metre or two away. I got up and retrieved it. It seemed to be intact.

A little later I came to the bottom of the hill. The going should have been easier on the flat, but the ground was criss-crossed with ditches—probably peat diggings—some deep, some shallow, and I found myself perpetually climbing in and out of them. At last I hit a dirt road that seemed to be going in the right direction and thankfully transferred myself to it. It was then that exhaustion really began to tell. There was no strength left in my legs. I was putting one foot in front of the other with the agonising slowness of a dream.

The only thing that kept me going was a jubilant inner consciousness of triumph. I'd done it. I'd stolen the icon. I'd taken the mainspring out of Father Zakhar's crusade. I'd beaten him and I'd beaten Alik. And I'd saved Lyuba.

I patted the Lady of Lebedevo affectionately through her canvas shroud. If she was historically interesting, I might give her to the Andrey Rublev museum. Or I might just hang her on the wall of my room and watch for thaumaturgic effects.

The dirt road turned to a metalled surface. I noticed the fact, but didn't take in its significance. It was only when the first street-lamp appeared in the distance that I realised I'd nearly completed the journey.

Tanya was asleep on a chair in the hotel lobby. A pile of magazines and an ashtray full of cigarette butts were on the low table at her side. She woke up as I bent over her.

"My God, it's you, Vanya. I thought I'd never see you again." She reached up, took my head in her hands and looked at me. "Are you all right?"

"More or less." Now that I'd stopped walking I realised how cold and wet I was. Reaction was beginning to set in. I started to shiver uncontrollably. "I need a hot shower. And something to eat."

"Come upstairs. I'll get you something." She got to her feet and leant against me for a moment. "I'm glad you're back. Don't do it again, Vanya, will you. I don't think I could stand it."

Half an hour later I was in her bed, drinking hot tea and eating bread and cheese. In between mouthfuls I told Tanya what had happened since we'd parted on the ridge above the monastery two days before. I saved the best to the end.

"Give me that parcel over there, will you?"

She brought the icon over to me.

"Have you got a pair of scissors?"

"Somewhere, yes." She went over to the dressing-table and came back with a tiny pair of nail scissors.

I took them and began to cut through the stitching at one end. When the hole was big enough, I put my hands in and ripped the seam apart. I laid the package down on the blanket and pulled the icon out carefully. It was face down. I was looking at the rough unplaned boards of its back. I took a deep breath and turned it over.

It was obvious why Father Zakhar hadn't bothered to send his hounds out after me. The front was exactly the same as the back. I'd stolen a fake. The real Lady was still somewhere in the valley.

23

The angle of the sunlight coming through the window told me that it was late morning. Tanya was no longer beside me in the bed. I lay there listening to the sound of her shower next door and thinking how marvellous she'd been. The shock of realising that I hadn't actually achieved anything, other than making a fool of myself, coupled with extreme physical exhaustion, had shattered me. But, comforting and consoling, she'd put me slowly together again, fragment by fragment, and when I'd eventually gone to sleep I had been reasonably at peace with myself.

She came through out of the bathroom and interrupted my thoughts with a smile. She had one towel wound round her and another tied like a turban on her head. She began to wander about the room, picking up and discarding articles of clothing. I watched her with loving amusement. In less than forty-eight hours she'd imprinted her personality forcibly on her surroundings, turning an anonymous, even rather restrained hotel room into something that was more like a boudoir than was absolutely proper in a socialist society. The heavy fragrance of her favourite French scent, obtained from the West at God knows what cost, in money or in kind, hung on the air. I breathed it in luxuriously. Everything was so normal that I felt the tensions within me seeping away. I was relaxed, physically comfortable for the first time in days.

Perhaps by contrast, my thoughts turned to the previous evening. I didn't know what magic lantern tricks Father Zakhar employed to obtain his effects, but the results were certainly impressive. And, in conjunction with hallucinogenic drugs, devastating. I still had the bite-marks to prove it.

Gradually isolated recollections of the orgiastic ritual that had followed came back to me. I shivered. I wasn't surprised that Lyuba had reacted so violently, that the experience had pushed her off-balance. It was rank, dark meat which only a strong stomach could take. But undoubtedly habit-forming. That Father Zakhar should have been able to bring her back to the *skit* and reconcile her with the White Swan was a tribute to the force of his personality.

Looked at academically, the sect was, of course, an interesting reversion to the old *dvoeverie*, the duality of belief which, according to some historians, had persisted among the people right up to the end of the eighteenth century. But there was an important difference between that phenomenon and the cult practised by the White Swan. Earlier the peasant had been an official Christian by day, but a popular pagan by night: *dvoeverie* described an opposition, a conflict between two beliefs. The White Swan's unique—as far as I knew—contribution to the history of sectarianism was to abolish the conflict, to yoke the two—the ascetic and the orgiastic—together into a symbiotic relationship, in which each was dependent on the other.

The orgy of lust would be followed by an equally fervid orgy of repentance; worship of the White Swan would be replaced by adoration of the Blessed Lady. Then temptation would gradually grow again, slowly building up into an irresistible force, until it finally released itself again in darkness and bestiality. And with each repetition of the cycle the members of the sect would be, through shared ecstasy, guilt and confession, more closely bound to one another, more grateful, more loyal and more subservient to their leader. This answered the question Bradley had put to me in the *shashlychnaya*. I could have told him now how Father Zakhar recruited his troops and ensured their devotion.

The whole subject was fascinating. If I got out of this mess with a whole skin, and had some time to spare, I'd write a paper on the cult. In present circumstances it would of course have to be for my drawer, rather than publication. Among other things it would be interesting to explore the connection with *Khovanshchina*. Earlier I'd thought, understandably but wrongly, that the sect had taken its name from the opera. Perhaps it was the other way round.

Tanya, half-dressed, was sitting at the dressing-table, staring intently into the mirror. Then, as if deciding that she'd put up with the features she'd been issued with for a little longer, she turned away abruptly and lit a cigarette.

"Vanya?" Her voice seemed louder than was necessary.

I rolled over and sat up with a vague feeling of disquiet.

"There's something I didn't tell you last night. You had enough to cope with." She hesitated. I didn't say anything and she went on. "Alik's here. He came yesterday. He's got a job for me and the crew. I don't know what it is yet. He knows you're here. I don't know how he found out. He's terribly pleased about it. I told you he wanted to get us all together again. He said he had to see you when you got back. 'If he gets back' was what he actually said. He was laughing at me."

I got up. I felt surprisingly calm. There was really

nothing more I could do. I couldn't get back to the monastery, couldn't influence Father Zakhar's decisions or change Lyuba's mind for her. And my impotence wasn't frustrating, but rather consoling. Though I was desperately sorry for Lyuba and the others, my sympathy was becoming curiously detached. I felt for them almost as one feels for sufferers removed from one by time or space: the condemned Decembrists in their cells in the Peter-Paul fortress, for example, or the victims of some remote South American earthquake.

Alik had quartered himself, as by right, in what must earlier have been the bridal suite of the hotel—though the thought that anyone could, even in pre-revolutionary times, voluntarily have chosen Vologda as a honeymoon resort was a startling one.

A delicately moulded plaster cornice ran round under the high ceiling, from the middle of which a dusty chandelier with many of its crystal drops missing hung down over a collection of heavy armchairs and sofas, all shrouded in the usual white dust covers.

At the moment, however, the room looked like the headquarters of a unit not too far behind the front line. A communications set stood on a table near the window. Larger than the one I'd seen in Father Zakhar's room, it was yet recognisably of the same family. On the other side of the room maps and diagrams were pinned to a huge sheet of plywood that leant against the wall. Most of the tables were covered with heaps of paper and files. Whatever space was left was filled with piles of dirty crockery, plates of half-eaten food, empty and half-empty glasses, bottles of wine, vodka and mineral water, overflowing ashtrays. The floor, too, was littered with cigarette ends and in places thick with mud. A pile of dirty clothes lay in one corner. The room stank of cigarette smoke, alcohol and sweat.

I had ample time to observe the details, as Alik kept me

waiting for a good ten minutes under the surveillance of my old friend Fedya. When he opened the door to me I recoiled rather hastily, but he made no immediate attempt at violence. Perhaps he bore me no malice for our last meeting. I was willing to let bygones be bygones if he was.

"Morning, Fedya," I said. "Is the colonel here?"

"He'll be back soon. Sit down and wait. And you call me 'comrade sergeant,' young man. Or, seeing as we've met quite often, I'll stretch a point and allow 'Fedor Evstafevich' as well."

There was an element of dry humour about him. I wondered whether Alik had been right when he'd called him "as thick as a Tambov peasant."

"Where's your friend?" I asked. "Aren't you working as a team any longer?"

"He's still in Moscow. He broke his ankle when he fell over some trash cans."

I tried to keep a straight face.

He eyed me sourly. "You'd laugh all the way to Vorkuta, you would."

We sat in silence until Alik arrived. He slipped into the room and nodded at Fedya, who got up and went out. I looked after him thoughtfully. He'd unwittingly given me an interesting piece of information, but I'd been caught before, reading meaning into what turned out to be merely coincidence. I wasn't going to stick my neck out on this without some more evidence.

Alik came towards me, smiling. The change in his appearance was startling. He had never carried much weight, but in the last month he'd fined down almost to emaciation and looked to be at the limits of physical and mental exhaustion. His face was chalk-white, his eyes sunk in his head, surrounded by dark-brown and purplish rings, and there was a strange, feverish glitter in them which reminded me uncomfortably of Lyuba.

"Congratulations, Vanya. You're not rating too badly on initiative for a man of letters. The escape was very ingenious. And there was a touch of brilliance about the theft. Too bad it didn't come off."

I wasn't worried by him any longer. There was nothing he could threaten me with. Indeed, the tables were turned, for I now knew enough about him to put a severe crimp in his career as a KGB officer.

"Why did you want to see me, Alik?"

"Why did I want to see you? You owe me a report, Vanya. I want to know what you've found out about the White Swan. How are we going to deal with it?"

I began to get a little angry. "If you wanted to know about the White Swan, why didn't you ask one of its members? It would have been easy enough to find one, wouldn't it?"

He said nothing.

"How would you care to be addressed? As Your Excellency? Or Your Lordship? Your Imperial Majesty is looking a bit far forward, I suppose. But you'll have to start thinking what title to take. It'll be Aleksey II, won't it? Counting, that is, from Aleksey Mikhaylovich. He was Peter the Great's father, so he must be your grandfather—"

He'd listened with surprising patience, but now he waved a tired hand at me. "Cut the buffoonery, Vanya."

I changed tack. "What was the point of that charade over lunch at the Aragvi? All that rubbish about computers and the sob-story about Lyuba. And those pathetic testimonies. Did you really go to the trouble of having them faked up for me?"

"They were all genuine, if nothing else was."

"Even Kozlova's? She knows about Father Zakhar and the sect. But the testimony gives the impression she's completely in the dark."

"Of course it does, you fool. She was writing for the authorities. But even if they'd all been obvious fakes, it wouldn't have made any difference. You'd have lapped them up all the same. All that academic brilliance, that critical flair they used to talk about didn't help you to see that I was handing you a plate of stinking shit. The story wouldn't have deceived an eight-year-old Pioneer. You couldn't have believed that we needed your help, could you?" He gestured towards the window. "A sparrow couldn't fart out there without us homing in on it. How long do you think a religious sect could remain hidden?"

I was confused by the way his personality seemed to switch from pretender to the imperial throne to KGB officer. And my earlier detachment from events was slowly being eroded, being replaced by the premonition of an appalling, imminent catastrophe.

"For God's sake, Alik. Tell me what's happening," I said.

There was a long silence. He stared out of the window. Snow had began to fall, slowly and gently. He suddenly turned back.

"All right. I will. At least it will show you that we're not all as stupid as you think. Some of us can actually do our flies up without help. Not all the brains in the country are in universities, you know."

He began to walk jerkily about the room, dragging on his cigarette and expelling the smoke in two plumes through his nostrils. The cigarette was only half-finished when he ground it out in a dirty plate, and lit another with a big shiny chromium lighter. I noticed with some surprise that he'd given up the brand he'd smoked as long as I'd known him—the cheap rough Dukat in their orange paper packet—and was now smoking American cigarettes—extra-long Parliaments.

"Here's a simple question for you: what's going to be the greatest danger to the Soviet system in the future?"

I shrugged my shoulders. "The United States? China?"

"Wrong, wrong, comrade professor. You've been read-

ing the newspapers. We've got a perfectly good understanding with the Americans. Their politicians and ours
may shout at each other in public, but in private they go
along pretty well together. It's all a question of spheres of
influence. Why do you think they did nothing when we
went into Hungary in '56? Or why we held off while they
were messing around in the Lebanon? As for the Chinks,
they're really crazy enough to try something in the Far
East, but we can take them out with one hand tied behind
our back, without even breaking into a light sweat.'' He
wagged a finger at me. ''No, think again, Vanya. I'll give
you a clue. The danger isn't an external one.''

''The dissidents?'' I said in surprise.

He roared with delighted laughter. ''You're the man for
whom propaganda was invented. You believe all the rubbish in *Pravda* and the even worse rubbish in the Western
papers. There are more dissidents in London and Washington than there are over here. We could round them up and
cart them off in five minutes if we wanted, but it's not
worth the trouble. No, the danger's much more real and
substantial than that.''

He lit another cigarette and sat down opposite me.
''Some time ago one of our research groups did an appreciation of future developments in the Near East. Ordinarily
their report would just have been filed and forgotten, but
luckily someone who could put two and two together saw
it.'' He paused.

I asked the obvious question. ''You?''

He nodded. ''I realised immediately that there were
serious implications for our own internal situation in their
conclusions.''

''What were they?''

He paid no attention to my interruption, but continued
along his own path. I remembered the trait from his earlier
lecture to me.

''What does one think about when the Near East is

mentioned? Arabs and Israelis, right? Well, the research group went into that situation in detail and came up with the kind of answers research groups always come up with. Anyone with any sense could have produced them himself after two minutes' thought. Situation unlikely to change, neither side capable of producing initiative towards de-escalation of conflict, and so on, blah, blah, blah. And then right at the end, as a kind of unimportant after-thought, came something else.''

His voice moved into a higher, fluting register and took on the condescending tones of an expert preaching on his subject to the uninitiated.

''It is extremely probable that this local conflict will be overshadowed by more general and widespread unrest in the Near and Middle East, caused primarily by a growth of nationalism in the states concerned. Some models also suggest that this will be accompanied by a simultaneous renascence of traditional Moslem values, especially in the area of religion, which will be an important factor in the situation. Marxist-Leninist analysis, however, shows that fraternal Socialist parties will speedily emerge and gain control, taking over from the bourgeois nationalists and the obscurantist religious groups.''

He banged his hand down hard on the table and the plates jumped and clattered under the blow. ''When I read that, I nearly fell off my chair. Those stupid, self-satisfied pricks in research. They never get off their arses and out of their offices to see what life's like in the field. All they are is a lot of hot air and half-baked theories. And most of the time they can't even see the significance of what they're saying.''

I was as shocked to hear Alik utter these blasphemies as I would have been had I seen Father Zakhar take an axe to his icon.

''Are you saying that their Marxist-Leninist analysis is wrong, then?''

He glanced sideways at me, and gave a bitter smile. "That sounds more like one of my lines than yours. No, it's right in the long term. But the time span's all wrong. You can't write off Arab nationalism and Moslem religious feeling as easily as that. Especially not the last."

"But I still don't see the relevance . . ."

He sighed gustily and demonstratively. "You want me to spell it out for you? Let me give you some facts. For a start, do you know how many Moslems there are in our great Soviet motherland? One Soviet citizen in five has a Moslem background. The Soviet Union is the fourth largest Moslem state in the world. Before 1917 only Constantinople and Cairo were more important centres of Moslem thought than Kazan. And the situation's steadily changing to our disadvantage. We Russians have caught the Western disease. Our birthrate's right down, below replacement level even. We get divorced, prefer small families, practice contraception, our wives and mistresses have abortions." His glance flickered for a moment. "The average Russian woman has six to eight; some clock up fifteen. But the Tatars, the Uzbeks, the Tadzhiks, the Kazakhs and all the other minor Moslem nationalities are still patriarchal societies. They breed like rabbits. They're going up by about three per cent a year—that'll double the Moslem population in a generation. We'll cease to be a European nation, and will turn into an Eastern one. Perhaps it's inevitable, perhaps not. It's certainly a problem that's been interminably discussed at a very high level. We may yet have enforced sterilisation in the Moslem republics." The thought struck him as funny.

"All this is fascinating, but . . ."

He waved a hand. "Patience, Vanya, patience. We're getting to the meat. Have you got something better to do than sit here and listen to me?"

I shrugged, and he went on.

"We've never had much difficulty with the Moslems in

the past. There was some trouble in Azerbaidjan just after the revolution. Then there were the *Basmachi* in Turkestan. We were hunting them right through the '20s and '30s. We only got rid of them during the war. And about the same time—1943—we shipped a whole tribe of fanatical Sunni Moslems—the Chechens—off to Siberia. They should have stayed there, but after *his* death someone decided to bring them back. But all this was only locally significant. Pinpricks, in the final analysis. Of course, we've always organised them carefully. We carved up Central Asia very cunningly in 1924, putting the Uzbeks in a number of different little parcels. But think of the future. The population explosion, and one of the predictions of that report coming up. Suppose a fanatical Moslem revivalist movement starts up just across the border. A spark blows over to us, lands in a clump of dry grass, and starts a fire which spreads right through the Moslem territories from Kazan to Krasnoyarsk. And who would you call on to put it out? The Red Army? With nearly half its yearly intake of recruits from the Moslem nationalities? And the proportion constantly increasing?"

I listened to him with growing astonishment. "Are you being serious?"

"Of course. It's a serious subject. I reported my conclusions to my boss, General Manilov. You've met Vadim Valerianovich, haven't you?"

"Not socially."

He ignored the remark. "I was authorised to set up a team to look into the problem. The first thing we realised, as soon as we got down to thinking about it, was that we didn't know a bloody thing about how religious societies worked: power structures, patterns of behaviour, conflicts of allegiance and so on. We'd done such a good job convincing ourselves they couldn't have any real existence that we'd actually come to believe it."

He leant forward and tapped me on the knee. "Take my

word for it, Vanya. It's a terrible mistake to get ideology
mixed up with the hard facts of life. You can work out
your general strategy by it, but whatever you do, keep it
out of tactics.''

Another blasphemy. There was something slightly worrying about the way in which Alik was laying himself bare
to me, almost as if he thought it no longer mattered.

''Well, we dug up a lot of pre-revolutionary material
from the Third Department's archives, got a couple of
analysts to work on it, imported a sociologist from another
directorate—appalling old hag she was, too—booked a lot
of computer time and sat back to wait for results. Everything seemed to go swimmingly for a couple of months,
but gradually it became obvious we weren't getting anywhere. We'd come up with a few interesting details. The
sociologist—another bloody academic—had used the time
to write some immense paper with a damn fool title like''—he
fell into the parodic mode again—''*The Shaman, the
Witchdoctor and the Priest: A Study in Comparative Popular Credulity*. She wanted permission to publish it. I
refused, and had all the copies shredded for a breach of the
security regulations. That gave me a lot of pleasure.'' He
laughed again.

''Then I was sitting at my desk one afternoon, reading
through the latest lot of reports, when I suddenly realised
that the whole project was a load of crap. We'd started at
the wrong end. You don't have to know how a car works in
order to be able to drive it. And that's just what we wanted
to do if anything started up. Drive it quickly away to the
scrapyard, keeping well clear of any danger. And then into
the car crusher and—crunch. We didn't need a lot of airy-
fairy theoretical knowledge to do that. What we wanted was
practical expertise. Driving lessons, not lectures.''

He made a significant pause and lit another cigarette. It
was obvious that he wanted to be prompted to continue,
and I had no objection to giving him that small satisfaction.

"So?"

"So I found the perfect vehicle for the learner driver."

"Which was?"

"Can't you guess?"

I shook my head.

"The White Swan, of course. Just marvellous for a controlled experiment in a test-tube. Small, isolated, independent. Turn the Bunsen burner up. Turn the Bunsen burner down. Add a pinch of this, a dollop of that. Watch what happens, see how far you can predict reactions. And if the experiment goes sour, and you have to throw the mess in the test-tube away, who the hell cares?"

I stared at him for a moment, trying to come to terms with this new interpretation of the situation. A thought presented itself to my stunned mind. "But if anything they're Old Believers, not Moslems."

He waved the objection aside impatiently. "Old Believers, Orthodox, Catholic, Moslem. What does it matter? The fanaticism's the same. That's one of the few useful things we did get from our research."

"You mean all this wasn't for real? It was just an experiment dreamt up by you and the organs? You cold-blooded shit, Alik. And I thought you cared for Lyuba, too."

"I do." He fell silent, staring abstractedly at the full ashtray in front of him.

I felt rather ill as I brooded over the latest revelations. They sounded like the truth. There was a certain outré, even ludicrous quality about the scheme which seemed in keeping with what I knew of the KGB's activities. Then I grew slowly angry. I remembered the joy on Lyuba's face, the pleasant girl who'd brought me food, the children who'd called greetings after us. I got up and stood in front of Alik.

"What's going to happen now? Is the experiment over? Chuck the test-tubes in the dustbin and set up something else on the bench?"

I thought he hadn't been listening to me. Then he said: "I don't know." He looked at his watch. "I should hear any time now."

"Don't you realise you've created something that's out of control? You can't turn it off and on like a tap. These are people, not inorganic substances."

I bent down and shouted at him. "You've bungled the whole thing, haven't you? The scientist isn't supposed to be part of his experiment, but you're right in the middle of yours. How are you going to explain that Lyuba thinks you're a cross between the Messiah and the last of the Romanovs, and that Father Zakhar gives out the parish news to you over the short waves? If they go down, you go down with them."

The door opened and Fedor Evstafevich appeared. He clicked his heels in front of Alik and gave him an envelope. Alik tore it open and read the enclosure. He seemed to turn even paler and put a hand out to support himself for an instant on the table.

I took him by the shoulder. "What are you going to do?"

He knocked my arm away, and turned on me furiously, eyes blazing in a bloodless face. "What the hell has it got to do with you, you mother-fucking idiot? Get out!"

Then, with an abrupt change of mood, he stepped right up to me and tapped me on the chest with his forefinger. "You're irrelevant now, Vanya. In fact, come to think of it, you've been irrelevant for most of your life. Just go and lose yourself. I've got work to do. You want to know what's going to happen? Remember your Lenin? 'We must not do away with terror,' he said. How right he was."

24

High and long, with a row of immense, floor-to-ceiling windows down one wall, the hotel restaurant was another faded monument to imperial splendour. It was far from full at the moment; indeed, probably never had been full since the last provincial governor gave his last official banquet. The liveliest note now was provided by the waitresses giggling round a table near the entrance, pointedly ignoring the scattered customers.

I found Tanya and her film crew at a table down at the far end. I slid in next to her on the faded maroon plush banquette. Influence, bribery or sheer doggedness had succeeded in producing enough food and drink. I pulled a plate of crab salad over and poured myself a glass of vodka.

Tanya looked at me anxiously. "Is everything all right?"

"I don't know," I said. "I'll tell you later. I don't want to think about it now. Let's talk about something else."

She nodded.

I forked up some more crab salad. It wasn't up to the standard of some Moscow restaurants, but wasn't too bad for the periphery. In fact, on reflection it was amazing to find anything like this in Vologda at this time of the year. Everyone knows that the best of everything goes to Moscow and Leningrad, in that order, and the provinces get what's left over. Not much, usually. A friend of mine lived on cabbage soup for two months in the Murmansk district. A thought began to flicker at the back of my mind. I asked Tanya a question.

She looked surprised, but answered. "Chicken Kiev. I didn't know whether you'd be here or not, but I ordered beef Stroganov for you, just in case."

I nodded across the table at the crew. "What are they having?"

"I can't really remember. Cutlets of some sort, kebab perhaps. Why don't you ask them? Why do you want to know, anyway?"

I didn't say anything, and a moment later her eyes opened wide.

"You're right, Vanya. It's amazing. It can't be just because of Alik. The local council? No, not enough weight. Only someone terribly important could produce chicken Kiev in a dump like this. The All-Russian basketball team? The Kirov ballet company? The Minister of Heavy Engineering? A foreign delegation? What do you think?"

"I don't know. Wait and see." I ate some more crab salad. "Have you found out where you're filming yet?"

She wrinkled her nose. "Nothing definite, but we're to be ready to go tomorrow afternoon."

Things were coming together, but every new detail made the picture less pleasant.

Something caught my ear in the conversation of the film crew. "What's got Stasik so excited?" I asked.

"They've got some new kind of film to play with. Very hush-hush. Handed over under the seal of secrecy, only to be used on specific instructions from above, not to be processed in unauthorised laboratories and so on and so on.'' She poked Lyova in the ribs. ''Tell Vanya about your new toy.''

Lyova bent down, fished around near his feet, then lifted the edge of the tablecloth and with a glance invited me to look down. On the floor I saw an open cardboard box filled with yellow film cans. He dropped the edge of the tablecloth again.

''What is it?''

''The latest American film stock.'' He breathed it as if he'd been intoning a prayer.

''Good is it then?''

''Fantastic.'' He indicated its superlative quality by a circle made with his thumb and forefinger. ''About five times faster than anything we can get.''

''Colour?''

''No. Black and white.'' He sounded aggrieved, almost as if he had a personal stake in defending the achievements of private enterprise.

''What would you use it for?''

''Well, not for making feature films. There you can always control the light. Easy in a studio, more difficult on location, but it can still be done. So you don't need a terribly fast film. But it'd be great for documentaries, or news films. Anything where you're working under adverse light conditions. I could get you results with it in situations you wouldn't believe. A bit grainy, mind you, and perhaps not too great on contrast, but perfectly acceptable all the same.''

''Could you get a picture of something at midnight?''

''Not with no light at all. You can't expect miracles.''

Miracles were, in fact, just what would be needed about the time that Lyova pointed his camera at the sect's Easter service. I hoped Father Zakhar could produce them on cue.

"But if there were some artificial light? And if you were filming, say, a torchlight procession?"

"I should be able to get something. Especially if there's some snow around to reflect the light. But I wouldn't guarantee results. What you want in conditions like that is a team from the organs. They've really got everything: image intensifiers, infra-red film, the lot."

Tanya nudged me, and, when I turned in her direction, gave an almost imperceptible shake of the head. I shrugged my shoulders in reply. Lyova might wonder what the purpose of my questions was, and begin to put two and two together, but I doubted it. All three members of the crew seemed abnormally incurious about anything outside their narrow world of cameras and cards. They'd film an ant's progress along a twig and a public execution with the same absorption in the technical problems involved, and the same lack of interest in the significance of the events in front of their lens. In some respects it was a way of looking at the world which had a lot going for it.

The beef Stroganov arrived. It was hot and much more than just edible, but I got it down hurriedly, without appreciation. My sense of impending doom was growing and I wanted to get away and be alone with Tanya. As I sat there waiting for her to finish I noticed a bustle down at the other end of the room. A man in a black suit with a white shirt and a slim black tie—the get-up with which we've replaced the decadent Western dinner jacket—was shooing the waitresses away from their table. Like startled ducks they rose and scuttled off in different directions, to reappear a moment or two later in a state of frantic busyness.

Under the direction of the man in the black suit—the restaurant manager, presumably—tables were cleared and pushed together to form a long board running down the centre of the restaurant. The folds were shaken out of freshly laundered tablecloths; cutlery, plates and glasses appeared; clusters of bottles—wine, vodka, mineral water—

sprang up at metre intervals. The manager took a last walk round, making minute corrections in the alignment of a knife, the position of a glass. Four tall vases, each containing a bunch of plastic carnations, were brought to him. With his own hands he set them carefully in place, and then withdrew a step or two to eye his creation. Did he find it good? No: something had been forgotten. Two waitresses scurried off-stage. When they returned they brought with them a collection of miniature national flags which were then set up down the length of the table. I saw the Stars and Stripes, the West German black-red-yellow, the French tricolour, the Union Jack, the Italian flag, and a number of others I didn't recognise.

"You were right, Tanya," I said. "There's a foreign delegation here. That's why the food is edible."

"I hope they stay as long as we do."

A few minutes later the delegates started to trickle into the restaurant. They'd come, presumably, from some well-watered official reception, if not from a series of receptions. Faces were flushed, voices higher and louder than normal.

Suddenly I felt as though someone had kicked me in the stomach. One of the delegates, his back towards me, looked disturbingly familiar. As he sat down I caught him in profile. It was Bradley.

"Change places with me, will you, Tanya." She looked startled, but did as I asked. The move put her between Bradley and myself.

"What is it?"

"Bradley's here. No, don't look round. I'll point him out to you later."

"But does it matter if he sees you?"

I thought for a moment. In fact, it didn't. He hadn't got a hold on me any longer. But I didn't want to speak to him, and, more important, didn't want him to make any connection between Tanya and myself. I told her so.

She shrugged her shoulders. "It's not too disastrous even if he does. I meet an awful lot of foreigners in my job. I don't get the same black mark for it as you might. But perhaps you're right. I'll leave in a minute and take the boys with me."

Bradley was now talking to someone sitting beyond him. I couldn't see who the person was. Then Bradley reached out for a bottle of wine, poured two glasses and, picking his own up, leaned back in his chair. Next to him sat Nicola Booth.

I suppose I should have been prepared for this. After all, I'd known there was a link between them. But it was still surprising to see them together, especially here in Vologda.

Tanya gave me a strange look. "What are you staring at?"

I told her.

"The Englishwoman you were on the train with?" Tanya had been able to resist looking at Bradley, but it was too much to expect her to exercise the same restraint with Nicola. She swivelled round in the chair.

The movement must have caught Bradley's eye. He looked up. I could see him taking in Tanya with interest. His gaze flickered over me and then returned. He looked surprised for a moment and then a broad smile spread over his face. He raised a hand in greeting and turned to say something to Nicola.

I was caught. The only way out of the restaurant lay past Bradley's chair. But Tanya might be able to get away. I told her to go. She refused.

"I want to meet her," she said.

I gave up. "At least the crew ought to go. There's no point in getting them involved."

They filed out, Lyova carrying his precious box, just as Bradley bore down on us with Nicola bobbing in his wake.

"Vanya! Great to see you again." He swallowed my hand in his and crushed it to pulp. "You're the last person

I expected to see in this neck of the woods.'' He gave me an immense wink. ''Nicola, here, tells me you and she are old friends.'' For Tanya he put on an expression as if he was meeting Eisenstein and Dovzhenko rolled into one. ''Miss Tatarinova, this is wonderful. I had the very great pleasure of being introduced to you at the House of Friendship a month or so back.''

''*Dom druzhby*? I don't seem to . . .''

''We never really got talking. Something came up and I had to leave suddenly. But I'm a great admirer of yours. Can I tell you what a wonderful motion picture you've just made?''

He needn't have asked. Tanya was soaking the flattery up and expanding like a dry sponge in water.

''We must celebrate this.'' Bradley snapped his fingers. A waitress grew out of the floor at his elbow, and a few minutes later we were toasting international friendship in Russian champagne, *demi-sec*.

Bradley was obviously determined to be the life and soul of the party. He started telling us about some of the experiences the delegation—mainly composed of foreign journalists—had had on its tour. He made a hilarious story out of them, yet at the same time there was nothing in his narration which would have offended the most sensitive defender of Russian virtues. Perhaps he was cleverer than I'd thought.

Nicola was sitting next to me on the banquette. I was uneasily conscious of her thigh touching mine. She turned and smiled at me.

''It wasn't very polite of you, Vanya, not to get in touch with me after we came back from Leningrad together.''

I muttered some lame excuse and asked her about the tour.

''It's marvellous. I'm really enjoying myself. Martin got me on to it, you know. He says that the only difference between an author and a journalist is that one gets paid

crap for writing and the other gets paid for writing crap.
He's got a fantastic personality, hasn't he?''

"Have you known him long?"

"No, not really. We met at a party in Moscow, just
after I got back from Leningrad.'' She looked at me with
big, wide-open innocent eyes. She really was a great little
liar. "Isn't it exciting, Vanya. I'm getting to spend Easter
in Russia after all.''

I must have given her rather a queer look, for her tone
changed.

"You do remember, don't you, Vanya? Explaining to
me all about the calendar and Easter that morning in
Leningrad, over breakfast at the Astoria? It was much the
most useful conversation I've had in Russia. I've been able
to put heaps of people right on the subject ever since.
Anyway, it's Easter Sunday the day after tomorrow, isn't
it? Martin says he knows a church around here that's still
open, where we can see a real Orthodox service . . . Is
something the matter, Vanya?''

"No, not really. Excuse me a minute, will you?"

I slid out of the banquette and moved round behind
Bradley. I took hold of his upper arm and used my fingers
on it.

"Jesus, Vanya!"

"Could I have a word with you?"

I led him out into the passage that went down to the
men's lavatory. I heard someone open the door at the
bottom, and the smell of urine and strong disinfectant rose
to meet us. Bradley leant against the wall and lit one of his
extra-long Parliaments.

"Well?'' he asked.

"I thought you were going back home to cover the
presidential election campaign. Did they find they could
do without you?''

"No hurry. There's a week or so yet.''

I waited as a fat man in a transparent nylon shirt and a

bright blue suit with a miniature medal in his button-hole waddled up the stairs and squeezed between us. His flies were undone, but I had enough to worry about myself without taking on other people's problems.

"What are you doing here?"

"Sight-seeing, Vanya. Just rubber-necking around. I told you I'd be coming up here, didn't I? You shouldn't be so surprised when I keep my word."

"And what have you been telling Nicola?"

"She's just wild to go to a real genuine old Russian Easter service, and that's what I've promised her."

"Where do you think you're going to find one?"

"The same place you are, I guess."

I waited for a moment until I'd got my temper under control. "Do you know what's going to happen at that service tomorrow night?"

"I've got a pretty good idea."

"Can't you do something about it?"

"Hell, boy," with a pronounced Southern accent. "I just write the news down. I don't make it."

"Come off it, Bradley. Everybody knows you're not a newspaperman. Your act stinks. I hope they catch you up there in the forest, while you're taking in the picturesque local ceremonies, and put you in the dampest, darkest cell they can find, and lock the door, and throw the fucking key away."

I marched back into the restaurant, caught Tanya's questioning look and beckoned angrily to her. Then I turned and left, without waiting to see whether she was following.

She came up to the hotel bedroom some twenty minutes later. "What was all that about? Why did you walk out like that?"

"I'd had enough of them."

"Really? I thought he was quite charming. And very knowledgeable about the cinema." She began to undress. "She wasn't very interesting. And not very pretty either.

Rather common in fact. A pause. "I can't understand why you went to bed with her."

"I did not go to bed with her. For God's sake, Tanya, how many times have I got to tell you that?"

"Mind you, she has a good figure. Of course, it could be artificial. What does she look like when she's undressed? Has she got nice breasts?"

"How should I know what her breasts are like? She's never paraded naked in front of me."

"Hasn't she, darling? How disappointing for you. I will, if you like."

"Are you drunk, Tanya?"

"I may be a little tipsy. That nice American bought us so much nice champagne. But I hope I can hold my liquor like a gentleman." She toppled gently against me.

I sat her down on the bed. "Do you know what you're going to be making a film of, tomorrow night?"

"Do you?" she said lightly.

I told her what I'd learnt from Alik and what I thought would happen. When I'd finished there was a long silence. Then she said: "I won't do it. I won't go. The boys will have to. But I won't. I don't care what happens."

"You must go, Tanya."

"Why?"

"Because you might be able to help if you do. If you don't go, you certainly won't be able to. And if it all comes out in the future, the more witnesses the better."

She considered what I'd said for a moment. "I suppose you're right. I'll go." She put her head in her hands. "But why, oh why couldn't he have brought in his own camera team? You heard what Lyova said. We might not even get a usable picture."

"For the same reason as he's got me down here. You put your finger on it that night in Moscow. He wants to recreate that summer. Demonstrate how powerful he is." I took my coat off. "Also, I think he's doing this all very much on the left-hand side, as they say. It's a bit of unofficial, private enterprise. So he obviously can't use an official KGB camera team.'' I got into bed and turned off the light. ''At least, I hope that's what he's doing. Because if it is, I'm going to use it to blow him up.''

''How?''

I told her.

25

There was no sign on the streets that the citizens of Vologda realised that the next day would be the anniversary of their Saviour's resurrection. I hoped Nicola wouldn't be too disappointed if she didn't find the local party secretary standing outside the district executive committee's offices handing out Easter eggs to the passers-by.

Not that he would have had many takers at the moment, for the streets were practically empty. I saw no one on my way over from the hotel, apart from a large black dog under the partial control of a small child, the latter so well wrapped up as to make its sex impossible to determine. They passed by on the other side of the street, travelling rather too slowly for the leader's, and rather too rapidly for the follower's taste, and vanished round a corner. If I'd been superstitious, I might have seen the pair as offering a crude symbolic parallel to my own situation. I hoped the child would get home safely, just in case.

It was a dark, lowering day. Yesterday's snow had

stopped during the night, but one felt that this was only a temporary break, and that it would be back with a good deal more in the near future. A wind straight from the Arctic circle was whistling round the buildings, bringing tears to my eyes and carving the skin from my cheeks with a blunt scalpel. Yet in some ways I welcomed the change to harshness in the weather. A snowstorm might hamper Alik's operations, might even, if severe enough, force him to call them off. And the change corresponded too to a change in my mood. The supineness of the previous morning had vanished. I felt fit, keyed-up and ready to make one final effort to redeem the situation.

The central militia station in Vologda was housed in a large neo-classical building in the main square. I went up a wide flight of steps, flanked by two lines of columns. The imposing double doors under the portico were locked. Indeed, they seemed very rarely, if ever, to be opened, since, for greater security—though who would want to break into a police station?—a heavy chain had been passed through both handles and fastened with an even heavier padlock. After a short search I found the entrance round at the side of the building. I pushed open the outer door and went through into a small dark lobby. For a moment, despite good resolutions, I stood there almost in indecision. No one had seen me. It would still be possible not to go through with it. But the possibility was more theoretical than real.

The inner door was thickly upholstered and covered with dark-brown, buttoned oil-cloth. It fitted tightly, almost hermetically in its frame and uttered a kind of squelching sigh as I opened it. Inside it was stiflingly hot.

Across the room ran some ten or twelve rows of backless wooden benches, worn and polished by the uneasy movements of innumerable suppliants. A few people were sitting there now. Most of them didn't bother to look at me as I walked down the room to the desk at the far end.

"Good morning, sergeant. I'd like to speak to General Manilov as soon as possible. It's urgent."

He was a broad, fleshy man with red cheeks and a coarsely veined nose. His cap was lying to one side of the desk and the hooks of his collar had been undone to give his neck the freedom it badly needed. He was transcribing something from a sheet of paper into a large occurrence book. He didn't speak until he'd got to the end of a sentence and completed it with a carefully placed full stop. Then he said, without looking up: "We're right out of General Manilovs for the moment."

He raised his head, took me in for a moment with bloodshot blue eyes, and then crooked his forefinger. A young policeman with fair hair and something of the look of the poet Esenin, who had been standing behind the counter of the cloakroom watching inquisitively, unlatched the half-door and began to come towards us, smiling.

I leant over the desk and began to speak rapidly, as impressively as I could. "General Manilov's with the security forces. From Moscow. He's here for a special operation. Tonight. I must see him. Call your superior officer at once."

He put down his pen. The young policeman came to a halt a few paces away. The sergeant looked at me again. He blinked a couple of times. I could read his thoughts as clearly as if they'd been carved on his forehead with a chisel.

The simplest, easiest, most sensible solution would be to have me thrown out. There was nothing about me to suggest a member of the KGB, even one in plain clothes. I hadn't produced an official identity card, and could therefore only be a member of the public, and a mad one at that, seized by some exhibitionist mania. But, on the other hand, if by some one in ten million chance, I did have something of importance to communicate, and it became known that he had failed to let me through . . .

He sighed, reached out and picked up a pad of forms printed on pale mauve paper. "Name, place of residence?"

In exchange for my coat and hat the young policeman gave me a cloakroom ticket. He obviously regretted that it wasn't a kick in the stomach. I sat down on one of the benches.

Now there really was no going back. I'd voluntarily offered myself up to the machine, and was about to be sucked in by it. The only question was what shape I'd be in when it decided to spit me out again.

Time went by. I began to feel sleepy in the heat. At long intervals the sergeant would call out a name. One of those waiting would go forward to the desk, and then out through a door behind it to the right. Some of them returned the same way later on, most with their expression unchanged. It was an expression which, allowing for physiognomical differences, was common to all. Not so much a look of hopeless despair as one of numbed indifference. I could feel my own features settling into the same mould as a defensive reaction to the surroundings. The pattern was broken only once when a fat peasant woman, wearing an old army greatcoat and felt boots, trundled back through the door with a radiant smile on her round flat face, pushing a sulky-looking youth in front of her.

My neighbour on the bench was a gaunt young man with a week's growth of beard. His thin check overcoat, probably once the property of a foreign tourist, must have migrated through a number of hands before eventually landing, torn and dirty, on his shoulders; it couldn't have been much of a protection from the Vologda climate. The same could be said of his shoes, which had the exaggeratedly pointed toes popular in Moscow a year or so back, and whose soles were coming away from the uppers. Every now and then he was shaken by a spasm of coughing which left him bent and wheezing. After one such attack he touched me on the arm.

"Have you got a cigarette, comrade? I've this terrible itch in my throat."

"Sorry."

He got up and moved away, but a few minutes later came back with a cigarette in his mouth.

"You're not local, are you?"

"What makes you say that?"

"Never seen you before. And you don't look as though you've come into town from a *kolkhoz*. I should think you're from Moscow. Staying at one of the hotels. Probably connected with that film crew that flew in the other day."

I grinned a little uneasily.

"Not wrong, am I?" And then, sliding a little closer on the bench and putting his mouth to my ear, he murmured: "Perhaps I can be of assistance. I know most of what's going on around here."

That might be true, but if so, I thought, it must be very much a buyer's market for information in Vologda at the moment. He didn't look as though he was making a fortune out of it. Of course, he might just be a stool-pigeon, planted by the KGB in the waiting-room to pick up trifles or provoke incidents.

"Well, what about it?"

There seemed nothing to lose. I could hardly get myself into more trouble.

"You know the district around here?"

"Try me."

"Up to the north-east?"

"Born there."

"Have you ever heard of the White Swan?"

He couldn't have withdrawn more quickly if I'd told him I was suffering from rabies. On his face I could see the shutters rattling down and the bolts being jammed into place.

"Well?" I said. At that moment the sergeant shouted

my name. As I got to my feet the man leant towards me and spat on the floor. One or two flecks of saliva landed on my shoes.

I had hoped to be taken to see Manilov immediately, but I should have known better. I found myself in a small room lined with dark-green filing cabinets. On the other side of the table sat my old friend Captain Lapshin. He seemed no more pleased to see me than I was to see him.

"You've put in an application for an interview with General Manilov." He picked up the form the sergeant had filled in and snapped it backwards and forwards between his fingers. "At this stage, of course, General Manilov can see no one. He is too occupied. However, as his operational assistant, I am willing to hear what you have to say. If anything seems important, I will report it to the general. But please be brief. I have other, urgent business." He picked up a pen—it was one of those imitation Parkers made by the Chinese, with a plastic body and chromium cap—and held it ready.

I had to see Manilov himself. He was the only person in the region with the power and authority necessary to act decisively, with sufficient speed to stop Alik's arbitrary actions before they led to disaster.

I weighed up the chances of persuading Lapshin to let me through. I couldn't use the same method on him as I'd used on the sergeant outside. Lapshin belonged to a younger generation, one which hadn't had all the initiative stamped out of it under the Georgian's heavy boot; which hadn't learnt, through fear, that inaction was better than action, "no" a more useful word than "yes." They hadn't seen the brightest and the best of their contemporaries rewarded for independence and intelligence, not by a pat on the head, but by a nine-gram bullet in the back of the neck.

It followed that I couldn't frighten Lapshin into letting me see Manilov, but something told me that he'd be eager to display his qualities as an interrogator, as an intelligence officer, to reconnoitre a situation and present an analysis of it. He'd try to extract from me everything I knew and hand it up to his superior on a plate, as his own work.

He was beginning to get impatient now. He rapped his pen imperiously on the desk. "Well, comrade Morozov?"

But the final deduction was already there. If he'd agreed to see me, so late in the day, it followed that he thought I might have something important to communicate. And what I had to do was, like a Japanese wrestler, to turn his own strength against him: let him think he was forcing the situation by getting me to see Manilov. I hoped he hadn't got any cleverer since we'd last met.

"It's true that I asked to see General Manilov, comrade captain, but that's because I didn't know that any of his staff were here. If I'd known I could speak to you instead, I'd certainly have asked to see you. I'd much rather tell you everything and let you report it to the general without me. It's far too important and delicate a matter for me, comrade captain." Was the note of cringing servility perhaps a little overdone? It didn't seem so. He was leaning forward with both hands on the table, looking excited.

"Out with it, man. What information have you got?"

"I can tell you, rather than the general? I won't have to see the general?"

"Yes, yes."

"It concerns a certain very highly placed member of the department. A close associate of General Manilov."

I paused and looked at him. He pursed his lips and nodded. He knew whom I was talking about.

"I think it could be shown that he has had dealings with a clandestine, counter-revolutionary organisation. And that he has been in communication with"—it couldn't just be another meaningless coincidence that Alik and Bradley shared a taste for the same brand of American cigarettes—"agents of the imperialist-capitalist bloc, that—"

"Stop!" He held up his hand. There was a long pause. His thoughts were, in fact, not much more difficult to read than those of the sergeant.

He could do himself a lot of good in the department with this information: he might even make it up to major on the strength of it. He'd cause a sensation by submitting a report on paper, but there'd be far more éclat in dragging a reluctant witness into the general's presence and forcing him to repeat his story there.

And there was another, more important—indeed vital— consideration which ought to occur to him in a moment. Since I was accusing a member of the security organs, it would be advisable for him to have a third party present as a witness when my statement was taken down: a precaution which would, of course, be ludicrous if I were denouncing an ordinary citizen. Furthermore, since the accusations were directed against an officer of superior rank to the captain, the witness ought to be, for safety's sake, of superior rank to the accused.

He sighed, capped his pen and clipped it back into the breast pocket of his tunic. I was glad to see that he still had a rudimentary feeling for self-preservation. It's a trait in us which must be the only surviving proof of Lysenko's theory that acquired characteristics can be heritable. Our fathers learnt the laws of survival in a society ruled by harsh, malignant and arbitrary force, and passed on their instincts to their children.

Manilov looked old, tired and ill. His eyes were red-rimmed, and his skin had a grey, leaden tinge. He dismissed Lapshin with a wave of his hand.

"But, comrade general . . ."

"I'll call you if I need you, Boris Mikhaylovich."

It looked as if Lapshin would never get to be present at a conversation between Manilov and myself. He drew himself up, crashed his heels together, turned about and stalked out of the room. Manilov smiled as he watched him go.

Then he pinched the bridge of his nose between his thumb and forefinger for a moment, closing his eyes as he did so.

"You know, Morozov, my intuitions are usually right. Before we came up from Moscow I got them to find your dossier. Had it put in with the rest of the paper work." He patted a thin cardboard file, open in front of him. "Here it is. Here you are." He pointed a finger at me. "And what do you have to say that's so important you have to disturb me?"

"Comrade general," I began. I could have done with a bigger audience. One performs better to a full house. "I consider it my duty, as a citizen of the Union of Soviet Socialist Republics, to inform you that your subordinate officer, Ostroumov, Aleksey Petrovich—"

"Ta-ta-ta," he interrupted me. "Less rhetoric, young man. You're not at a party meeting."

Subdued, I went on to tell him what I'd found out about the sect, about the relations with Father Zakhar which Alik had established, about my suspicions that there was a close link between him and Bradley.

I spoke for some time. When I'd finished there was a long silence. Manilov began to make himself a cigarette. He tore off a small square of newspaper, and rolled it into a narrow funnel, which he filled with *makhorka* from his pouch. Then he bent the thing at right angles, a third of the way from the narrow end, so that it looked like a mis-shapen pipe, lit it, and blew a cloud of smoke across the table at me.

"Interesting. Interesting. But what do you want out of it, eh? Not a *seksot* by nature, are you?"

I seized on the opening he'd given me. "I want you to—"

"I seem to remember, back in Moscow"—he rode over

me as efficiently as Alik. It must be something they learnt
at staff college—"telling you to keep your nose out of this
business. Perhaps it's as well you didn't. But it's a nasty
affair. Very nasty."

He puffed away for a moment or two. I was just about
to appeal to him again, when he began to speak, slowly
and ruminatively, in a style very unlike his usual conversational manner.

"There was a time, you know, when one was proud to
be called a *chekist*. I can remember how I felt the day my
probationary service came to an end, and I became a full
member of the department. It was like entering a monastic
order. The same commitment. The same dedication to an
ideal. We thought of ourselves as a secular priesthood, as
moral guardians of the state. That was long ago, of course,
in the days of Feliks Edmundovich." He paused for a
moment, looking out of the window. The snow had begun.
It was coming down in sharp, whirling flurries. "He was a
saint of the Revolution. As incorruptible as Robespierre.
As terrible as Saint-Just. We worshipped him, we tried to
live up to the standards he set. Since then things have
changed. We've suffocated under bureaucrats, our work
has been perverted by degenerates. The old cadres have
been swept away. There are few left whose memories go
back as far as mine. The former idealism, the sense of
duty, of obligation. All gone. All that's left of Feliks
Edmundovich now is his name on a blue and white street
sign in Moscow—Dzerzhinsky Square."

He came slowly back from the past. "Today the service
is full of technocrats who think that power grows out of a
computer terminal, of bully boys with their brains in their
fists, or of careerists like your friend Ostroumov, with one
eye on their work and the other on the main chance."
With a sudden, wolfish smile which for a moment made
him look young. "His song is sung, though. I've ordered
him to pack up his lunatic experiment. I should never have

agreed to it. But there were pressures. There always are.'' He brooded for an instant. "Today he's rounding up Father Zakhar and the rest of the sect. Tomorrow I'll put him and the American in the bag together.''

"Comrade general, might I ask whether you have given any special orders on how this operation on the sect is to be carried out?''

He looked at me in surprise, and then shook his head. "Nothing specific, no. He's done it scores of times before. He knows the drill. Minimum force. Minimum personnel.''

"He told me to remember Lenin's precepts on the use of terror. What could he have meant by that? And does the comrade general know that a camera crew has been assigned to cover the operation?''

"Nothing strange in that. Routine procedure. Could make a useful training film.''

"With respect, comrade general, is it routine to bring in an outside crew, together with the well-known film director Tatyana Tatarinova? To make a *training* film? In the snow, in the middle of the night? Of Leninist terror in action?''

He looked at me. "Well, what conclusion have you come to?''

"Comrade general, there are hundreds of innocent people up there in that valley, men, women and children. They may believe in God, they may worship in church, but according to our constitution these aren't crimes. They haven't done anything illegal, but they're going to be persecuted for their religion. Something terrible, something appalling is going to happen to them. I don't know what it will be, what form it will take, but I have the feeling that my friend Alik wants to destroy the whole sect. I don't think he's quite sane any longer.''

Manilov drummed his fingers on the table. "Religious persecution . . . a camera crew . . . an American observer. It all hangs together.'' He reached out for the telephone.

When he put the receiver down, ten minutes later, he seemed to have collapsed in on himself. He looked old and very frail.

"You're right. He's taken far too many troops. And equipment. All my men."

"Can't you stop him? Relieve him of his command? Have him arrested?"

"It's too late. They moved out half an hour ago. A training exercise of extreme severity. Simulation of battle conditions. Radio silence to be strictly maintained. No communications with base. I can't establish contact with them. If a message did get through, it would go straight to Ostroumov." He looked out of the window. The snow was still coming down. "They say conditions are too bad to put a helicopter up. There's nothing to be done."

"Nothing?"

He shook his head.

"But what about the people up there? Lyuba, the children?"

"They'll have to take their chance. I'm sorry, Morozov. A nasty, nasty business."

I looked at my watch. It was three o'clock. Alik had made his move very early, presumably in order to use the last hours of daylight and to avoid interference from above. But I was convinced that he wouldn't begin to move in until the service began. There might still be an outside chance of getting there, if I could get a lift, or the use of a vehicle. I stood up.

"Where are you going?"

I shrugged my shoulders.

"I can't allow it."

"But, comrade general—"

"No. The fewer people involved, the better. There's more to it than what you see. It's an affair of state now." He lifted the telephone again.

While he spoke I looked out of the window. The light

was fading outside. The snow had come, but too late. Though it had stopped Manilov, there wouldn't be enough to stop Alik's trucks. In my mind's eye I could see the convoy winding up the road towards the head of the valley. In the back of each the soldiers would be huddled together under the canvas tilt, cold and uncomfortable. There would be the reek of low-grade petrol, of cheap tobacco, of unwashed bodies. Someone would be telling a dirty joke. Then the trucks would halt, nose to tail. There'd be the clatter of weapons and equipment as the troops dismounted, a few stifled laughs and curses. The sergeants would form them up and then, section after section, they'd file off through the snow.

The door opened, Lapshin came in.

"Take Morozov to the airport, Boris Mikhaylovich. Put him on the next plane to Moscow."

It was obvious that Lapshin could have imagined no better way of spending the rest of the afternoon. He sprang to attention. "Certainly, comrade general." And then, after a pause: "Does the comrade general wish me to inform Moscow that he is arriving?"

I waited anxiously for Manilov's reply. He closed my file and tapped it a few times on the table. Then he turned it lengthways and tore it across and dumped the pieces in the waste-paper basket.

"No. Moscow has enough on its hands at the moment. Good-bye, Morozov."

As we walked away down the corridor Lapshin said: "Don't let the old man fool you with that trick of his. I've seen him play the scene fifty times before. Your file's still in Moscow archives. That was a duplicate he tore up."

26

The airport lounge was crowded with people and luggage. The snow must have stopped all flights. Lapshin went away, leaving me in the custody of his police driver. After a lengthy exchange of opinions with a peasant woman who was flying to Armavir to see her daughter-in-law and three grandchildren, I managed to persuade her to move one of her corded bundles, and sat down on a small corner of bench.

Lapshin came back again, looking pleased with himself. "They don't expect the snow to last for very long. But flights won't begin again until tomorrow morning. You've a long, uncomfortable wait in front of you. Airport security will be keeping an eye on you, so keep your nose clean." He wheeled round and left.

I sat there thinking about the affair. I was relieved that I'd persuaded Tanya to go with the film crew; at least there would be one objective, credible witness to the events. But I was also sorry I'd let her in for it. I tried not to let myself imagine what she might see.

I would have liked to be able to forget everything in sleep, but when I closed my eyes it was only to see troops in white camouflage smocks moving slowly through the forest, closing in on the valley from all sides. Alik, with a smart grey *papakha* on his head, and wearing a light-grey officer's greatcoat with a gold belt, was directing operations with a baton. There were shouts, the clatter of automatic weapons, one or two isolated blasts from a shotgun. A woman screamed violently. A girl ran past, floundering in the deep snow, followed by two laughing Red Army men. A child's wail of terror was cut off in midbreath. I woke up with a start, sweating heavily.

Someone was poking me in the ribs. I turned and noticed without surprise that the peasant woman had turned into Nicola Booth.

"Go to the lavatory," she said.

"What?"

"Go to the lavatory."

"I didn't know you spoke Russian."

She kicked me hard on the shin. I limped away.

Vologda could be proud of its airport lavatories. They were new, clean and smelt of pine disinfectant. Bright overhead lights shone on white tiles. Somewhere a cistern flushed.

Bradley was leaning against a basin, smoking. He threw me an old, dirty, workman's *telogreyka* and a cheap fur cap.

"Put these on. And pull the ear-muffs down." He looked at me. "OK. Now try these for size." A pair of boots skittered across the floor. I put them on. They fitted reasonably well.

"What about my things?"

"Igor will take care of them." He called. A man came out of one of the cubicles, buttoning up his coat. He grinned, and I recognised him as the sharp dresser who'd been sitting next to me in the police-station.

"When we're gone he'll put on your coat and hat and go and sit where you were. It should fool them for long enough."

He bustled me outside. A car came up to the entrance as we emerged. It was a Zaporozhets with the high-clearance suspension. Bradley pushed me into the back and ran round to the driving-seat as Nicola slid over to the right-hand side.

"Where are we going?"

"To the monastery. You want to be in at the death, don't you?"

"I don't much care for the way you put it. But yes, I do."

The arc lights on the airport gate lit up the inside of the car. Anxiety touched me for a moment, but the guard paid no attention to us. I leant forward and tapped Nicola on the shoulder. "What are you doing here? Are you coming too?"

"Didn't you believe me last night, when I told you I was going to an Easter service? I might pick up some local colour for the novel as well." She giggled.

We drove on some way in silence. The windscreen wipers clicked monotonously over the glass; the snow was still falling thickly. Bradley began to fiddle with the heating controls, cursing quietly to himself.

"Bradley," I said.

"Uh-huh?"

"Who's Igor?"

"Just an acquaintance. Who wants to turn an honest buck occasionally."

"Will anything happen to him?"

"Your guess is as good as mine. They might lean on him a bit, but if he says he found the clothes in the washroom, what can they do? And his brother-in-law is a lieutenant in the police, at that."

"Was he following me?"

"I asked him to keep an eye on you."

"Did you ask him to spit on my shoes?"

Bradley laughed. "He told me about that. He's a great little method actor, that boy. He said that's how he thought he'd behave, if he were really the person he was pretending to be."

He said no more, but concentrated on his driving. He was holding the centre of the road, and pushing the car along as fast as it would go, making the most of the small engine by taking the revs up in each gear until the valves began to chatter. With the high suspension it swayed wildly on the corners. I wedged myself into the back seat and hoped we wouldn't meet a lorry with no lights coming the other way.

Later Bradley turned off on to a side-road, and our progress slowed. I'd no idea where we were, but we weren't following the route Tanya and I had taken.

"I hope you know that your friend Alik is somewhere up here ahead of you with a small army," I said.

"*My* friend Alik?" said Bradley in a voice which had polite incomprehension chopped up and sprinkled all over it.

"Come off it, Bradley. I know you've got something going with Lieutenant-Colonel Ostroumov of the KGB. General Manilov knows it, his assistant knows it, and probably half the waitresses in the hotel restaurant know it. What I don't know, though I expect everyone else does, is what the hell you're up to together. Do you feel like telling me now?"

Bradley didn't say anything, but Nicola twisted round in her seat to face me.

"What do you know about Ostroumov's units?"

"Not very much, apart from the fact there's a bloody lot of them."

"We saw them moving off. This afternoon." Her voice tailed off, as though she'd realised she'd said something she shouldn't.

"Go on, tell him," said Bradley.

"In detail?"

"Why not?"

"All right." She paused and cleared her throat.

"A small reconnaissance unit left first, at 1426 hours. Six motor-cyclists, two BTR-40 scout cars. The old type, without amphibious capability. The main body followed just over five minutes later, at 1431. Ten armoured personnel carriers; three of them newish BTR-60P's—that's the wheeled, not the tracked variant—with canvas hoods, and the other seven BTR-152's: again the older model, on the ZIL-151 chassis. The rest of the troops were in soft-skinned vehicles, mainly Ural 375 and ZIL-157 trucks. There were seventeen of these, and one command car—a BTR-152U. Basically, therefore, a motor-rifle battalion without its artillery, armour and its support vehicles. But in addition there were six searchlight trucks towing mobile generators, and two BM14-17 rocket launchers, mounted on GAZ-63 light vehicles."

Nicola's technical expertise was both astounding and impressive, but for the moment I was too shocked by the information to be surprised by the manner in which it was given. Manilov, I felt, had rather understated matters.

"Does he think he's going to be fighting the Battle of Stalingrad all over again? He knows who's up there. He knows all about the White Swan. What the hell does he need so much fire-power for?"

Bradley came in, as if he'd received the right cue. His tone was unusually restrained. "That's what we'd like to know. We were rather hoping you might have some views on the subject."

"Sorry." Then a phrase of Manilov's occurred to me. "Of course, he could just have marched all the troops he could lay his hands on out of the barracks so that they couldn't be used against him. He needn't be going to bring the whole battalion into action against the White Swan."

"That's one possibility, but we're not sure it's the only explanation. You don't have any other ideas?"

"No." I caught his eye in the rear-view mirror. He was looking at me with some scepticism, as though he didn't quite believe me. He would have been right not to, for something else had come into my mind. Father Zakhar had been convinced that he was going to receive help from outside. Could Alik possibly be taking his troops to join in the crusade of the White Swan? The idea was so fantastic I was reluctant to mention it. Anyway, whose side were Bradley and Nicola on? Mine or theirs? If, indeed, there were sides to be on. Perhaps there weren't, or at least not in any way that I could make sense of.

I tapped Nicola on the shoulder. "What about Tanya and the camera crew? Did you see them?" I hoped that Alik had changed his mind about filming the events.

"Sorry. I forgot to mention them. Not really on the strength, are they? But they were there all right, in a small truck next to the command car."

The Zaporozhets tipped suddenly to one side, throwing me back into a corner of the seat. There was a jar, and something scraped along the side of the car. Bradley swore loudly, and spun the steering-wheel. A wall of snow filled the windscreen. I was flung forward against the front seat. The engine coughed weakly and then stopped. For a moment or two the only sound was the tinkle and crackle of hot, over-stressed metal contracting and cooling down.

There was obviously no hope of getting the car out of the deep ditch without a tow-truck. Nicola and I climbed up on to the road. Bradley joined us a little later with his arms full. There was a metallic chink as he put his burdens down.

"What's that?"

He rested his hand on my chest and prevented me from coming any nearer. "It's a hunting rifle." He turned round and picked it up. "A nice little gun. You must have seen them around. The civilian version of the Dragunov semi-automatic sniper's rifle. They call it the *Medved*—the Bear. A smaller magazine, no foresight protectors and a different stock, but otherwise exactly the same as army issue. It comes with quite a reasonable telescopic sight. I'd prefer an infra-red one for night work, but it's hardly the thing you can pick up off the shelf in the sports department of GUM.''

''What the hell do you think you're going to shoot with it up here?''

''Bears?''

He found his own joke so funny that it was some time before he could go on. Then he sorted through his bundles and gave us each a white coverall.

When we'd put them on he handed Nicola a small pack and shouldered one himself. Then he looked at his watch.

''It's half past seven. We're going to have to hike a bit further than I'd planned, but we should still manage to get there in good time, if we keep moving. Let's get this show on the road, boys and girls.''

We moved off into the forest.

27

Although the new snow made walking difficult, Bradley set a cracking pace from the start. I managed to keep up without too much trouble as long as we kept to level ground, but later, when we left the valley floor and began to crab our way diagonally up its steep right-hand wall, I found myself in difficulties. Nicola and Bradley seemed unaffected. They trod on ahead lightly and easily while I panted and stumbled in their wake.

When we climbed out on to the summit of the ridge, I felt almost as exhausted as I had two nights before, when I'd left the monastery. I didn't seem to be getting any fitter, despite the exercise I was taking. My tendons were stretched agonisingly, my eyes were so full of tears I could hardly see anything, and I was gasping for breath.

Luckily, Bradley decided to take a short rest. He consulted his compass, had a word or two with Nicola, and led us off again. The going was easier up here—the wind hadn't allowed the snow to settle—but it was also colder. I pulled the flaps of my hat down and tied the strings under my chin. With head down and shoulders hunched, aware only of Nicola's feet moving backwards and forwards at the periphery of my vision, I trudged on. Soon I'd settled into a rhythm, and then, as time went by, I walked myself into a kind of daze.

Cold, hunger, fatigue—all ceased to be pressing, receded somewhere into the darkness. Other, less physical concerns became more insistent. What did Bradley think we could do when we got there? How could we help Lyuba and the others? The questions went round and round in my head without producing any answers. Maybe there weren't any answers. And I found myself becoming uncertain, too, of the questions. Later I fell into repeating the same snatch of verse over and over again:

> "I look behind the dark veil
> And see the shore enchanted
> And the enchanted distance."

One foot went down into a hollow full of soft snow, the other scraped along the frozen crust.

> "I look behind the dark veil
> And see the shore enchanted
> And the enchanted distance."

Nicola's boots were still going on ahead, tirelessly left right left right left right left . . .

> "I look behind the dark veil
> And see the shore enchanted—"

I bumped into an obstruction.

"And the enchanted distance," said Bradley's voice. "Look where you're going, man, you nearly had me over.

Come down here." He pulled me in behind a fallen tree which acted as a windbreak. Nicola was already there, squatting down and looking through her rucksack with a torch. She handed me an open thermos flask. I took a gulp of molten lava, flavoured with coffee. My mind and body came back together with a jerk.

" 'In the evenings, above the restaurants.' " Bradley quoted the first line of the poem thoughtfully. "You go for Blok, then?" He broke a bar of chocolate and handed the pieces round.

"Sometimes."

"All a bit too up in the air for me. He hadn't really any idea of what it was all about, did he? I like something with a bit more steel in it. Mandelshtam. Or Tsvetaeva. They both knew what the score was. And wrote about it."

I giggled. There was definitely something ludicrous about the situation: sitting on a snow-covered hill in the middle of the night discussing Russian verse with an American agent. But perhaps this poetry lover was the real Bradley; or was, at least, closer to the real Bradley than the carica-tural newspaperman he'd been masquerading as up to now. I wished he'd revealed this persona earlier. I could have done, too, with a bit more literary criticism now—how did he stand on the Dostoevsky/Tolstoy question, for example— and was disappointed when he decided to get back to business.

"Gather round, will you?"

He dug into the breast of his jacket, brought out a map and spread it, folded, over his knee. Nicola directed the beam of her torch on to it.

"I should have done this earlier on in more comfortable surroundings. Driving the car off the road like that threw me a bit out of kilter. I thought we'd really have to hightail it along to get here before the balloon went up. But we seem to have a bit of time in hand. It's just before eleven."

He traced a route on the map with a stubby gloved

forefinger. "This is where we went off the road. Then we came up this re-entrant, climbed up on to the spur, and followed it along to the main ridge. I figure now that we're about here. Just below the summit and about twenty minutes away from the head of the valley. What we want to know now is how Ostroumov is going to run his operation. You've seen the layout, Vanya. Give us a run-down on it."

I bent forward and looked at the map. With its different shades of purple and green and neat contour lines it seemed a very inadequate representation of the reality I remembered. But the general picture was clear enough.

"The monastery is right up at the head of this valley. It'll be just beneath us when we come down off the ridge. A track runs up to it along the valley bottom from this village down here. That's the only way Alik will be able to bring his transport in. Just opposite the monastery there's a path over into the next valley on the east. That's the way I came last time."

"And the west?"

"That's the way I left. There's no path there. It's steep, but not impossible."

"The head of the valley?"

"Sheer cliff. No one could get up it unless they had some mountain goat in them."

Bradley pondered for a moment. "Made for the job. You couldn't design a better terrain if you worked on it for a year. Well, it's obvious what he'll do. He'll halt about here, somewhere above the village. Send off two patrols to cordon off the east and west slopes." His thumb and forefinger moved up the map, separating as they went. "When they're in position, he'll push the main body up the centre and snap the jaws together." He tucked the map away and rose to his feet.

I'd stiffened up during the rest and for some time couldn't do much more than hobble. Luckily Bradley no longer seemed in a hurry. Indeed, after quarter of an hour he brought us to another halt. This time he went on ahead by himself, saying that he was going to "do the Indian scout bit."

I tried massaging my calves, but it didn't appear to have any effect. For the moment they were as hard as two blocks of wood and about as much use. Nicola offered me the thermos again.

"Thanks." I took a drink. "Rather different from our other journey together, isn't it?"

"Colder, certainly."

"But you're used to that, aren't you?"

"What do you mean?"

"Well, this is obviously the kind of thing you really spend your time on. Night exercises, winter survival techniques, unarmed combat, weapons training. That sort of thing. All that stuff about being the great female novelist, up there with Iris Murdoch and the rest, was just bullshit, wasn't it? I don't believe you've ever written a line of fiction in your life apart from an intelligence report."

She screwed the top back on the thermos flask. "You better had believe it, buster, because it happens to be true. If you ever get back to Moscow, go and look me up in the catalogue at the Lenin Library. You'll find me there, just after Boadicea and before the Brontë sisters and Fanny Burney." She prodded my knee with a finger. "I know you're under a strain at the moment, but all the same don't make cracks about my art. I'm sensitive about it, and you're liable to end up with a broken arm. Or worse."

"What are you doing with Bradley?" I remembered her passport. "You're not American."

"No. Hundred per cent English. Cheltenham Ladies College and Cambridge. But this isn't my show. If he wants you to know what's going on, he'll tell you, all in his own good time."

"Which isn't just yet." Bradley surged out of the darkness. "Come on. There's no one posted up this end."

We lay on the edge of the cliff, peering down into the valley. It must have been very near the place from which Tanya and I had first seen the *skit*. Yellow candlelight spilt out of the high, narrow windows of the church, falling here and there on a face in the mass of worshippers surrounding the building. They stood motionless, with heads bared and bent. The sound of chanting, muffled by snow, thin and indistinct, could be heard. It swelled up, and then died away.

Bradley whispered something in my ear.

"What?"

"Five minutes to go."

In five minutes the priest and congregation would emerge from the church and move round it in solemn procession with the icon, the Most Blessed Lady of Lebedevo, borne triumphantly in front of them.

For Father Zakhar, for Lyuba, for the other sectarians the ceremony would mark the birth of a new era, the symbolic overthrow of Antichrist and his hordes, the establishment of divine harmony on earth.

Would it, could it possibly mean that for Alik as well? Or would it merely mark the end of an unsuccessful experiment, tell him it was time to clear the debris off the laboratory bench in order to make way for some new apparatus?

I closed my eyes and pressed my forehead into the snow. It was cooling, calming. I could almost forget where I was.

The chanting began again and grew louder. I looked up. The crowd outside the church had begun to stir.

Suddenly the whole scene leapt out in stark black and white, frozen and immobile for an instant. Alik had turned his searchlights on. They were arranged in a semi-circle, blazing away from somewhere near the main monastery buildings. The camera truck must be there too. I looked hurriedly away, but for a moment or two was blinded by the after effect of the glare.

When my sight came back the scene by the church had changed. A ring of soldiers had sprung up round the congregation. The head of the procession had appeared round the corner of the church and was now halted. In front two young boys held poles aloft. Between them, hanging from a wooden cross-piece, was the icon. But it was edge-on to me and I could see nothing of the painting. Behind the icon-bearers stood Father Zakhar, in priestly regalia, and behind him, in a long white dress with a veil, was Lyuba. Peredonov stood protectively at her shoulder.

Alik appeared, walking briskly and confidently towards the church. My subconscious in my dream had earlier— perhaps significantly—dressed him rather above his rank, in the winter parade uniform of a Marshal of the Soviet Union. In actual fact he was wearing an ordinary officer's padded jacket, with belt and cross-strap, jack-boots and a fur hat.

The crowd parted to let him through. He came up to Father Zakhar, saluted, and began to speak, gesturing energetically with one hand.

"I could wipe your nose for you, you snotty bastard," Bradley grunted. He was prone on the snow, the rifle cuddled to his shoulder, his eye to the telescopic sight.

I fell on him, with both hands pushing the barrel down into the snow.

"What the hell? Nicola!"

She plucked me off his back and dumped me on the ground. Bradley picked himself up and came towards me, looking sour and angry.

"Look at that!" Nicola's arm shot out.

Bradley stopped and turned. "Jesus H. Christ!"

I pulled myself up on to my knees.

Down below the crowd had turned into a seething,

heaving, fighting mass, into which the procession, Lyuba, Father Zakhar and Alik had vanished. The cordon of troops round the circumference of the crowd were containing it with vicious use of rifle butts and muzzles. The followers of the White Swan were fighting back. I saw one soldier drop his rifle and reel away with his hands to his face. Weakened, the cordon bulged at this point, then broke completely. A small phalanx of sectarians crashed through and then broke up, its members running in different directions out of the light and into the darkness. The cordon re-formed, beating back a weaker assault.

The icon still swayed, like a ship in a stormy sea, above the heads of the crowd. Then one of the poles must have snapped. I even thought I heard the sharp crack above the dull, confused roar of the riot. The cross piece folded down and the icon vanished.

I found myself on my feet, running off to the right, towards the path that led down to the monastery. Bradley shouted something after me, but I paid no attention.

I ran on. The noise from below increased. A figure in white suddenly popped up in front of me.

"Halt!"

I swerved violently away from the fixed bayonet and ran straight over the edge of the cliff.

28

I came down on my back with an appalling thump which jarred every bone in my body. In fact, the drop wasn't very great. I landed on the steep scree below the sheer face of the cliff and immediately took off down the slope in an uncontrolled glissade, arriving at the bottom in the middle of a small avalanche. I was bruised, shaken and dizzy, but otherwise unharmed. Some time later I picked myself up and ran unsteadily towards the church.

The fighting was already over. The snow, trampled down over a large area, here and there stained and dirty, was littered with the debris of battle: fur hats, caps, torn clothes, sticks, makeshift clubs and missiles. I saw the poles on which the icon had hung, shattered and bloodied from their use as weapons. There was no sign of the icon itself.

Further down the valley, near the monastery buildings, the troops were loading Father Zakhar's supporters into lorries. Nobody paid any attention to me as I picked my way through a small knot of soldiers gathered near the front of the church.

Two officers were standing slightly apart from the rest. The younger, small, swarthy, with slant eyes and a pencil moustache, held a walkie-talkie. He was alternately speaking into it and listening to the distorted, metallic tones emanating from the receiver.

His companion, a big, beefy man, had his hands clasped behind his back and was rocking gently from heel to toe as he looked up at the cupola of the church, shining under the light of the searchlights.

"Well?" he said.

The other lowered his set. "All in order, comrade commander. Three hundred and sixty-two under arrest. B company are mopping up the group that got away up the east slope. V Company are searching the buildings. That just leaves—" He noticed me standing in front of him.

"Sergeant!" There was a clatter behind as someone jumped to his feet. "There's one here you missed. Come and take it away."

"No, no, comrade lieutenant. Excuse me, but you're wrong. I've nothing to do with the White Swan. I've only just arrived. I must see Colonel Ostroumov."

His superior—a major, I noticed—brought an eye down from the summit of the church and rolled it at me consideringly. "Not a counter-revolutionary, you say. No. I don't suppose you are, if you want to see Colonel Ostroumov. There's no difficulty about that. You can see him straightaway. Whether he'll be able to see you is another matter."

He exchanged glances with the lieutenant, who was trying to keep a straight face after hearing what he obviously considered to be the funniest line of the year. I didn't see the wit of it, myself.

"Over there." The major nodded towards the church.

The soldiers made way for me. Alik was lying on the ground, propped up against one of the huge carved pillars of the porch. His head was resting on a rolled-up soldier's greatcoat, and another was spread over him. His face was waxy, with great drops of sweat on his forehead. His eyes were closed. I dropped on my knees beside him.

"Alik."

His eyes fluttered half-open and his head turned towards me.

"Vanya?"

"What happened, Alik? What happened? Where's Lyuba?"

He closed his eyes again. "I'm done for, Vanya, done for." He spoke slowly and painfully, with long pauses between words. "It was Peredonov. He was too quick for me. I didn't expect it. Not from him. It's ironic. Really ironic."

"What is, Alik?"

He didn't seem to hear me.

In a minute he said: "The Tambov peasants win in the end." A laugh turned into a cough. His eyes shut, and his head rolled slowly to one side. I thought that death had come. I began to get up.

Suddenly he said: "Lift my head. I want to see."

I put my hand under his neck, and raised it from the pillow. He looked round. "It should have worked. I forgot to allow for chance. For the individual." He began to cough again and I let his head down.

A little bloody foam had appeared at the corner of his mouth. I wiped it away. He said nothing for some minutes. And then: "But it went well, my last operation. I should have liked to see the film. It would have been Tanya's triumph. The most influential of her works."

"Where's Lyuba, Alik?"

"Look after her, Vanya. She needs protection." He fell silent again. Then his eyes opened. He looked straight up into the sky above him. Perhaps he no longer knew I was there. "Not the New Jerusalem this time, Father. I'm sorry.'' His hand crept up and fumblingly made the sign of the cross. Quietly, but clearly and distinctly, he said: ''Receive, O Lord, the soul of Thy servant, Aleksis.'' His head fell sideways and a gush of blood poured out on to the snow.

A little later I got stiffly to my feet. The snow had stopped. From further down the valley I could hear the monotonous thudding of the generators. I wondered why the searchlights hadn't been turned off. There wasn't much action going on for Tanya to film.

I turned away and began to move off with the intention of looking for her. Suddenly the noise of a distant engine blew up into an ear-splitting roar. A helicopter leapt over the side of the basin, banked round the church with a deafening chatter of rotors, and landed about two hundred metres away.

Bent double, the young lieutenant scuttled out to it, opened the door, and obsequiously helped the passenger out. The rotors swished slowly to a halt.

Manilov came striding towards the church, acknowledging salutes with a wave of his swagger stick. He saw me and beckoned.

''Ivan Vasilevich, what a surprise! How did you get here? No, don't tell me. I might not believe you.'' To the young officer: ''Comrade lieutenant, oblige me by sending a patrol out to pick up this man's friends. An American writer and an English lady novelist.'' He looked round. ''They'll probably be up there. On the valley rim. Be kind to them. They represent the world of art and culture.''

A remarkable change had come over him. He looked as though he'd shed forty years in the last few hours. He was fizzing with life and energy. He danced rather than walked, and words sprayed out of him, as though forced up by some irresistible pressure from beneath.

''I suppose I should have told Lapshin to handcuff himself to you, eh? If he didn't want to lose you? A blockhead, an idiot, an incompetent fool. But—'' he poked me in the ribs with his stick. ''He's got an uncle in such a high position.'' He laughed, then drew his face out into mock seriousness. ''You're displaying some uncomfortable qualities, Morozov. Usually confined to the deity. Omnipresence, for example, I shall look very carefully under my bed tonight, to make sure you're not there. Omniscience, too.''

''I beg your pardon, comrade general?''

''You were right. I was wrong. I freely admit it. Manilov can be magnanimous. I wanted to send you to Moscow. You wanted to stay here. It turns out you might be of use.''

''In what way, comrade general?''

''Don't you know? Haven't they told you?'' He sighed dramatically. ''With subordinates like mine God would have been hard put to it to finish the creation in seven years.'' His eye fell on Alik's body. ''He was different of course.'' He waved his stick at it. ''Could have had a brilliant career. Might even have succeeded to my post.'' He laughed, as though at some private joke. ''But a fatal flaw. Incurably infected with bourgeois individualism, poor chap.'' He turned away. ''Clear that mess up at the double, sergeant.''

Taking a confidential hold of my arm, he began to walk me up and down in front of the church.

''The trouble is, Ivan Vasilevich, that some of your misguided friends have locked themselves up. In the church. Before we could persuade them not to. Of course, they're bound to come out sooner or later. Got no food. No water. Question is: how long? Forty days and forty nights? I doubt it, but these fanatics can be pretty obstinate. As you know.'' He swung me round. ''See the doors? They aren't made of paper. And the quartermaster hasn't had any battering-rams for some time. And then, it may not be Kizhi. But it's still a monument of popular culture. Part of our national heritage, as they say. Carved by the adzes of

honest proletarian carpenters from the dreaming forests of
Mother Russia. We don't want to knock it down. But this
operation will be over at dawn. So you can tell your
friends. If they don't come out—'' he looked at his watch
''—in the next two hours, the walls of their sanctuary will
have to come down. I'll play Joshua to their Jericho. They
should understand that.'' He patted me on the shoulder.
''Go on, Ivan Vasilevich. They might listen to you.''

When I'd last seen the church porch it had been spot-
lessly clean. Now it was littered with rubbish, the floor
covered with snow and dirt. Red Army men had used one
corner, out of the wind, as a convenient lavatory and,
possibly in annoyance at the unexpected resistance, had
daubed excrement on the walls. The wrought iron bracket
on which a lantern had hung had been torn down, and the
lantern itself was bent and broken. I picked up the bracket
and hammered on the door with it.

''Father Zakhar. It's Ivan Morozov. I must talk to you.''
There was no reply. I hammered and shouted again.

Then, startling me by his proximity—he must have been
just on the other side of the door—he spoke: ''What is it,
my son?''

''Is Lyuba with you?''

''Lyubov Dmitrievna? Yes, she is here. Do you wish to
give her a message?''

I'd known that she must be, as soon as Manilov had told
me of the situation. It didn't really make much difference.
If she wasn't a prisoner now, she would be very shortly.

''I have a message for you, Father. From General
Manilov.'' I gave him Manilov's ultimatum. There was
silence for a moment, and then a shout—it sounded like
the red-haired Valery—''Tell him to go fuck himself!''
Father Zakhar spoke smoothly, as though the interruption
had not occurred. ''We must consider this carefully. In a
little time we will give our answer.''

While I'd been talking they'd driven Alik's command

car up the path from the monastery buildings and parked it close to the church. Manilov was sitting inside, smoking another of his hand-rolled goat's-legs. He squinted at me through the smoke.

"All right, we wait. But not more than two hours."

When I'd delivered this message to Father Zakhar I hunted up the young lieutenant. He told me the camera truck had left for Vologda some time ago. "A nice piece of crackling, eh?" He winked and kissed his fingers.

I liberated a Red Army greatcoat from a pile, wrapped myself in it, and sat down on the bottom step of the porch. I felt hungry, physically exhausted and emotionally empty.

There were only a few troops left by the church. Most of them had gone down to the monastery buildings. Someone brought me a mug of hot, sweet coffee. Below the lorries, one after another, rumbled away along the valley. Nicola and Bradley appeared in the distance with an escort of soldiers. They vanished into Manilov's command car and didn't reappear. I rested my head against the pillar and, like Alik, looked up into the sky. But I couldn't see anything there.

The troops down in the monastery buildings must have relit the stoves. The magical smell of woodsmoke drifted into my senses again, charged, as before, with so many happy memories of the past. Perhaps, when all this was over, I'd go and live in the country. Give up academic life, take a job as a caretaker at some rest home, some converted noble mansion in the provinces. One really didn't need much. Warmth, a few books, food, vodka . . .

But the sectarians would never have allowed their fires to go out. They'd have made them up with enough to last the night. Why hadn't I smelt woodsmoke before? Had the wind changed?

I got up and walked a few steps into the open. The wind was blowing down the valley, not up it. I turned round and looked at the church. The light in the windows seemed darker, ruddier than before.

I leapt up the steps and hammered at the door. "Lyuba! For God's sake!" The smell of woodsmoke was stronger, more pungent. I thought I could hear the crackle of flames.

Suddenly, from inside, came singing. Feeble and wavering to begin with, then firmer and stronger with every moment.

I couldn't believe it. It was self-immolation. Straight out of the last act of *Khovanshchina*. But things like this belonged to history. They were dead now, over and done with. It couldn't be happening. I hammered on the door again. And again.

Later the singing stopped. A powerful bass—was it Peredonov?—intoned a line. The congregation replied. Another line followed; and another response. It went on for some time.

The singing began again. It seemed more hesitant, interrupted now by fits of coughing. Smoke was pouring out round the door, and it was getting hot in the porch.

Manilov appeared beside me for a moment, and then vanished again.

Only one or two voices were singing now. There was a loud crash from inside. I heard Lyuba's voice:

"Vanya! Vanya! Help me! Please help me! I'm burning!"

The studs on the door were too hot to touch now. I ran down the steps and looked up. Flames were shooting high into the air above the cupola. The gold cross sank sideways and fell into the fire.

"Give me a grenade!"

The corporal looked astonished. He had the broad flat face of a Samoyed.

"Do what he says, soldier." I hadn't noticed that Manilov was at my side again.

Nicola would probably have known what type it was, the weight of the charge, the length of the delay fuse, and the fragmentation radius. I didn't care. I pulled the pin out and lobbed it up into the porch.

A moment later I followed it up and crawled through the wrecked door.

The church was full of flames and smoke. The remaining members of the White Swan were huddled together under the iconostasis. Several had collapsed to the floor, but the others were clinging to one another, holding each other upright. Their mouths were opening and shutting, but if they were singing the sound was lost in the roar of the fire. I saw Lyuba, Father Zakhar, Peredonov. Behind them I thought I saw the icon, hanging in its former place.

I began to edge towards them. There was a groaning and creaking overhead. A moment later what was left of the cupola, together with the drum beneath it, crashed to the floor between us. I staggered to my feet. Lyuba and I were separated by an abatis of blackened and burning timber. I couldn't see her any more. A flame rippled down the wall. My padded jacket was smouldering. I beat at it with my hand. I thought I heard Lyuba scream. A terrifying, panic-stricken shriek. I thrust forward. Something gave way beneath my foot. I dived down, down, deep, deep into darkness.

29

Against a continuous background of pain days and nights flickered past, the one indistinguishable from the other.

They gave me medicines, fed me, picked me up, washed me, put me back together again. Gradually my burns healed, my bones knitted together.

When the sedation started to taper off, and I began to come back to a real consciousness of self, I was already convalescent. Dressed in hospital pyjamas, with a shaven head, I had a room to myself and lay in bed looking out over an esplanade lined with palm trees to the blue sea beyond.

I remembered what had happened, but it seemed unimportant and far away. I felt detached from everything. Day followed day, each with the same, unchanging routine. I must have lain there for weeks, incuriously gazing at the exotic, sub-tropical scenery, before a nurse told me that I was in a military sanatorium near Sochi, on the Black Sea.

Gradually colours became brighter, sounds clearer, smells more distinct. The taste of food returned. And gradually I came to take an interest again in the affairs of the outside world. I read the newspaper, listened to the wireless at the head of my bed, watched television in the patients' lounge.

Things had changed during my absence, but not much. A different Middle Eastern premier had just been greeted at Moscow airport by jubilant, flag-waving crowds; a new nuclear power station had been opened near Minsk; our football team had lost to the Tunisians; the American presidential election campaign was still in progress; a former CIA agent had revealed the story of his agency's inept attempts at political assassination; the leader of a Ukrainian nationalist organisation in exile had had a fatal heart attack on a Paris street.

I began to make preparations to leave. I wrote to the secretary of the department and to the concierge of the apartment house, asking them to send on my mail; I wrote to the professor, Nikolay Stepanovich, asking him what courses I would be teaching in the coming semester—if what I'd experienced had been life, I couldn't wait to get back to literature.

Results were not long in arriving. A week or so later the nurse brought in, together with my midday meal, a bundle of letters and put them on the tray in front of me. I began to flip through them as I drank my soup. Out-dated invitations, form letters, departmental memos, outstanding bills. The most interesting was a note from the house committee at the apartments, calling attention to the exorbitant consumption of electricity in the public areas: citizens were requested to make sure that they extinguished the light on leaving the lavatory.

Suddenly, from the space reserved for the sender's name and address on an ordinary envelope, decorated, like so many million others, with a coloured picture of a Soviet sputnik, a name from the dead leapt out at me: *Peredonov*.

For an instant I felt sheer, unreasoning panic. Then I noticed the initials: not M. E., but F. E. I opened the letter.

Honoured Comrade Morozov!

The undersigned, former senior sergeant Peredonov, Fedor Evstafevich, holder of two citations for bravery and a long-service medal, recently retired from the army and occupying himself presently in his native region of Tambov with the propagation of the Gospel and the teachings of our Lord Jesus Christ, in which endeavour he is subject to constant persecution, both on the part of the local executive committee and the local party authorities, considers it his duty to put forward the following facts:

1) On several occasions while serving with his former superior officer the late Lieutenant-Colonel Ostroumov, Aleksey Petrovich, he heard the latter assert that one of the purposes of his actions (all the others being wicked and some even blasphemous) was to take his revenge on you, comrade Morozov, on comrade Tatarinova, and on his late wife, Lyubov Dmitrievna Ostroumova, for the manner in which these personages had insulted and humiliated him in the past.

2) In view of the facts set out above the undersigned feels that although his late brother of blessed memory, Peredonov Mikhail Evstafevich, was formally guilty of the death by stabbing of the above mentioned late Lieutenant-Colonel Ostroumov, his crime was to a certain extent mitigated by the above mentioned circumstances and he himself was moreover without doubt ex-

culpated of guilt for the crime by his heroic
death as a martyr in defence of the one true faith.
Amen.

> With great respect
> (signed) Peredonov, Fedor Evstafevich

Now I remembered that when the sergeant had told me
his patronymic for a moment I'd suspected a connection
with Peredonov. But then I'd dismissed the idea as too
far-fetched. I should learn to trust my instincts more. But
why had he written to me? From some obscure desire to
clear his brother's name? To establish, for the sake of
future historians, the truth of what had happened? Or did
he have the vain hope that I might be able to lean on his
local executive committee and party authorities?

I read the letter again and put it down. Religion, love,
jealousy. In the end these had been the motivating factors.
I'd never know now what incident—which must at the
time have seemed so trifling and insignificant as not to be
worth remembering for an instant—had inflicted such an
appalling psychic wound on Alik. Whatever it was, it had
certainly taken a toll in destruction incommensurate with
its size.

A day or two later I was lying in bed, half-asleep,
towards the end of the afternoon, when there was a knock
on the door and Bradley came in.

I found myself wringing his hand, patting him on the
back, sitting him down in the armchair. Would he like
some mineral-water, a biscuit, an apple? Should I send out
for tea, coffee, beer, wine, vodka, something to eat? How
was he? How did he come to be here?

"Thanks, Vanya, I'm fine. Don't bother about me. But
how are you? You look a little rough."

"Much better. I'll be leaving soon."

Bradley walked over to the window. "A great view you
have here, Vanya. On a clear day you must be able to see

right across to the NATO bases in Turkey." He was silent for a while and then, still looking out of the window, said: "Did they tell you what happened?"

"No," I said. "Nobody told me anything."

"They all died. No bodies were found."

"How did I get out?"

"Manilov sent a couple of soldiers in after you. You hadn't gone very far. But the church collapsed on top of the other poor sods. They never had a chance."

"Perhaps they didn't want one."

But as I said it I wondered. Was it true? Had they all consciously chosen death rather than life? Father Zakhar perhaps. Peredonov too. But did Lyuba—I couldn't forget that last despairing childlike cry for help—really want a martyr's crown?

Bradley appeared to be making preparations to leave already. He took a carton of cigarettes out of one pocket, a bottle of whisky out of another, and put them on the bedside table.

"Well, Vanya, I guess—"

"Why did you come here, Martin?"

"To say good-bye. I'm going home next week."

"How did you know I was here?"

He looked sheepish. "Manilov told me. I think the old buzzard thought you'd had a rough deal. He told me to come and see you and fill you in on the details. If I do, I come off clean. There's no comeback. No stink which could hurt me, careerwise."

"Well?"

He shrugged. "Handing out information gratuitously goes against the grain for an old spook like me."

Then he told me.

It all began, he said, about six months ago in a smart duplex in Washington. Working on a game strategy to put the President back in the White House. He was trailing in the polls; might not even get his party's nomination at the autumn convention. They decided to play the old cards: honesty, sincerity, integrity. To milk the Christian, religious angle for everything it had got.

So they kicked it around a bit more, and someone came up with the idea that the man could give his image a bit of a shine by attacking religious oppression. In the Soviet Union, for instance.

The only trouble was, said Bradley, that there weren't any oppressed believers obviously around at the time. "Well, they could have tossed the idea into the trash can, and pursued something more rewarding, like fabricating charges of child molestation against the other candidate, but they'd invested a good deal of thought—about five minutes' worth—in the concept, so they called me in to see what could be done. And I got hold of Alik."

"Did you know him?"

"I'd met him a couple of times. But at that level it's like pro football. All the players know each other well enough to nod to."

"I see."

"I was really looking for persecuted Baptists—they go down better with the press. But then Alik handed me this wonderful set-up on a plate, and I was happy to take Old Believers instead. It was odds-on they'd turn up as Baptists in most write-ups, anyway."

"What set-up?"

"For some reason—he never told me why—he'd been running this little sect. Growing it, like a culture on a glass dish in a lab. With Manilov's knowledge and approval. But the thing was that he was mustard-keen to get Manilov's job. He thought he could do that by making Manilov fall flat on his face in public. So our aims jelled together beautifully."

I didn't get it.

Bradley sighed patiently. "As Manilov's subordinate and on his orders, Alik brutally suppresses the White

Swan. On behalf of the free nations of the world, I witness
the atrocity. So does my companion, a gracious English
authoress. By sheer coincidence, we happen to have a film
of the incident, taken by a well-known Soviet director.
The President calls the wrath of God down on Russia and
takes the Indiana primary. A lot of Ukrainians in Indiana.
Manilov has caused a scandal, the Soviet Union has lost
face. He's lucky if he ends up driving a tractor in
Verkhneudinsk. Alik steps into his job. That was the
scenario."

"But it didn't work."

"No, it didn't. It went like magic to begin with. Manilov
was the only person who could stop us. He knew vaguely
that something was up, but not what it was—until you told
him. And even then the snow kept him grounded in Vologda.
We figured anyway that he'd rather let the operation go
through than risk a showdown with Alik in front of the
troops. What I didn't know until too late was that Alik had
gone stark raving bananas. He kept his cards very close to
his chest. There was no way I'd have gone along with it if
I'd known that he was trying to decide between becoming
head of the KGB and Tsar of All Russia. He didn't
understand that there weren't any options. There was no
choice to make. Only one thing could happen. And then,
while he was still playing both ends against the middle, he
gets knocked off by a sectarian, the snow stops, Manilov
waltzes in and turns the whole operation round in a flash.
No publicity. Nothing for the President. And that was
that."

And that was that. It seemed, somehow, an inadequate
epitaph.

I showed him Peredonov's letter. He nodded wisely
over it.

"What did I tell you? Bananas."

I remembered something that had puzzled me.

"How did Nicola come to be there?"

"The Brits lent her to us. They wanted to know what was going on. And we needed a good impartial witness." He grinned.

"And why did you want me? If you were getting everything from Alik?"

"I didn't trust him. Did you? I needed an alternative way in."

"Would you really have shot him then? If a riot hadn't developed naturally?"

"You must be joking."

We sat there in silence for some time. On the horizon the sun was going down. A black fishing-boat moved slowly over a golden ocean.

Bradley got to his feet. He wanted to shake hands. I let him. At the door he turned round.

"Remember Igor?"

I nodded.

"I saw him in Moscow the other day. He'd got a story about the icon. Seems it was saved from the fire. Now it's healing the faithful in another little church up there. Crazy." He shook his head in disbelief, opened the door and went out.

A moment later he poked his head in again.

"By the way, I came down with another friend of yours. I sent her away while I talked to you, but she's back now with a lorry-load of grapes. Shall I let her in?"

Tanya stood in the doorway. She looked wonderful. I smiled at her.

Peace to the dead. Life to the living.

BESTSELLING BOOKS FROM TOR

MORE BESTSELLERS FROM TOR

GRAHAM MASTERTON

- [ ] 52195-1 CONDOR $3.50
  52196-X   Canada $3.95

- [ ] 52191-9 IKON $3.95
  52192-7   Canada $4.50

- [ ] 52193-5 THE PARIAH $3.50
  52194-3   Canada $3.95

- [ ] 52189-7 SOLITAIRE $3.95
  52190-0   Canada $4.50

- [ ] 48067-9 THE SPHINX $2.95

- [ ] 48061-X TENGU $3.50

- [ ] 48042-3 THE WELLS OF HELL $2.95

- [ ] 52199-4 PICTURE OF EVIL $3.95
  52200-1   Canada $4.95

Buy them at your local bookstore or use this handy coupon:
Clip and mail this page with your order

TOR BOOKS—Reader Service Dept.
P.O. Box 690, Rockville Centre, N.Y. 11571

Please send me the book(s) I have checked above. I am enclosing $_____ (please add $1.00 to cover postage and handling). Send check or money order only—no cash or C.O.D.'s.

Mr./Mrs./Miss _____

Address _____

City _____ State/Zip _____

Please allow six weeks for delivery. Prices subject to change without notice.

Ramsey Campbell

☐ 51652-4	DARK COMPANIONS		$3.50
51653-2		Canada	$3.95
☐ 51654-0	THE DOLL WHO ATE HIS		$3.50
51655-9	MOTHER	Canada	$3.95
☐ 51658-3	THE FACE THAT MUST DIE		$3.95
51659-1		Canada	$4.95
☐ 51650-8	INCARNATE		$3.95
51651-6		Canada	$4.50
☐ 58125-3	THE NAMELESS		$3.50
58126-1		Canada	$3.95
☐ 51656-7	OBSESSION		$3.95
51657-5		Canada	$4.95

Buy them at your local bookstore or use this handy coupon:
Clip and mail this page with your order

TOR BOOKS—Reader Service Dept.
P.O. Box 690, Rockville Centre, N.Y. 11571

Please send me the book(s) I have checked above. I am enclosing
$_____ (please add $1.00 to cover postage and handling).
Send check or money order only—no cash or C.O.D.'s.

Mr./Mrs./Miss _____
Address _____
City _____ State/Zip _____
Please allow six weeks for delivery. Prices subject to change
without notice.